D1824474

A Novel by **Wendy Mason**

St. Francis

An Instrument of Peace

novum pro

This book is also
available as
e-book.

www.novum-publishing.co.uk

© 2018 novum publishing

ISBN 978-3-99064-376-1
Editing: Hugo Chandler, BA
Cover photo:
Incomible | Dreamstime.com
Cover design, layout & typesetting:
novum publishing

www.novum-publishing.co.uk

PART ONE

CHAPTER ONE

CHILDHOOD IN ASSISI

I heard Mother sigh with relief at the town-crier's announcement. The merchants' cavalcade had been spotted earlier, on the road between Spoleto and Assisi. Since then she had cleaned the house from top to bottom, prepared Father's favourite meal and made everything perfect for his return. He was expected any time now.

The smell of freshly baked bread wafted down the stairs. My tummy rumbled.

'Francesco, do you see your father yet?'

I smiled. 'How many times, Mother? No, not yet.'

'Let me know the instant he arrives, Francesco.'

'Yes, Mother. I said that I would.'

'Or if any customers want serving. Call me at once. Do you hear, Francesco?'

'Yes, Mother, I promise – Father, customers, gangs of robbers – I swear to call you.'

She let out a low chuckle.

I listened to Mother's footsteps tip-tapping on the ceiling above me. They crossed the room, passed the dining table, and paused beside the cooking range. The oven door clunked as she checked on the bread. The chain rattled on the cooking pot hanging over the open fire. She must have stirred the stew because I could now smell the heady fragrance of the lamb ragout. Mother's footsteps moved over to the comfy benches where we sat in the evenings.

I imagined her plumping up the heaps of brightly coloured cushions, made with leftover scraps of material from my father's shop.

I turned to Angelo, who at three years old barely reached the height of my seven-year-old chest. 'Angelo, stay here while I climb the tree to get a better view.'

'Angelo come too?'

'You are too little. Keep watch, and warn me if Mother appears.'

The highest branches of the poplar tree made the perfect lookout for me to see over the wall and into the street that led to the Piazza. There was no sign of Father yet, but I spotted Enricho, his best friend who lived two houses down from us.

'Enricho!' I waved my arms to attract his attention.

'Francesco.' He returned my wave. 'Take care not to fall.'

'I am like a cat.' I grinned and waved both arms high above my head.

'So I see. I hear your father will soon be home.'

'Any moment now. Mother is frantic.'

'Then I will see you all tomorrow for supper when I might have a little something for you boys.'

'Is it the camels?'

Last year Enricho had built Angelo and me a wooden ark and had since carved us a number of toy animals. On his last trip, Father met a spice trader from Africa who gave him a picture of a strange exotic creature called a camel. We gave it to Enricho and begged him to make us a pair for the ark.

I shuffled forward on the branch to catch his reply.

'You must learn patience, Francesco. You will see soon enough.' He waved again and wandered off in the direction of the Piazza.

I do not remember life without Enricho. Mother said he had been grief-stricken when his wife died in childbirth. Already slight in build, the flesh had melted from his bones. Father, fearing his friend might die, invited him to share our evening meal. Now he dines with us every Friday; he is a part of our family, an uncle to my brother and me.

'What can you see, Francesco?'

I looked down between my feet, through the branches and still further to where Angelo was struggling to climb the tree. Shafts of sunlight shone through the leaves onto his angelic face. Little wonder he was my father's favourite. Angelic by name and by nature, his dark brown almond-shaped eyes, framed by thick black lashes, shone with the excitement of the climb. Even his nose was handsome. How could Mother have produced the two of us, one beautiful in looks with such a sunny personality, and the other so plain and disappointing?

'Be careful, Angelo, you will fall, and it will be my fault. Remember, I am supposed to be taking care of you.'

Too late, I heard a branch snap. Angelo tumbled backwards. He turned a complete somersault in the air, grabbed at a branch and missed, crashed through a few twigs and landed in a crumpled heap at the base of the tree.

'Angelo, are you alright?' I yelled.

Dear God, let him live, or my parents will never forgive me.

Confirmation that my prayer was answered came with a loud wail from Angelo.

Mother rushed from the house just as I reached the ground. 'Angelo, darling, my baby. Francesco, whatever were you doing? He is far too young to climb trees. He could have been killed.' She cradled Angelo in her arms and rocked him until his sobs settled down to an occasional sniff. 'Let me look at you. Oh dear, a grazed knee and this red mark on your arm will no doubt become a colourful bruise by tomorrow – but otherwise, I think you will live.' She kissed his forehead. 'Do you want to come inside and help me to get things ready?'

Angelo sniffed and mumbled, 'Stay with Francesco and wait for Father.'

'Then no more climbing.' Mother patted his head and glowered at me. 'Neither of you, do you hear? Stand on this doorstep, and do not move from it.'

'I could go to the Piazza,' I offered, in the hope of distracting Mother's attention from my failure. 'That way we will know how close they are.'

'You will stay where you are and look after your brother. Remember to shout up to me if any customers want serving. I want to make sure that your father's meal is on the table the moment he arrives.'

I looked around the shop and sighed. Racks of shelving lined the walls, filled with bolts of richly coloured textiles. Each one had a corner turned back, so that customers could see at a glance the colour and pattern of the cloth. Towards the front entrance was a large bench where the material could be unrolled and examined in greater detail. I stroked the nearest cloth, hoping to find more pleasure in it than I usually did.

Hearing the steady clip-clop of horses' hooves, I looked eagerly towards the gate.

'Here he is, Mother!' I yelled.

Father was a large man, not fat, but tall and thickset. As he rode into the yard, I noticed that his black hair and beard had grown during the month he had been away. He smiled broadly and waved.

'Mother!' I shouted again.

She arrived, out of breath, as Father dismounted.

'Pica, my dear, you look as lovely as ever.'

'And you, Pietro Bernardone, are full of charm, as usual. Little wonder I was swept off my feet and enticed away from my beloved France.'

'No regrets?'

In answer, Mother threw herself into his arms. Angelo and I shuffled our feet and blushed as Father hugged her tightly, then kissed her passionately. Eventually, she made her escape, and he turned to us.

'And who are these fine young men?'

'It is I, Father, Francesco.'

'And I, Angelo.'

'Heavens above, how you have both grown. I did not recognise you.' He grinned and ruffled our hair. 'I have a gift for you, boys.'

Father took a bundle of cloth out of his pocket and peeled aside its layers to reveal two gold rings, each set with a shiny black stone.

'They are jet stones,' he explained. The rings will be too large for you now, but you'll grow into them soon enough. Until then,' he dangled two leather strings, 'you may wear them on these.'

Before Angelo had even grasped his ring, I had threaded and knotted mine onto the cord and draped it proudly around my neck.

'Thank you, Father,' I beamed.

'Let me help you, Angelo,' Father said.

Two of Father's men entered the courtyard, leading two large horses, each one pulling a trailer bursting with huge bundles.

'More than enough to pay the Duke his taxes,' Father nodded at the loads, 'and plenty left to see us through the winter. Take note, Francesco, we must always be sure to pay Duke Conrad his share if we wish to live peacefully in Assisi.'

'But why should we pay taxes to a German Duke?' I asked.

'It is his reward for services to the Emperor.'

'But that is so unfair. Everybody hates him.'

'That may well be, but it is the law, and the law must be obeyed.'

I did not agree, but I knew better than to argue with my father.

Father turned back to his men. 'Well done my fine fellows.' He handed them both a leather pouch. 'Now, would you unload these trailers and put the material into the store shed, all except for these few bolts wrapped in muslin, which I need in the shop.' He patted the horses, dug into his pocket and gave each one an apple. 'Look after these horses; they have served us well. Wash them down and then turn them out into the large paddock.'

We waited, and our patience was rewarded when he returned his attention back to us.

'Come on, boys, let us go and see what your mother has prepared for us.'

He swung me onto his back, scooped Angelo into his arms and carried us into the shop. I ducked my head to avoid the door frame and nuzzled into my father's neck. I rarely got the chance to get this close to him. I breathed in his distinctive smell – a mixture of sweat, horse and leather.

Father climbed the stairs to the large hall, the main room of our home, and gently lowered each of us to the floor. Before we could scramble into our seats, my mother placed four steaming bowls of stew on the table and handed my father his golden goblet of wine.

After we had eaten, Angelo and I changed into our nightshirts and snuggled together at Father's feet. Bathed in the soft glow produced by the log fire and candles, we listened to the exciting stories he had harvested from those he had met on his journey – tales of faraway places and brave knights with noble causes. His voice was soft and gentle, full of admiration for these brave men. I vowed, then and there, that one day I would become such a hero and win my father's affection.

Father lifted us into his arms, elbowed aside the colourful tapestry curtain and carried us up the staircase to the sleeping areas, where he and Mother shared one room, Angelo and I the other. I forced myself to stay awake so that I could take comfort from the way he tucked us in, kissed our foreheads and left us cocooned in our warm blankets.

I loved it when my father returned; being away seemed to make his heart grow fonder of me. I drifted off into a deep sleep and I dreamt that I was a brave knight, just like the ones my father spoke so highly of. All night long I fought dragons and rescued fair maidens.

The next morning, I was awake long before Angelo or my parents. Thinking it would please my father; I snuck downstairs to the shop and began to unpack some of the bundles of cloth he had bought. A dark green velvet fabric, with a pattern of gold thread, fell to the floor and unravelled. I lifted one end over my shoulder and paraded up and down in front of the mirror, every inch the rich and noble lord I longed to be.

'What do you think you are playing at? Give it back at once!'

Father pounced, grabbed the fabric from my shoulders and pushed me to the ground. I heard the fabric rip and realised with horror that my robe had snagged on the corner of the bench. Father held up the velvet. I could see the ragged slash in the cloth where it had torn as he wrenched it free.

'I am sorry, Father.' My voice shook as I scrambled to my feet. 'It was only a game. I was pretending to be Lord Francesco, dressed for my victory ball after defeating Duke Conrad and rescuing the town from rebels.'

Father's face twisted with anger. 'Your head is full of romantic rubbish.' He raised a hand and slapped my face: a stinging blow that knocked me back to the floor in a heap.

'Pietro. Please, leave him be.'

Mother ran towards me, but Father placed a hand on her arm and stopped her from reaching my cowering body.

'This is your fault, Pica. You spoil him outrageously.'

'He is a sensitive boy, Pietro. He needs–'

'What he needs is discipline, and by God, I will see that he gets it.' He turned to me. 'Just look at this fabric. How am I going to sell it now?'

'I am sorry,' I whimpered, shaking under his fury.

'See?' He turned to my mother who hung her head and refused to look at me. 'See how he whines like a dog? What kind of son will he make if I allow this to go on? No, Pica, do not interfere.' He pushed my mother away. 'You do him harm with your pampering and misguided belief that he is special. No more. The boy must learn.'

He reached down and pulled the leather string from my neck. 'I will sell this ring to pay for some of the damage you have done.'

He grasped my arm, yanked me to my feet and hauled me out of the door. My cheeks flamed with embarrassment as he dragged me down the street and into the church, then pushed me onto a pew.

'Wait here while I find out which priest is confessor for today.'

My hands trembled as I awaited my fate. Perhaps Father would change his mind. He must realise that I was only playing. Surely he would have had fun with such games when he was a boy?

I prayed that the priest taking confession would be my old friend, Father Tommo: I knew that he would treat me kindly. But no, it was the senior priest, Father Tiberio. He was also a teacher at our school, where we boys called him the *Dragon*.

Father Tiberio showed us into the vestry. I sat on a stool with my head hung in shame while my father explained the *wilful* destruction of his valuable material.

'And what do you have to say about this, Francesco?' Father Tiberio demanded.

'Please, Father, it was an accident.' My eyes sought out my father's, but he fixed his gaze on the priest. I fought back tears. 'I meant no harm.'

'It was theft,' Father Tiberio snapped. 'You deprived your father of goods that belonged to him. What does the good book say? *Thou shalt not steal.*' He came nearer and bent down, his face so close that his spittle speckled my face. 'You disrespected your father. Again, what does the good book say? *Thou shalt honour thy mother and thy father.* Wicked. Quite wicked.'

Shame burned through me as a few tears escaped and rolled down my cheeks.

'It was a game. I did not mean to be wicked.'

'You need to beg forgiveness, learn obedience and mend your ways, my boy, or you will die a sinner and burn in the eternal flames of Hell.'

I shook with fear. The thought of burning in Hell terrified me. Tears flowed unchecked down my face. My father shook his head, his obvious disappointment in me more painful than a thousand slaps. I sniffed, and then wiped away my tears with my sleeve.

Father Tiberio turned his back on me, walked across the room and sank to his knees. His mumbled prayers for my sorry soul destroyed any hope I had for mercy.

'I am very sorry, Father,' I whispered. 'I meant no harm.'

'You never do, do you, Francesco?' My father kept his gaze on the bent shoulders of the priest, whose mumblings grew louder.

'I beg your forgiveness, Father.'

'Stop snivelling, Francesco.'

'Kneel beside me,' Father Tiberio demanded.

Hastily, I crossed the room, dropped to my knees, hung my head and placed my hands together for prayer.

'Well, speak, boy. God is listening.'

'Bless me Father for I have sinned.' My voice shook. 'I am heartily sorry for the offences I have caused.'

'Is that all you have to say for your wickedness?'

'My God, I detest all of my sins, because I dread the loss of Heaven and the pains of Hell, but most of all because I have offended You, my God, who is all good and deserving of all my love. I firmly resolve, with the help of Your grace, to confess my sins, to do penance and to amend my life. Amen.'

The priest gave me absolution and forgiveness, but his voice remained harsh and cold. He did not sound as if he meant it. I stayed on my knees while I waited for him to tell me my penance. It was usually a prayer, or at worst, a few, so his next words came as a shock.

'You will stay here today and make copies of the Ten Commandments until the evening service, when your father will return to collect you.'

'But what of breakfast?' I blurted out, my growing hunger overcoming my good sense.

Father Tiberio glared. Out of the corner of my eye, I saw my father hang his head with the weight of his shame.

'You will not eat again until you leave church this evening.' Father Tiberio rose to his feet. 'Come with me.'

I followed, without looking back at my father. I did not want him to see my tears.

The priest led me away to a small dark room with no window. The only light came from a candle. He gave me a copy of the Ten Commandments, a few sheets of parchment, a pen and inkwell and then left me on my own. I knew I was supposed to feel regret, to repent my wicked ways, but I was hungry, cold and angry. This was so unfair. I gripped the pen and scribbled the commandments in a hand so heavy that the paper ripped. I hated writing, I hated Father Tiberio and I hated my father.

My friend Dimitri lived next door. His father made leather goods; belts, shoes, and horses' tack. His mother sold the items from their shop, which, like ours, was on the ground floor of their home. We played together all the time, along with Angelo and another friend, Elias.

Elias lived in a small village a few hours walk from Assisi. His parents were farmers who worked every hour of daylight, harvesting their crops. Elias must have been even more of a disappointment to his father than I was to mine. If he went anywhere near grass or flowers, he would cough and sneeze, his eyes would stream with tears and he would find it difficult to catch his breath. His father decided it was best for Elias to spend summers with his aunt. She did not have any children and enjoyed his company. As did we.

Elias and I were the same age, but he was always the quiet, thoughtful member of my gang. Obviously, with Dimitri two years younger and willing to follow me anywhere, and with Angelo four years younger, it was always left to me to make the decision about which game to play.

'We will be soldiers today and rescue the town from the evil Duke and his supporters, those pesky Perugians.'

'Can I be the leader today?' asked Angelo. 'Please, Francesco, please say I can.'

'You are too little.' I turned away so I did not have to watch those big beautiful eyes fill with tears.

Before long, I had all three boys lined up, armed with sticks, and marching up and down the yard in time with my instructions. 'One two, one two, halt.' The ragged group came to a stop. 'About turn,' I commanded.

Angelo turned the wrong way and caught Dimitri with his stick.

'Angelo, you ass.' Dimitri rubbed his shoulder. 'You are supposed to turn to your right.'

'I am sorry, Dimitri. I got muddled.'

The next attempt was much better, and for once Angelo turned to his right.

'Perfect, now we are ready to face our enemy,' I declared. 'Charge!'

We raced across the yard to a bag of sand tied to one of the lower branches of the poplar tree, then stabbed and whacked at it with our sticks.

'Here you go, boys.' My mother arrived with a tray, on which sat cups of freshly squeezed orange juice and some sweet almond biscuits, fresh from the oven. The smell was heavenly. 'It is hot today. You will need refreshment after all that running around. Come and sit here, out of the sun.'

The portico made a nice shady place for us to sit. A climbing rose bush clambered over the railings, and as we raced into its welcome shelter, I noticed a wonderful sweet smell: a few early pink rosebuds had burst open. Elias sneezed.

Mother placed the tray on the table. We scrambled onto the chairs and dived into the biscuits. They were still warm and tasted delicious.

'How is your mother today, Dimitri?' asked Mother. 'I have not seen her, and I noticed that the shop is closed.'

Dimitri paused his nibbling. 'She has a headache, and her face is all swollen up. She is lying down and sent me out to play so she can sleep for a while.'

'The poor thing, I' make one of my cold lavender compresses for her. It will soothe her head and take down the swelling. Remember to collect it before you leave.'

Two days later, I found my parents huddled around the breakfast table. They were talking in whispers but broke off as I arrived.

'What is it? Is something wrong? Mother?' My mind raced through the possible causes. What had I done this time? Was it bad enough for me to be dragged before Father Tiberio again? I hoped not.

'It is your friend Dimitri.' My father's voice was quiet and stern.

'Dimitri?'

'You can no longer play with him.'

'But we agreed to meet today for a game of soldiers.'

'He will not come to play today, or ever. You will never mention his name again.'

I looked from my mother to my father to try to see where the joke lay, but this was clearly not a laughing matter. 'But why? I do not understand?'

'His parents were arrested last night.' My father paused. 'The whole family is in the town gaol awaiting trial.'

'No.' I shook my head. 'His parents are good people.'

My mother's eyes filled with tears. 'They were arrested and charged with heresy.'

'That cannot be. They are our friends.'

'You must never say that to anyone,' my father snapped. 'They have offended the Holy Roman Catholic Church with their Cathar beliefs.' My father stood, gripped my shoulders and shook me until my teeth rattled. 'Remember this, boy, remember this well. You never knew this family, they are dead to you. They never existed.'

'What will happen to Dimitri?'

'Have I not told you, *never* use that name again? When will you ever learn to do as you are told?' He sighed and shook his head. 'With God's grace and if the Church is merciful, they will be saved from death and punished by banishment. Go out and play. Forget you ever knew that child.'

I ran from the room, staggered down the stairs, through the shop and stumbled out into the hot, dry yard. I did not want to play. Not without Dimitri. I swore I would not forget my friend.

For weeks, Elias and I watched for a sign of our friend or his family, but it seemed my father was right. They vanished overnight, and nobody would talk about them. It was as though they had never existed. *Damnatio memoriae.* They had simply disappeared from memory.

CHAPTER TWO
SEARCHING FOR A FATHER'S LOVE

'Silvia, where *are* you?' I called crossly. 'Come out now, this instant, or I will be late for school.'

Silvia was my pet snake. She was dark green with rows of spots running down her body, a yellow collar behind her head, and was as long as my arm, from the tip of my middle finger to my elbow. She liked to sit on my hand with her tail wrapped loosely around my wrist, swaying gently, her head held high and her tongue flicking from side to side as she tasted the air. Her black eyes stared back at me knowingly when I spoke to her. She understood every word I said.

I hated to leave her at home while I was away. The cleaning lady, who helped my mother to keep our home spotless, might find her and scream in terror. I feared the handyman would then be brought in to throw Silvia outside, where the hens could peck at her, or she could fall prey to a falcon.

'Oh, there you are, at last.'

Silvia slithered towards me and with a rush of relief, I picked her up, placed her gently into my tunic pocket and headed downstairs to join my mother, who waited patiently to kiss me goodbye.

'Where is your cloak, Francesco?'

'I do not need it, Mother.'

'Oh yes you do. It is cold today.'

I sighed and fetched my cloak from its hook.

'Be a good boy for the priests.'

My mother kissed me goodbye and tucked my packed lunch under my arm. It was Tuesday, which meant homemade goats cheese, olives and freshly baked bread, all wrapped in a cloth. I marched up the road towards the Piazza and then turned and trudged down the path towards San Giorgio.

Tuesday was one of the worst days: Latin with Father Tiberio, ugh! I could at least take comfort from the fire this morning; the pot-bellied stove would be full of blazing firewood. With luck, I might be chosen to add extra logs during the morning. I knew how to lift the top carefully with a long metal prong, hooked at one end to fit under the clasp on the lid, and then throw new logs into the fire. I liked to see the sparks fly up in response and to breathe in the wonderful smell of burning wood as it wafted through the classroom.

'Good morning, boys,' Father Tiberio said as we settled into our seats. He slapped his cane into his palm with a menacing swish.

'Good morning, Father Tiberio,' we all chimed.

'Today we are going to read the song of Oliver and Roland, in Latin. I will be asking each of you to read a short passage and then translate it back.'

My heart leapt. I might yet escape the cane. These were my favourite verses, and I knew them virtually word for word.

'Francesco, will you start us off?'

Even better, the first few verses. I absolutely knew these, word perfect. I began to read, but then something brushed against my thigh. Silvia slipped from my pocket onto the floor and slithered towards Father Tiberio. He spotted her immediately.

'Stand back, boys.' He pushed back his chair and raised his cane. 'I will save you from this wicked and vile creature.'

'No, Sir.' I leapt to my feet and moved towards Silvia. 'She is a pet – perfectly harmless.'

Father Tiberio moved faster than I. He scooped up Silvia with his cane, picked up the prong, pulled up the lid and threw her into the flames. The air hissed and sizzled. He replaced the lid, and her twitching body thumped against the sides of the pot. Then silence fell in the room.

'Silvia!'

Father Tiberio turned on me. 'Are you responsible for this abomination? Did you bring this creature of Satan into our school?'

'She was my pet. I loved her. You killed her, you … you … dragon.'

'Love is to obey, boy. Hold out your hand. I will teach you about love.'

The cane came down hard on my outstretched palm. I jerked my hand away and blew on it to stop the pain.

'Put your hand back out, boy.' Father Tiberio's voice was seriously grave. 'Do as you are told. I will show you what happens to those who disobey.'

The cane tore across my flesh, brought up welts and eventually bloodied my hand. The pain was unbearable, but I knew that if I screamed or cried out, it would make him angrier. It was only after the tenth lash when the blood oozed over my fingers and formed a pool on the tiled floor that Father Tiberio appeared to notice the damage he had caused. He stopped, red in the face and breathing heavily.

'Get out of my class, boy. Do not come back until you learn to obey.' He glared at me and growled. 'Go to the Abbot and explain how sinful you are. He will decide your punishment.'

I stomped through the cloisters towards the Abbot's office, mourning for my beloved Sylvia. Father Tiberio had committed murder, the worst of sins. I would tell the Abbot, and he would have him excommunicated. He would disappear like Dimitri and his family, never to be spoken of again.

When I explained to the Abbot, he was furious, but he was furious with *me*. Instead of banishing Father Tiberio, he sent me home with a letter.

My father frowned as he read it.

'What is the meaning of this, Francesco?'

I gave him the full story, knowing full well that he would understand how badly I had been treated. Instead, he took off his shoe and put me over his knee.

'How could you embarrass me like this, calling a priest names?'

Whack. The shoe came down hard, a stinging blow.

'It is blasphemy.'

Whack.

'A sin.'

Whack.

'I will not have you corrupting your brother.'

Whack.

'Now go to your room and stay there until I say that you can come out.'

I climbed the stairs and threw myself down on my bed, ablaze with the pain of my grief for Silvia, the pain the cane had caused to my hand and the pain of the spanking delivered by my father. Huge racking sobs shook my body. I would show them. One day they would all be sorry.

My mother arrived with salve for my hand. 'Francesco, my love, my first-born, what have you done? Causing all this upset – whatever gets into you? Your father is so angry. It will make him ill. You must learn to respect your father. And the priests. You must obey them.'

'But Father Tiberio murdered Silvia, a poor defenceless creature. Why should I obey a murderer?'

'Shush, Francesco, you cannot say such things.'

'I speak the truth.' I wiped my sleeve across my teary face. 'My father should believe me. He should take my side, but he does not. I hate him, and I hate the priests.'

'No, Francesco.' My mother shook her head and gently laid my injured hand in her lap. 'You were in the wrong, my son. You must always accept the priests' judgement. You must always show respect to a man of the cloth.' I winced as she pressed the salve into my wounds. 'And you must never again cause your father such embarrassment.'

'I will run away, take Angelo with me, and travel the world and then Father will be sorry. I will disappear from his life as surely as Dimitri has disappeared from mine.'

Mother reached across and pulled the blanket over me. 'You will not leave me, will you? Not until you find a nice girl, settle down and have a family of your own.' She gently tucked the blanket around me and kissed my forehead. 'Unless you decide instead to enter the church: perhaps you will become a priest or a monk?'

'Never! I hate the Church. I will die before I grow up to be either.'

Mother frowned. 'You must learn to curb your tongue, Francesco. You cannot speak of the Church in this way. And anyway, I am sure that you will see things differently when you are older.' She stroked my brow, pushing my hair back from my face. 'I know that one day you will be famous across the world as a man of God. You will see.'

By the time I was thirteen, and Angelo nine, we were both the same height, and he no longer looked up to me as his big brother. Father was away on another buying trip. Mother was busy, as usual, and I was left to look after the shop. Of late this responsibility was forced upon me more often than merited my pleasure.

The shop was unusually quiet, and I spent the morning hanging around, bored and restless. Angelo joined me, but even his smile failed to lighten my mood. He stroked and fussed over bundles of cloth and arranged them in rows just as Father liked them to be. He fingered a piece of fine red silk.

'How smooth it feels. See how shiny it is, Francesco?'

I turned my back on him and poked a stick into a crack in the wall, dislodging a black beetle with glossy black wings that shone dark green in a shaft of sunlight. It was infinitely more interesting than any textiles could ever be.

'He is here,' Angelo cried out as my father's horse turned into the open gateway.

Father's bearded face broke into smiles of joy as he spotted my mother hurrying across the yard towards him. Greetings over, he announced that he had brought back a special gift. He asked Angelo and me to turn around, so he could tie scarves over our eyes.

'What have you brought?' I asked. I could hear hooves clip-clopping into the yard and the wheels of the carts scrape to a halt. I strained to see what treasures they held for us, but the blindfold prevented me. 'What is it, Father?'

My father did not answer, and Mother nudged me and bade me shush as she guided me out into the yard.

'Mind the chicken, Francesco,' she said.

Too late. I caught the bird with my foot, and she fluttered across the yard, squawking in protest. One must have escaped when I penned them in earlier. Father would no doubt have something to say about that later.

'Are we there yet?' I asked, hoping to distract him from my failure.

Father sighed and untied the knot. The scarf fell from my eyes. I gasped. Before me stood two horses; one black, the other brown.

'Are they for us?' I clapped my hands in gleeful anticipation.

'The black one is for you, Angelo,' Father said. The black horse was fine-featured, with a long neck, and a thick mane and tail. A perfect white star emblazoned the centre of his forehead.

'Thank you, Father.' Angelo quietly patted his horse's neck.

Father handed him the reins, gave him a leg up into the saddle and finally turned to me.

'The brown one is for you.'

My eyes prickled with tears, and before I could stop myself, I threw my arms around my father and gave him a big hug. He stiffened and backed away. I quickly released him, turned, and instead threw my arms around the horse's neck. I buried my nose in his long black mane, stroked his soft brown coat and breathed in that distinctive smell of horse. The horse pawed at the ground, tossed his head and twitched his ragged black tail. A crooked white blaze ran down his nose, and several white scars marked his rump. He was nowhere near as pretty as the horse Angelo sat astride, but he had this lively gleam in his eyes. I loved him at once.

Father gave me a leg up, and then led us both out through the rear gates, across the road and into the large paddock where our horses and ponies grazed. The ground sloped away gently into the distance, and beyond I could see my father's extensive fields of fruit trees and vines.

'Come on, Angelo!' I shouted. 'Race you to the far side.'

We were both well-versed in horsemanship. We already owned ponies, and each of us rode my father's horse whenever he allowed it, but it was so exciting to know that this magnificent creature belonged to me. We raced across the field, my horse instinctively knowing what I expected of him. He swerved this way and that to avoid bushes, with only the slightest pressure from my knee. I thrashed Angelo and then turned back to try my new steed over a few tree trunks that lay in the paddock. He cleared them easily. What a wonderful horse. What good friends we would be.

'I will call him Willow because he bends so easily,' I told Mother when I reached her side.

'You make a perfect pair.' Mother's wide grin matched my own.

'And I will call mine Jet,' Angelo fingered the well-worn leather cord that hung around his neck, 'after the stone in my ring.'

Father beamed at him.

I could scarcely believe that the powerful beast beneath me was mine. Laying my face close to Willow's neck, I whispered, 'I promise to take good care of you always, fair Willow. Always and forever.'

I listened to Angelo's gentle snoring as I lay awake, desperate. I knew that I should have used the latrine one last time before I came up to bed, but I had not. I could use the chamber pot in our bedroom, but I hated the embarrassment of slopping out the next morning.

I crept downstairs and paused at the tapestry curtain. Should I walk through to where Father and Enricho sat enjoying a goblet of wine? But if I did, I would need to explain why I was going outside, and then Father would ask why I did not use the chamber pot instead. That would be even more embarrassing. I continued to linger behind the curtain, uncomfortable and undecided. I could clearly hear my father's voice.

'I tell you, Enricho, I will never say this to anyone else, especially not his mother, but I despair of that boy.'

I cringed. Of course, he was referring to me. He would never speak of Angelo in this way.

'But Pietro,' Enricho sounded surprised, 'you should be proud to have a son like Francesco. He is kind, thoughtful and gentle. What more can you want?'

'The boy has no ambition. Look at me. I am prosperous, respected by everyone, and fabled for my ability to drive a hard bargain. How will he ever take over from me and be a success?'

'Perhaps his talents lie elsewhere. Have you seen how the other children adore him? They would follow him anywhere. Perchance he will be a great leader one day.'

'Leader of what? He is disobedient, so the Church will not have him. He despises learning, so the universities are no place for him. He hates the shop, and unlike Angelo, he takes no interest in the textiles. I despair. Whatever will become of him?'

My head bowed under the heaviness of my father's sigh.

'What of his mother – what does she say?'

'His mother simply spoils him.' I heard the sploshing of liquid. 'More?'

'Thank you, no.'

'I have never spoken of this, but when she was giving birth, Pica saw some sort of vision. As a result, she believes that Francesco is special and destined for greatness.' Father paused. 'You must understand; it was a terrible labour. She lay wracked with pain. Delirious. She became convinced the baby would die unless we moved her down to the stable, as if she believed she was delivering our Lord Jesus himself. Of course, I did as she asked. You do anything to calm them in those circumstances.'

'Yes,' Enricho said quietly. 'I remember.'

I could hear the pain in Enricho's voice, and I felt so sorry for him. Had Father forgotten the tragic circumstances of his friend's loss?

'I sometimes wonder what would have happened if I had refused to move her. What if I had pointed out that she was in great pain and talking nonsense? He might have died at birth, leaving the way clear for Angelo to become my first-born and inherit everything.'

'Pietro, how can you say such a thing?' Enricho cried.

'I would say it to nobody but you, my friend.'

'Then I beseech you, do not. You have two healthy sons. Our Lord God has seen fit to bless you, and here you are, wallowing in self-pity.' Something, it sounded like Enricho's goblet, banged against the surface of the table. 'I want no more of this conversation.'

'Enricho, I did not–'

'Francesco is a fine boy. I should be proud to have him for a son. As should you be.' A chair scraped back. 'You are a fool, Pietro. You do not recognise good fortune unless it carries a price tag.'

'Enricho, my friend, please sit down. Have some more wine.'

'I will drink with you on the morrow, but for now, I must bid you good night before I utter words I may later regret.'

As Enricho stormed across the room, my legs found motion, and I flew back up the stairs to my bedroom. Angelo snored gently, oblivious to the deafening pounding of my heart. I made use of the despised chamber pot and clambered in beside him.

Angelo whimpered in his sleep. A bad dream no doubt.

'Hush, Angelo, you are safe, I am here.' I stroked his head. 'Hush little one.'

My father's harsh words echoed round and round in my head. Sleep evaded me. As I lay there, I swore an oath that one day my father would regret wishing I had died at birth. One day I would make him proud.

CHAPTER THREE
SEARCHING FOR A CAUSE

When I reached the age of fifteen, Father announced he had successfully enrolled me in the group, *Societas Iuvenum*. It was a youth group that met every week, usually in rotation at each member's home, to enjoy fine food and entertainment.

'I do not want to go,' I sulked.

'But Francesco, you will be mixing with the sons of nobles and lords.' Mother glanced across at Father and continued. 'We are honoured that they have accepted you into their group.'

'They accept me only because of my money.'

'That would be my money,' Father said.

'I would rather play with Elias.'

'Do not be ridiculous,' Father snapped. 'Elias is the son of a farmer. He will never be allowed to enrol in such an elite group.'

'Then I will not either.'

Father threw his hands in the air and stormed out of the room.

'You will do as your father bids,' Mother said in a voice sterner than I was used to.

With little choice in the matter, I joined the group, and before long became elected *Provosti,* responsible for organising activities. I still occasionally saw Elias, but with less in common, we drifted apart.

My new best friends, Sergio, Josepo and the ever-thoughtful and more serious member of our group, Antonio, were all the sons of nobles. Sergio's father was a lord who had fought in the

Crusades, and Sergio vowed to one day follow in his footsteps. Josepo's father was a count and, as the eldest son, Josepo would inherit the title. Antonio's father was also a count, but he was the third son and so had determined to take his vows and become a monk. The proposition of being locked away from the world did not appear to fill him with the same horror that it did me.

Oh, how I envied them. Here was I, the son of a merchant, set to inherit a shop full of textiles that held no interest for me. Whenever anybody asked me about my future, I would recall my father's words, 'I despair of that boy.' Instead of giving them an answer, I would try to distract them with my songs and lute playing, or, as I grew older, by buying another round of ale.

Prestigious as the families of my new friends might have been, I was the wealthiest amongst us. My father relished my newfound connections and lavished me with a generous allowance that allowed me to dress in the finest finery, to drink the finest wine and to entertain in the finest fashion. As we grew into adulthood and traversed the boisterous circuits of the various taverns, I played my lute, sang the loudest, drank the most and picked up the tab on every occasion. Never had the son of a merchant been so well-loved by the noble youth of Assisi. And yet, as time went on and the bouts of gaming and drinking blurred one into another, emptiness festered, and at times threatened to overwhelm me.

'Francesco.' Sergio staggered across the tavern holding onto one of the barmaids for support. 'What are you doing stuck in the corner on your own? Why so gloomy?' He released the barmaid and patted her bottom affectionately as she made her escape. 'I shall see you later.' He winked at her, and then slapped me on the shoulder so vigorously that wine spilt from my goblet. 'Come, my friend. Join us.'

He dragged me to my feet and pulled me towards a group of our friends. Furniture crashed to the floor as we wove our chaotic way across the room.

'Sit,' my friend insisted. 'No point in being miserable on your own. Come on, give us a tune.' He looked at me and frowned. 'Where's your lute?'

'At home. I did not feel like singing tonight.' I flopped down next to Josepo, ordered another round of drinks and tried to join in with the banter.

Josepo grabbed a barmaid as she passed by, desperately trying to balance her tray. 'Come here, my lovely, give me a kiss.'

'Let me go.' The barmaid struggled to escape from his embrace and her elbow knocked my goblet. Wine splashed over the floor and splattered her skirt.

'Do not worry,' Josepo laughed. 'My friend here will compensate you for the loss of your fine dress.'

I blushed with embarrassment at his insensitivity. 'Leave her be,' I said.

Josepo released her while I dabbed at her hemline with my silk scarf.

'Get off me,' she snapped.

I held out a coin. 'Recompense for the damage.'

'You are all the same, you lot. Do nothing all day, then spend more on wine in a night than I earn in a week. You think you can buy anything.' She turned and pushed away through the laughing crowd, ignoring my proffered coin.

I stared gloomily into my empty goblet, clutching the refused coin in my palm.

'Oh come, now,' Josepo said. 'What ails you tonight, my friend?'

'She speaks the truth, does she not?' Quiet fell over the tavern. I looked around to establish the cause. A monk had entered, holding out his bowl. I recognised the Almoner from the Abbey, collecting money for the poor. He shuffled his way through the tables. The crowds parted to allow him access to every purse in the room. He passed by my table, and I carelessly tossed the rejected coin into his bowl. The barmaid dug a hand into her purse and handed over what must be, to her, a day's wage. Her generosity intensified my shame.

Within minutes, bowl rattling, the monk departed from the room, and the noise resumed its habitual roar.

'This will cheer you,' Sergio cried as the tavern erupted into applause at the arrival of a group of troubadours. They jostled their way through the crowd and settled into a space just in front of our group. An expectant hush fell. Sergio leaned across and replenished my wine with some of his own.

Usually, I loved the troubadours, with their songs of the dashing King Arthur, the Holy Martyrs Roland and Oliver, and the Crusaders. But on this night, their tales of chivalry and heroism only served to deepen my depression. Their stories reeked of bold heroes, brave adventures and chivalrous deeds. What had I ever done? What was the point of my sorry little life?

A suckling pig roasted on a spit over the fire. The skin blistered. Fat trickled over the carcass in small brown streaks and fell onto the burning logs, causing the flames to flare. The oil hissed and crackled, and visions of my once-beloved Silvia trapped in the pot-bellied stove returned to haunt me. The smell of the burnt fat mingled with the stench of the spilt drinks, unwashed bodies and cheap perfume. My stomach lurched, and my head swam in protest.

'What is it, Francesco? Why have you stopped drinking?'

I looked up at Sergio, who was once again standing before me, his expression full of concern. His arm was around another of the barmaids as he drank from his goblet. Red wine stains streaked down his dishevelled tunic. He swayed on his feet as he clung to the barmaid, his eyes unfocused. He leaned forward to speak to me, and I was conscious that his breath stank of stale wine, and suddenly I was seeing how I must look to my parents when I staggered home from these rowdy nights. My mother; whose heart had so convinced her that her first-born son was destined for greatness, and my father; who believed no such thing.

'Forgive me, Sergio. I am unwell. Something I ate. I need some fresh air.'

'Let me help you, Francesco.'

'I need to be on my own.' I threw some coins on the table. 'Enjoy the entertainment. I will see you again when I am worthy of your company.'

Outside, the evening was pleasantly cool. There were no clouds to detract from the magnificent night sky. Bright stars hung in the inky-black heavens and twinkled like distant candle flames. A full moon shone and lit my surroundings with a soft honeyed glow. A small stream trickled down the hillside into the valley below, providing the perfect setting for tree frogs. The air resounded with their amorous love songs.

I thought back over the stories of the knights who had fought to bring the Christian word of God to the heathens, to protect their lands and to win the love of beautiful women. What did their parents see when they looked upon their sons whose lives promised such purpose, justice, and honour? The thought continued to trouble me long after I had slept off the effects of the wine.

Father was about to leave on one of his buying trips, and I was, yet again, tasked with looking after the shop.

'It will be good practice for you.' He patted me on the back, kissed my mother farewell, nodded at Angelo and departed to join the other merchants who gathered in the town square to receive the Bishop's blessing.

Mother wept as he rode away. The passing of the years saw her worry far more about Father's safety as he travelled along the dangerous roads of the region.

Angelo placed his arm around her shoulder. 'Come, Mother, he will be safe in the cavalcade.'

'But the gangs know that they carry large sums of money as they travel to market, and valuable items on their return.'

'That is why they travel together; for protection.'

Mother struggled to muffle her sobs as Angelo escorted her upstairs, leaving me alone in the shop. I too was filled with despair, but for a different reason. I gazed around at the bundles of cloth, and at the bench with its measuring rod and cutting tools. This role as a merchant was my future, was what my father expected of me, was what I must do if I were to prove Father's words to his friend Enricho to be false. And yet, I could not bear it. There must be another way, but if there was, it cruelly eluded me.

I pondered my options. I was perfectly capable of extending my education. I could enter the University of Bologna to study law or the University of Salerno to study medicine, but I despised puffed-up academics and their book-learning. Since the day Silvia sizzled in that pot-bellied stove, I had not opened a book, nor wished to.

I could follow my mother's suggestion, enter the church and become a priest, but I still felt angry when I thought of my past encounters. I had been treated unjustly by Father Tiberio and remained resentful at the loss of my pet.

I could take my vows and become a monk, like my friend Antonio, but the monks tended to remain within the confines of their Abbey, and the thought of being cooped up and contained in that way filled me with dread. So here I was, toiling in my father's shop.

Two long, dull weeks passed by, and I was daydreaming about sitting outside my favourite tavern, Frenelli's, breathing in the heady fragrance of the roses, when a beggar appeared. He hovered in the shop entrance, his big brown eyes full of hope and his hand stretched out towards me. His nails were broken and black with dirt, his ragged clothes filthy, his hands and feet covered in sores. Whatever smell emanated from him, it most assuredly was not that of flowers.

I shooed him away like a stray dog. 'Be off with you.'

Before he retreated, I saw the light of hope in his eyes grow dim. He limped away; head hung low. As I returned to the shop, I glimpsed my reflection in the mirror: healthy, well-fed, dressed in fine clothes. Without thinking, but aware that I burned with the shame of my un-chivalrous behaviour, I snatched up the day's takings and ran after him.

'Please,' I gasped as I caught up with the bedraggled fellow, 'take this and buy yourself clothes and a decent meal. It was not my intention to be discourteous. I apologise. Please forgive me.'

'It is not my place to forgive you,' he said through broken teeth. 'That is something only God can do.'

I pushed the money into his calloused hand. 'Then let us trust that He will.'

He smiled and took the money. As I watched him hobble down the steep pathway and out of sight, a strange sensation of warmth enveloped my very being. Is this what it feels like to do right? Is this what it takes to earn God's approval?

'How could you do such a thing, Francesco?' My father's face burned with the heat of his rage as I recounted my good deed to him on his return. 'That's a week's profit gone.'

'But, Father, the poor man's need was so great, whereas mine is small.'

'If your need is small, Francesco, 'tis only because I act responsibly. Unlike you, I work hard to put good food in your mouth and fancy clothes on your back.' My mother rushed into the room, but my father ignored her and continued to berate me. 'Look at you, so proud of what you have done. Do you not realise, it was not even your money to give away? Where is the gift in that?

'But Father—'

'No, I will not listen to your nonsense any longer. Or yours, Pica. I despair of him. Go, Francesco. Be gone from my sight.'

I grabbed my lute and left for the nearest tavern, head bowed, my brief sense of pride crushed. But no matter how many jokes I told, how many songs I sang, or how much ale I consumed, nothing came close to matching the warmth and joy I had felt on giving to that beggar.

At least Father's return gave me back some freedom. I sat outside Frenelli's tavern entertaining Sergio with a tale about a dog, a duck and a careless cheese-maker, when news arrived that the newly appointed Pope Innocent III, had defied the Emperor and ordered the hated Duke Conrad to surrender his castle and lands in Assisi to the Church. Oh, such joy and celebration surged through the town, the likes of which I had never witnessed before. Musicians played until they fainted with exhaustion, only to be replaced with further fiddlers and yet more drummers. I danced until the rhythm of the drum hammered in my chest and echoed the pounding beat of my heart. The common people of Assisi showed more stamina than I had ever suspected them of possessing, and I matched them dance for dance, song for song and drink for drink.

When the day of the Duke's departure arrived, I returned to Frenelli's and watched the once mighty Conrad ride from his castle. The Piazza heaved with excited, hung-over bodies, all eager to boo the tyrant from our land.

The Duke was not alone in his entourage; a host of richly robed families followed him, many of whom I recognised.

'Why do they all leave, Sergio?' I asked as we quenched our thirst with cold beer.

'Who, them? They are friends of the Duke. Riders of his rich coattails.' Sergio spat into the dust and wiped his mouth with the back of his sleeve. 'Their homes have already been looted and occupied. What choices have they? Some will return with him to Germany. Others will no doubt take refuge in Perugia.'

Amongst the followers, I noticed a young girl with long blonde hair. Ten or eleven years old, I would guess. She sat regally, side-saddle, on a magnificent white horse.

'I have seen that girl before, Sergio. Who is she?'

'Ah, her. She is Chiara, daughter of Count Favarone di Offreduccio. He is a friend of my father and despises the Duke, but I hear that her father is sending her to Perugia for a while, as a precautionary measure, to stay with an aunt until the troubles settle down.'

I watched the girl ride out of the town, and despite my joy at the Duke's departure, a twinge of sadness touched my heart.

More celebrations followed, but they were short-lived, and as the town sobered up, a new awareness seeped into everyone's consciousness. The exiled Duke may have returned to Germany, and his loyal supporters might have taken their leave, but many, as Sergio had predicted, remained nearby in Perugia. The vast riches of land and property they left behind them brought the danger that, one day, they would return to re-stake their claim. With neither an army nor an outer wall, our town was vulnerable to attack. The new town leaders quickly concluded that we must build a wall to enclose the town and protect ourselves as best we could.

As the son of a respected merchant, I was appointed as one of the overseers for building the wall. I spent a few weeks working alongside a master stonemason. He taught me how to choose the correct blocks and trim them to fit snugly together. He showed me how to grind down the chippings and mix them with volcanic ash, lime, sand and water to produce a mortar for binding the stones together and filling any small gaps. Once I was proficient – and to everybody's surprise, not least my own, I was indeed proficient – the Master Builder allocated a team of men to assist me, and a section of the wall's construction was placed under my authority.

Amongst the men allocated to my team was my old friend Elias, who avoided the taverns, and so for many years I had only seen occasionally. Spending so much time with him again reminded me of how much I enjoyed his quiet, shy spirit. His companionship uplifted me in a way no amount of ale ever managed.

Our team quickly became the most productive. We worked like demons to produce the straightest and strongest results in the shortest space of time. Building a wall did not hold the glory of taking part in a crusade or bloody battle, but it was noble work for a just cause. I discovered talents I never knew I possessed: the heavy manual labour made me physically fit; the finished result gave me a sense of pride; my role in the process brought me esteem from the townsfolk, and my new physique brought me much admiration from the ladies. More importantly, my father's pride in me was restored. He also expressed the welcome opinion that my younger brother, Angelo, demonstrated far more competence and enthusiasm for the family shop and the textile trade than I.

When, as we feared it would, the town came under attack, my father concluded that he could spare me from returning to the drudgery of the shop. He encouraged me to follow my dreams, to join the battle and fight to defend our town.

Mother wept as I prepared to ride off into battle, but for once they were tears of pride. Father also looked at me with a new light in his eyes. Happy to be funding a more noble enterprise than my tavern bill, he presented me with a suit of shiny armour and a beautiful black war horse. I would have preferred to take my faithful Willow, but he was too delicate for such endeavours; unable to carry the considerable weight of the armour and lance.

In the packed town square, I knelt beside Sergio as the priest wafted incense while the Bishop led the prayers for our victory and safe return. My horse pawed the ground and tugged at his reins, anxious to be on his way. I was once again a boy, playing at soldiers, putting Elias, Dimitri, and Angelo through their paces as we charged the evil Duke with our sticks. The priest gave his final blessing, and we rode out of town, buoyed up by the cheers of the crowd. More than one maiden bid a tearful farewell to Sergio, who promised each one that his victory would be for her alone.

Our fresh horses thundered across the plain, spurred on by our excitement. My beautiful beast devoured the ground, and Sergio's magnificent stallion matched us stride for stride. The smell of horse sweat filled my nostrils and heightened my sense of exhilaration. My heart pounded as I caught sight of the battlefield at Collestrada; a grassy meadow close to the Ponte San Giovanni Bridge. As we galloped towards certain glory, I thought only of my father's pride when we returned victorious.

Alas, it was not to be. We were hopelessly outnumbered and outmanoeuvred. Lacking experience, I was hit a glancing blow and knocked from my horse on the very first charge. Fear surged through me as I lay in the mud, winded but otherwise unhurt. All around me, others fell, their screams piercing an indifferent world. Hooves thundered over the fallen bodies, and twice as I attempted to rise, a hoof caught me and sent me hurtling back to the ground.

I crawled over the bodies, seeking out Sergio's familiar face. I found him, but barely recognised my friend. He lay half buried in mud, his arms dismembered. Never again would he enfold a barmaid in his embrace. His face shone white with fear as I lifted his head onto my lap.

'Help me, Francesco,' he gasped. 'I am so cold.'

'All will be well, Sergio. I will get you away from this hellish place.'

Wrapping my cloak around him, I watched, helpless, as his eyes dulled and then glazed over. His face took on that ghastly pallor that only comes with death. A deep cry tore through me, the pain of loss unbearable. He was twenty-one; the same age as me. He should have his whole life ahead of him. How could this make any sense? I gazed at the sea of mutilated corpses that surrounded me, sickened by the cloying stench of blood.

'Why?' I cried. 'Such a senseless waste, so many young lives lost, and for what purpose?'

I heard the thunder of hooves behind me. I tried to stand, but I was too late. I barely registered the blow before I lost consciousness.

I woke up, but immediately wished that I had not. A thunderstorm raged inside my head. I tried to open my eyes, but the floor beneath me tilted. Oh my, how much did I drink last night? And then it all flooded back to me, the battle, the fear and the humiliation, and worst of all, the death of my good friend Sergio. Why did I continue to exist when he had died? He was such a kind and honourable young man; so many ambitions to achieve and so much to offer.

I lay still and tried to collect my thoughts. I was still alive. My father's extravagance with his choice of armour must have saved me from serious injury. For whatever reason, I had survived, and now I needed to do something with my life and justify my continued existence. But first of all, where was I?

I opened first one eye, and then the other. Totally black. Had the blow to my head rendered me blind? But no, I could make out a shape next to me. A man. As my eyes adjusted to the darkness I could see his face, but it was not one I recognised. I reached over and prodded his arm.

'Where are we, what happened?' I asked.

He opened his eyes and peered at me. 'Oh, you have come round. We thought you were a goner.' He looked me up and down. 'Francesco Bernardone, I'm told. One of the others recognised you.'

'Others?'

'There are about twenty of us.'

'But we must have numbered two hundred. What happened to the rest?'

'Some retreated and got away. The poor and badly injured were slaughtered where they lay and left to the wolves, but we – I guess the better-clad survivors – were brought to Perugia. They must think that we have wealthy families and intend to hold us for ransom.'

'Where are we?'

'Perugia's main dungeon underneath the Palazzo in the town's square.' He yawned, turned away from me, and within the blink of an eye, loud snores announced that he was once more asleep.

As the giddiness abated, I lifted myself onto one elbow and looked around. At first, my eyes still struggled with the lack of natural light. The only source of illumination came from beyond the metal grill in the door of our cell. As my eyesight adjusted further, I could see, as my neighbour had predicted, that there were about twenty sleeping forms surrounding me. One groaned in his sleep. One stood, shuffled and stumbled over the slumbering bodies until he reached the far wall of the cell, where he relieved himself. I guessed there must be a pit in the corner that served as a communal latrine. The appalling stench that came from it mingled with the stink of unwashed bodies. Tying my neck scarf over my mouth and nose, I sank back to the floor and fell into an exhausted sleep.

The changing of the guards and our twice daily meals were the only clues by which we could measure the passing of days. We quickly grew tired of our diet, which consisted of bread, occasionally supplemented by a few olives or items of fruit. The guards handed out sacks filled with straw for us to sleep on; infested with insects and mice. After a couple of nights of being bitten by both, I decided it was more comfortable to sleep directly on the sandy floor of the cell.

Our captors said that negotiations for our release were underway, but time dragged on, and our health suffered.

In a bid to retain some level of fitness, I spent my days walking round and round the small cell, stumbling over my companions' feet as I circuited the tiny space. At first, they shouted at me to stop, but gradually they joined me. Over the course of a day we would walk several leagues, an activity that induced a trance-like state. Despite our dire circumstance, through quiet reflection, I found I was able to escape my prison walls. I dreamed again of becoming a famous knight and performing deeds of chivalry.

While I thought of my noble future, I also reflected on my less than noble past. What pain I had caused my mother with my selfish, debauched behaviour. How must she have felt, wondering if I lay amongst the broken bodies on the battlefield? I prayed that by now my father had been approached for ransom, thus alerting her to the fact that I was alive. As I thought about my mother's fears and anxieties, I vowed that I would never again be the cause of her distress. I *would* make my parents proud of me.

But first, I needed to survive.

'One day I will be famous across the world as a man of God,' I sighed.

'You arrogant donkey, who do you think you are, Jesus Christ?' snapped Lois, a fellow prisoner who sat beside me and overheard my lament.

'Forgive me. I have no desire to be famous and no intention towards arrogance. I am simply repeating what my dear mother saw in her vision of my future. Her belief that I have one gives me some confidence in our survival.'

'Ah, mothers,' Lois grinned. 'Such is their faith; each one of us is a God.'

I became very friendly with one prisoner. He was clearly of noble birth and went by the name of Giovanni. The other prisoners mistrusted his expensive clothes and callous-free hands. In these cramped conditions, we were all aware how simple it would be to arrange an accidental trip into the latrine, or to drown someone in the water barrel while the guards were distracted. So, when Lois, the self-appointed leader of our group, accused Giovanni of being a spy, I leapt to my new friend's defence.

'Come now,' I said, 'how could he do that? He is never out of our sight.'

'He could pass them secret messages with his gestures when they bring us our food. See how they favour him.' Lois pointed at Giovanni, who crouched in the corner, an olive in each hand, supposedly lending weight to Lois' suspicions.

'I'm sure, Lois, that each of us here is impressed you could think of such an obscure method of secret communication, but anyone of us could do that.' I pointed a finger at him. 'Could you not?' A few of the group sniggered as Lois flushed. 'Friends, I will vouch for this man, Giovanni. He has a noble heart and a loyal spirit. Let us not forget who our enemies are, for only our enemies win if we turn on each other.'

'Francesco is right, Lois.'

'We must stick together.'

'Let us walk together and pray,' I said. 'Giovanni, will you walk with me?'

Giovanni leapt to his feet and fell into step behind me. The others joined us one by one until only Lois remained sitting.

'Come, my friend, we will soon be free. Let us remain strong and united so that our loved ones may welcome us back, each and everyone, with no further shame or grief.'

For a moment, I thought he would reject my peace offering, but he rose slowly to his feet, joined the chain of bodies, and together we walked.

Months dragged by and winter approached. Our dungeon grew cold beyond bearing. A rasping cough racked my body. Before I could drink from the water barrel, I needed to break through a layer of ice, but then the freezing cold water chilled my stomach and gave me cramps. After several visits to the latrine, I was exhausted and lay slumped against the damp wall.

'Francesco, you must walk,' Giovanni said, his face full of concern.

'I cannot.' Another bout of coughing tore through me. When I wiped my mouth, my hand came away speckled with blood.

'Get up.' Giovanni hauled me to my feet, wrapped my arm around his shoulder and supported me in the morning shuffle until my legs collapsed from under me. As I hung on Giovanni's neck, I became aware that our fellow prisoners had gathered around the cell doorway. Giovanni shouldered his way to the front, dragging me with him.

Two women stood outside the gate, one a very young maid. Her innocence lit up the cell like a holy beacon. Our group fell silent as we gazed on her simple beauty until another painful bout of coughing bent me double and broke the spell. A guard unlocked the cell door, and while he and his comrades, swords drawn, guarded the entrance, the two women entered. I looked up into the face of the young maid, her brow furrowed with concern.

'I know your face,' I said when my coughing ceased.

It was the young maid who had sat so regally on her horse the day the Duke rode from the town. Her name came to me in a rush – Chiara.

'Is there anything we can bring you to ease your suffering?' she asked.

'This is no place for a young maid,' I replied.

'My aunt and I are here to help, in any way that we can.'

Her face was so close to mine; her sweet breath caressed my cheek. I wanted to reach up and touch her, but I was afraid that she might take fright. The way she looked at me, her expression filled with compassion, reminded me of my mother.

'Is there any way you can get a message to my mother? Tell her I am well, that I will be released soon?'

'Gladly.' She smiled, and the walls of my cell melted to nothing. 'Your freedom is not far away now. Take heart.'

Her aunt pushed small parcels of food – nuts, dried meat, and cheese – at each of us. We devoured them shamelessly.

A week later, Chiara and her aunt returned and pressed more food parcels into our hands.

'Your mother is well. She sends her love and this jar of soothing syrup for your cough.' Chiara pressed the welcome pot into my hand. 'Fear not, you will soon be home.'

'I thank you for your kind words. You cannot know how much comfort they bring me.'

She tilted her head and regarded me closely. 'I know not why, but I am certain that this will not be the last time I bring words of comfort into your life.'

I believed her.

It seemed like much longer, but after a year in prison, a deal was at last reached between the exiled nobles and the townsfolk of Assisi. The aristocrats returned to their property and positions of power, but the merchants, such as my father, were to be granted a much greater involvement in the administration of the town. Our families paid a handsome ransom, and we – the sons of the wealthy – were released.

Our gaolers threw open the doors to our prison and danced with us as we staggered out into bright sunlight. The heat from the sun's rays streamed down on my ragged body and filled me with elation. My heart leapt when I saw my parents in the crowd. I stumbled towards my mother's waiting arms. Tears of joy ran down our cheeks as we embraced for the first time in over a year.

My recovery was a slow process, but I defied the doctor who said that I was unlikely to survive. In time, I returned to some semblance of my former self. My friends claimed to have missed me, but few visited, and I came to believe that they missed the copious wine my allowance paid for, rather than my company. My health may have improved, but whenever I thought about my life so far, my heart remained heavy. What a mess I had made of it.

CHAPTER FOUR

THE CONVERSION

During my long convalescence, I acquired the habit of taking rambling meditative walks and elicited some joy from the fact that I no longer needed to do so in tiny cell-sized circles. I returned home from one such walk to find Giovanni, my prison companion, sitting at the dining-room table with my father, enjoying a goblet of wine.

'Francesco, my friend.'

He stood to greet me, and I raced over and threw my arms around him with such enthusiasm that we fell to the floor in a heap. We lay there and laughed until our sides hurt.

'What brings you here?' I asked once we recovered and took our seats.

'You, of course. I am off to join Gaultier de Brienne's army. He is on a crusade to rescue Sicily from the Germans. I have come to see if you want to join me and earn your spurs as a knight?'

'Gaultier is my hero, one of the best-known knights in Italy. I would be honoured to join you.'

'Bravo.' My father patted Giovanni on the back. 'This is just what Francesco needs – to be useful again.'

My chest swelled with pleasure. Today was the first occasion where Father had demonstrated any pride in me since the day I rode out of Assisi to challenge the Perugians.

'Please, Francesco, do not go,' my mother begged. 'You are not well enough. Look how you have already suffered.'

'If this is my calling, Mother, I must answer it.' I hugged her hard. 'You would not have me do otherwise, would you?'

'But how do you know it is, Francesco? How do you know?'

Although I assured him it was not necessary, my father once again spent a small fortune on armour and a new war horse. He paraded me around in front of all the neighbours, proud of his first-born son once more.

On the evening before we left for the battlefields I experienced a vivid dream. I approached my father's house on horseback, but strangely it was not the house of my youth. Instead, it was transformed into a splendid castle. I entered the hall, and I could see the walls festooned with brightly coloured banners. Two crossed swords hung on the wall in the shape of a crucifix and before me was a beautiful bride, also on horseback. Surely this was a premonition of how I would be received when I returned from the battles as a victorious and brave knight. But even as a part of me rejoiced in the picture before me, another part sneered. Was this all that glory meant to me – a luxurious castle and a beautiful maid?

As I urged my horse forward, a hand tugged at my spurs and slowed my horse to a halt. Below my towering steed stood the barmaid whom I had once insulted with my spilt wine and proffered coin. In her hand, she clutched a rein, and beside her stood my beloved Willow.

'So,' she said, her voice a faint whisper that forced to me to lean low in my saddle to catch her words. 'You have learned nothing, Francesco. Nothing at all.' She turned and walked away, taking Willow with her.

I woke in a sweat, and when Giovanni arrived to collect me, I knew what I must do.

'Please, take my armour,' I begged. 'Accept it in recognition of my gratitude.'

'It is beautiful armour, but I cannot possibly take it. Your father bought it for you.'

Remembering my father's anger when I gave his money to the beggar, I considered this point carefully before concluding: 'He gave it to me as a gift. It belongs to me now, and therefore I can do with it as I please.' I struggled out of the outfit. 'It pleases me that you have it. You have earned the right to wear the very best.'

We swapped armour, and I felt proud to wear Giovanni's older, simpler attire while he shone so brightly in my former finery. Being a knight, I realised, was not dressing to look the part, but more about achieving inner nobility.

Six other would-be knights joined us, and together we rode through town with our heads held high, the white Crusaders' cross emblazoned across our chests. Flags waved, children danced around our horses, young women threw flowers and ran up to tie their scarves to our lances, then blew us kisses as we rode out through the town gate.

I searched for my father's face in the crowd, and my heart leapt as I spotted him. He stared at me in my simple attire and then looked at Giovanni in the new armour. I watched as he slowly shook his head before he turned and walked away.

By the time we made our first camp, doubts about our mission were already creeping into my mind. My new companions had become loud and bawdy, worse than the tavern friends I thought I had left behind. Giovanni increased his volume and level of coarseness to match theirs.

'Will Gaultier ride alongside us once we are there?' I asked Giovanni.

'Gaultier will be too busy at home pleasuring his rich wife. After all, it is her extensive lands in Sicily he seeks to preserve.'

I shook my head, puzzled. 'He seeks to save the Christians of Sicily from the invading Germans, does he not? I thought the Pope declared his mission a crusade.'

'The Pope can be easily convinced where Crusades are concerned,' Giovanni said.

'I care not,' laughed Marcello, a big bearded fellow with arms strong enough to break an infidel's neck without even trying. 'So long as there are maids aplenty for the victors to enjoy, then I am game.'

'What do you mean?' I asked.

My enquiry met with raucous laughter, and more vivid descriptions of past examples of their conquests than I could stomach.

I slipped away to the lakeside and knelt down to drink the cool, clear water, struggling to collect my thoughts. The boastings of my companions bore little resemblance to the noble tales of chivalrous knights told by the troubadours. Nothing I had heard today supported the idea that we were here to do God's work. My mother's words came back to me: *How do you know, Francesco?* I splashed water on my face and groaned. Had the attractions of glory and the need for my father's approval so blinded me?

Green and silver ripples played across the surface of the lake. I remained on my knees, seeking answers until giddiness overcame me and the lake misted over. The distant voices of my companions faded from my hearing; the noise replaced by a dove gently cooing in the trees behind me. The bushes around me shivered as a light breeze rustled through their leaves. The voice, when it came, was as clear as any I had ever heard.

'You are wrong. You are wrong. Turn back.'

I trembled with the shock of it and searched the area for the owner of the voice. I found only the wind and the trees and the dove, which cocked its head up and down and then took to the air, wings flapping wildly. I struggled to breathe as a cold black cloud enveloped me.

When I came round, the world had grown dark, and my arms lay loosely across the shoulders of two of my colleagues as they supported me along the path leading back to the campsite.

'Are you ill, Francesco?' Giovanni asked as they laid me down and covered me with a cloak.

'I know not. I was … there was … I must have passed out.'

When I woke the next morning, my head burned with fever, and I was too weak to stand.

'You must go on without me,' I told Giovanni. 'I will catch you up in a few days when the fever has abated. Fear not, I have plenty of food and water.'

'Are you sure, Francesco? I will stay with you if you wish.'

'I do not,' I said, noting the relief that washed over Giovanni's face.

My brief companions in glory saddled their horses, wished me well and left me alone with my troubled thoughts.

My parents had encouraged me to attend church regularly. School had ensured that I was well-versed in the Bible, said my prayers daily, and went to confession once a week. Despite this, I would never have described myself as *religious*. And yet, here I was, like Saul on the road to Damascus, hearing a voice telling me what I should do. Was I ill, or had God spoken to me? My brain burned as the fever raged and I slipped in and out of consciousness. Days drifted by.

Eventually, I grew strong enough to eat, and then well enough to mount my horse. At a walking pace, we made our way home. My horse trundled through the town gate where I was confronted by a small group of youths. They pointed at me and laughed.

'Look at Francesco now.'

'He is no knight. He's a simple coward, returning to his mother.'

They taunted me and poked sticks at my horse, then laughed as he reared and I fell from his back in a crumpled heap at their feet.

'See how he tumbles.'

'Look, the town fool.'

One youth kicked me as I lay on the ground. The rest joined in. I curled myself into a ball. Boots rammed into me until I fainted with pain and exhaustion.

Weeks passed, and once more my mother nursed me back to good health. She would sit by my bedside, bathe my forehead with a lavender compress soaked in cold water, and offer words of endearment.

'Do not fret. Rest and get better,' she sighed. 'One day, God willing, you will become a good Christian.'

I saw nothing of my tavern friends, but my good friend Elias often frequented my bedside. As my health improved, Elias would accompany me on short walks into the Piazza, where we would sit by the fountain and watch the old men gossip and slap each other on the back as they laughed and told their bawdy stories.

My health gradually improved, and my spirits lifted. One morning, feeling so much better, I decided to take a walk down the pathway that ran from the Piazza towards the town gate. Unlike others in the town, it was not steep and would take me out onto the hillside where I could enjoy some fresh country air.

Traders bustled around their shop fronts, crying out to passers-by, trying to persuade them to sample their wares. A donkey and his owner ambled towards me, hauling a wide cart loaded with sacks of vegetables. Forced to step back from the pathway, I sought refuge in the entrance to the butcher's shop. The rhythmic sound of his cleaver striking the carcass of a dead animal assaulted my ears and drew my eye. Sickened, by the gory sight, I turned away, and my foot knocked against a bucket that swam with entrails waiting to be collected by the pig farmer. I recoiled at the image of the young animals feeding on the remains of their slaughtered mother. As the loaded cart passed by, it was with a sense of relief that I stood back down onto the pathway and staggered on my way. I stepped aside to avoid a pile of steaming donkey dung, turned a corner and came to the small yard that housed the workshop of the town blacksmith; Mario.

'Francesco, my boy, you look decidedly unwell?' Mario, wearing his distinctive leather apron, loomed over me. 'Come and sit with me for a while and drink some water.'

I followed him into the smithy, a cool dark space with stone walls and the comforting smell of smouldering coals and hot metal.

'We have not seen you about town for some time, Francesco. I hear you have been very sick?'

'Yes, but by God's grace, I am now well.'

'Hmm. I think you had better sit here before you fall.'

I sank with gratitude onto the stool that he indicated and accepted the water he offered. 'I will rest a short while.'

'You must not exert yourself.'

'I yearn to walk out onto the hill and enjoy some fresh air.'

Mario put his finger under his chin and gazed upwards. 'I was there myself last week. Or was it the week before?' He closed one eye, pursed his lips and then shrugged his shoulders. 'It was when they hung the heathen they caught stealing the golden chalice from San Pietro. Take care of yourself, Francesco. It is a gentle walk, but you must not overdo it.'

I promised to take heed, bade him goodbye and trudged on until I reached the hill.

The mountainside towered above the town, covered in a light mist, with its peak bathed in pastel hues. The sky was bright blue and sprinkled with wispy white clouds. Below me lay the plains, so flat that I could see far away into the distance. I remembered how we rode across them on the fateful day of that futile battle. What difference had it made, apart from those who had lost their lives, their loved ones, or their health?

A light wind blew across the hilltop, stirring me from my reflections. I yearned for the fresh air to clear my head after the stench from the town, but instead, another putrid smell invaded my senses. I turned and then stopped in my tracks, heart pounding. Before me, a body dangled from the gallows. I realised who he was – or had been; the thief that Mario had spoken of. So now, here he hung.

Three crows pecked at his head. Maggots spilled from the two black holes that once housed a pair of eyes. Flies buzzed around the macabre scene. I gagged and fell to my knees. Dear God, whatever happens, whatever your intention for me, do not let me end up here. No wonder they call it *Collo d'Inferno*, the hill of Hell.

The birds took to the sky and circled above my bowed head, caw-cawing their annoyance as I first prayed for the soul of the thief, and then begged God to let me know what direction my life must take. Nobody but the crows replied.

I worked my way slowly back towards the noise of the busy town, my ears still filled with the sound of the crows.

I stepped over the gully where Assisi's householders emptied their slop buckets each morning. It ran with excrement, but my nose burned only with the stench of the thief's rotting corpse.

When I reached the smithy, Mario rushed forward and frowned. 'Francesco, my boy, I told you not to overdo it.'

I sank once more onto the stool.

'You are very pale, my friend. Rest for a while and I will help you home.'

Concerned about the fragility of my health, Mother insisted that I venture beyond the walls of the town only when escorted by Elias, and to save her further heartache, I agreed. Elias and I were on one such walk when we came across a small grotto. I stood at the entrance to the cave and peered into the darkness. It was impossible to make out any details.

'Be careful, Francesco – sometimes these caves are inhabited by wolves.' He reached into his shoulder bag. 'Take my flint box and this pack of candles. I purchased them for my aunt in town this morning. I can easily get some more before I return.'

We made a small fire and used it to light one of the candles. I begged Elias to stay in the glade while I explored the cave alone. Soft flickering candlelight reflected on the glistening walls that were the colour of creamy milk. Despite a slight scent of dankness, my feet sank into the dry sand, and the cave showed no sign of being used by wolves or any other animal. The silence was like none I had ever experienced, and the urge to pray overwhelmed me. I tilted my candle and allowed it to drip onto a small rock. Then I stood it upright in the pool of molten wax until it hardened, freeing my hands for prayer. I sat enveloped in the silence and thought back over my life.

I remembered my selfish, indulgent and excessive lifestyle. I cringed when I reflected on my attempts to become a heroic and chivalrous knight, and how they had ended in failure. I flushed with embarrassment at the thought of my proud boasts predicting my return as a famous knight. Instead, I was a failure, a coward, and a fool. Oh God, what a muddle I had made of my life so far. I groaned.

'Are you alright, Francesco?'

I crawled back to the mouth of the cave to reassure Elias that I was well. The sun was dipping behind the town below, staining the grey tendrils of clouds pink. A few early bats flew from crevices in the rocks. Hours must have passed.

'I am sorry, Elias, I lost track of time.'

'It is of no matter.'

'I do not know why, but I feel this place is very special to me. I need to stay longer. But do not let me keep you. You return home, and I will come and find you when I am done.'

Elias smiled at me. 'I will return to the town, tell your mother you are safe, and then return here with food and wait for you.' When I raised my hand in protest, he shrugged. 'I will be comfortable here with this stone as my pillow, the leaves as my mattress and the stars as my mantle. Take as long as you need.'

I returned to the cave, where I replenished my candle and knelt to pray.

Dear God, help me to understand. What is it that I need to do? My whole life has been a failure. I have been such an ass. How can I redeem myself? My thoughts went round and round in my head, over and over again until I was exhausted. Please, my God, if you have a purpose for me, speak. I promise to listen.

I focused on the candle and stared into the flickering flame which gradually grew bigger and bigger until it filled my vision. The warmth from the flame wrapped itself around me like an affectionate embrace. Calmness engulfed me as God's love poured into my very soul. Without being able to explain how or why, for the first time in my life I felt complete, whole, and cleansed. God was with me, a part of me, showing me that I was forgiven and that I could start anew. I wept copious tears of gratitude and relief, thanked Him, curled into a ball and fell into a deep sleep.

When I woke the next morning, I was hungry but so alive and filled with joy. I crawled out of the cave, shook Elias awake, and rushed home to tell my parents how I planned to turn away from my old life.

'I promise you, Father, I will never embarrass you again. My drunken revelry is a thing of my past.'

'Thank God, Francesco,' wept my mother.

'So, what will you do with your life?' my father asked.

'I know not the details yet, Father, but I do know it will be God's work.'

My mother's smile lit the room. 'It is as my vision revealed it would be. My son will become famous across the world as a man of God.'

Father sighed. 'So, you will join the priesthood, Francesco? Or a monastery?'

'I will not,' I replied.

'Then let us celebrate the event of your calling when we have full cause.' My father turned his back on me and left the room.

As unimpressed as he appeared to be by my lack of a tangible direction, my father agreed to pay for one last celebration so that I could part from my old friends on good terms. He provided copious wine and excellent food and even arranged for a visiting group of troubadours to provide entertainment. I sat in the corner and watched everyone enjoying themselves, glad that this side of my life was finally behind me. I knew not what my future held, only that I wanted to share my experience in the cave – to share with others how it was to experience forgiveness and to begin a new life.

The musicians played on. All around me my friends cavorted and gorged themselves on the bountiful feast my father's sense of status obliged him to provide. As I watched the evening unfold, it struck me that what I was leaving behind was not so much these people – many of whom I still held a dear fondness for – but rather, I was leaving behind this life of excess. I recalled the sense of joy I had experienced upon giving the day's takings to the beggar, and I realised that what I truly wanted was to live my life as Jesus had. I wanted to live in poverty, rich only on the rewards that come from experiencing God's love.

'What is it, Francesco? Why are you so quiet?' Honorri asked, his voice full of concern.

Josepo joined us, placed his hand on Honorri's shoulder and tried to steer him away.

'Leave him be, Honorri; he's thinking of getting married, I can tell. He has that look about him.'

'Come on, Francesco,' begged Honorri. 'Who is it to be, what is she like?'

'I am indeed thinking of marrying a beautiful woman,' I replied.

'Come on then, tell us, do not keep us waiting, what's her name, is she rich?' asked Josepo. He was always on the lookout for a rich woman. His father might be a count, but he was not a wealthy one.

'Her name is Lady Poverty,' I said, 'and she is to become my lifetime bride.'

They looked at me as though I was mad, but what did I care. I simply ignored them and made my way out of doors, into the cool evening air. I turned my back on my former friends and my past life. The very next day I would begin my new life. I would start with the penance suggested at my last confession; a pilgrimage to Rome to give thanks at the tomb of St. Peter.

The vast, gloomy interior of the Basilica resembled a cross, with wide aisles lined by a forest of pale marble pillars. The walls, richly decorated with frescos, depicted scenes from the Old and New Testaments, but in contrast, the altar looked elegant; simply decorated with a linen cloth and three golden candlesticks.

I looked down through the grating into the crypt that housed St. Peter's tomb and thought about the apostle. In his weakness, Peter denied Jesus three times. Jesus forgave him, and from that day he followed Christ's example and dedicated his life to spreading the word of God.

But was this also what God wanted of me? How did He want me to spend the rest of my life? I knelt and asked God to show me how I could best serve Him? I waited for a sign, but none was forthcoming.

I continued to kneel as people squeezed past me to give alms in honour of St. Peter and carelessly tossed their offerings into the collection bowl. Many of these people were well-dressed and clearly of noble birth, so it shocked me to see how meagre their donations were. I walked up to the collection bowl and emptied the entire contents of my purse into it.

'If you truly love your God, you must give until it hurts,' I told them.

I walked out onto the Piazza, feeling a lightness I could not explain. Within moments, I was approached by a filthy beggar. I remembered the joy I had experienced from giving money to the poor old man who had approached me at the shop, but then realised I had nothing left to give.

'I do not have any money, my friend. I have given it all to St. Peter.'

He shrugged and turned away.

'Wait.' I looked down at my fine clothes. 'I will swap my clothes for your rags,' I told him.

If I expected eagerness or gratitude, I was to be sorely disappointed.

'I thank you, but no. Fine clothes are all well and good, but who would give money to someone dressed like that? I would starve in such garments.'

'Oh, yes, I see. Then let us barter. I will exchange clothes with you for the rest of the day, and take your place here, begging. You can enjoy your day and return this evening when we will swap back into our own clothes. I will also give you any money bestowed upon me.'

He looked dubious, as one would when confronted by a mad-man. His gaze lingered on the fine material of my tunic.

'I promise to beg well on your behalf,' I said. 'You will not be disappointed.'

He agreed. We quickly exchanged clothes and he left, prom-ising to return later.

The beggar's garments irritated my soft pampered skin. Sitting in the shadows of the Basilica, the begging bowl at my feet, I itched and scratched and imagined a million lice crawling over my body. But I stayed in place and begged my heart out, noting the various reactions that resulted from my pleas for charity. Some people completely ignored me and rushed past. Others smiled and dropped a coin into the bowl. Many chastised me, called me names, and told me I should be out seeking work. It dawned on me that although good fortune made this my first experience with a begging bowl, I had spent my whole life living on the charity of my parents. I resolved that however my future unfolded, I would never again expect something for nothing.

By midday, the sun was directly above. There was no shade. Rivers of sweat ran down my body. White blisters formed on my exposed skin. By the time the sun sank and disappeared behind the buildings, I was so thirsty that my head throbbed. I was extremely relieved when the beggar returned. We exchanged clothes, and I handed him back the bowl containing far fewer coins than I had hoped.

'You have done well,' he said. 'I thank you.'

'This is doing well?'

He peered again into the bowl. 'Oh yes, it is enough to buy food for tonight and breakfast on the morrow. Often I manage neither.'

'Then I am glad. How did your day fare?'

His face broke into a smile. 'Oh, I have swaggered about in your fine clothes. Men have greeted me kindly, and women have smiled at me shyly. I knew not that such things were possible for me.' He lifted his chin high and looked me straight in the eye for the first time. 'Tomorrow I will seek out a job, so I may buy a fine outfit and find me a good woman to settle down with.'

'Then it has been a good day,' I said, 'and we have both gained much from it.'

Several weeks after my return from Rome, I was out riding through verdant meadows, still decorated with a rich tapestry of late flowers. The weak sun broke through the clouds and flooded everything with a soft golden light. Willow snorted and twitched his ears as we ambled down a quiet grassy track. He brushed against a bush of rosemary. The aroma reminded me of the focaccia and cheese that Mother had packed in my saddle bag. My tummy rumbled, but I decided it was too early to stop for lunch yet. I allowed the reins to fall so I could turn the pages of my Bible and read:

'And now a leper approached him, bowed low and said 'Sir, if only you will, you can cleanse me.' Jesus stretched out his hand, touched him, and said, 'Indeed I will; be clean again.' And his leprosy was cured immediately. Matthew, 8, 1–4.'

A bell rang, putting me on instant alert. A leper must be nearby. Had I inadvertently strayed too close to San Salvatore delle Pareti, the local leprosy hospital? These disfigured creatures terrified and nauseated me. My hands were clammy as I picked up the reins and turned Willow around, intending to retrace our steps and vacate the area as quickly as possible.

We had not cantered far when the words I had just read returned to haunt me and forced me to rein in. What a hypocrite I was. These many months past, I had prayed and prayed to God for guidance, and now, when he had given it, I had run away.

I turned Willow back towards the leper. As I drew near, the stench of his rotting flesh assaulted my nostrils and challenged my resolve, but I thought of the example given by Jesus and forced myself to dismount. The leper's face broke into a toothless smile, and he reached out towards me with one bony arm and one blackened stump. Though I recoiled on the inside, my feet held firm as I emptied the coins from my purse into his outstretched palm.

'Thank you, kind sir.'

On an impulse that I might well have prevented, had I felt it coming, I grabbed his hand and kissed it. He leapt back, more startled by my action than I.

'You must not,' he cried. 'Do you not know what I am?'

'I know well how you suffer,' I replied. 'Please, take me to the lazaretto. I wish to visit.'

'But why? You are healthy. You must stay well away from us.'

'I must do God's work,' I told him. 'Right now, I feel sure that this is what he is calling me to do.'

I spent the next few days in the colony, caring for the terminally ill and marvelling at how a few kind words or simple deeds from me were so generously repaid with gracious thanks and looks of admiration. These people, who appeared to have nothing, were capable of giving such a wealth of spiritual gratitude. Truly humbled I left, not fully understanding why God had sent me there, but thankful that he had.

On my arrival home, I could hear Father shouting. I left Willow tied to a post in the yard and rushed inside.

My father stood beside the table; his face the colour of ripe plums; his fists tightly clenched, and with sweat trickling down his forehead. Mother sat with her elbows on the table and her head in her hands. I could see from her shaking shoulders that she was in tears and rushed to embrace her.

'No! Do not touch her', yelled my father. 'You have gone too far this time.' He moved around the table and came towards me, wagging his finger. 'It is bad enough that you spend all of your time moping about with your nose in that Bible, but now, I am told, you have given away more of my money.'

'But Father—'

'Shut up,' he snarled. 'You have given *my* money, to a *leper*.' Spittle drizzled down his chin. He wiped it away with his silk handkerchief.

'But Pietro, he has only goodness in his heart,' Mother pleaded.

'I will not allow you to bring that *filthy* disease into our home. You are no longer welcome here. Do you understand me?'

Mother stood and walked over to my father, grabbed his sleeve and sank to her knees. 'Pietro, I beg you to reconsider. Please, he is your son.'

Father shrugged her arm away. 'The whole town thinks he is mad, and we have to consider Angelo. I wish you had never been born. I wash my hands of you. It is done.' He turned back to face my mother. 'Never mention his name in my presence again.' He stormed from the room.

Once again, I was a mere boy, hearing my father wishing me dead. I walked over to where my mother still knelt, wrapped my arms around her shoulders and kissed her head. I could hear her sobs as I left. I stumbled down through the town, out by the east gate, and made my way towards the sanctuary of San Damiano, my favourite chapel.

Despite the hurt inflicted by my father's words, as the chapel came into view, my spirits lifted. Positioned halfway down a steep hill, San Damiano provided a wonderful view of the plain below. Surrounded by cypress, pine and olive trees, it was a safe haven for the myriad of birdlife that sang, accompanied by the cacophony of cicadas.

A priest cared for the church and lived in the small adjoining shack. Both buildings were in a poor state of repair. A pile of rubble lay where it had fallen the previous winter during a, particularly ferocious storm. The mortar had crumbled badly, and several large stones clung perilously to their positions, threatening to fall and join the ever-growing pile of debris. I gazed at the church, enraptured by its tired beauty and simplicity.

Broken hinges creaked and groaned as I entered. My eyes were drawn to the simple altar and then to the Byzantine crucifix decorated with pictures of salvation, and depicting an enchanting image of Christ suspended on the cross. His expression exuded love, encouragement, and forgiveness. I prayed for God to show me what I should now do. How should I use the lessons He had blessed me with to redirect my life? How could I best serve Him?

As I prayed, the shafts of light that streamed through the windows grew ever brighter until a soft glow surrounded the image of Christ on the crucifix. His halo glittered with renewed intensity as He looked down kindly upon me. His eyes shone, and He smiled. It was at that moment that I heard the voice:

'Francesco, go and repair my Church, for as you see, it is in poor condition.'

My heart pounded. At last, here was the direction I had prayed for – my quest – to rebuild the church, make it beautiful, and gain my Holy Father's approval in the process.

PART TWO

CHAPTER FIVE
THE JOURNEY BEGINS

'Willow stand still! We must finish this packing and get away before the family return from church.' I lifted another bolt of fine lace onto his back, tied it securely, and examined the selection – lace, silk, and velvet in a medley of colours. 'What say you, Willow? These textiles should be sufficient to raise the funds we need, do you not think?'

Willow nodded his head and pawed the ground.

'Good boy. Now stay here quietly while I leave a note for Father. By the time we return, I am sure his anger will have mellowed.'

I ran into the shop, grabbed some paper and Father's pen, and scribbled a quick note:

> *Father,*
> *I have been called by God to repair San Damiano Church. I*
> *have therefore borrowed some textiles, against my inheritance,*
> *to raise sufficient funds for the building materials required.*
> *God Bless, Francesco*

Satisfied with the justice of my actions, I covered the fabric with some clean sackcloth and patted Willow's burdened rump. We set off for Foligno, the best textile market in the region, where I would undoubtedly achieve the highest prices.

Two days later, I gathered my empty sackcloth into a bundle and prepared to return home. Willow nuzzled my elbow, and I turned to stroke his velvety soft nose. As he snorted hot breath into my outstretched hand, seeking the treats I so loved to give him, my chest grew tight. Tears rolled down my face. If I truly wanted to carry out God's work and repair His Church, I needed to raise money. A lot of money. I remembered my words in Rome: *If you truly love your God, you must give until it hurts.* Thus far I had sold only that which belonged to my father. The real sacrifice would come from giving up that which I valued most in this world – my beloved Willow. I pressed my face into his warm neck and breathed in his familiar smell.

It took me a further two days to find the right owner for Willow: a young boy whose eyes lit up with a joy I recognised, and whose father would pay the right price. I said goodbye and walked away, my heart aching but my head held high.

I had work to do.

I returned to San Damiano with a large bag of gold coins, sought out the priest and held out my offering, but instead of accepting it with gratitude he backed away and folded his arms across his chest, slowly shaking his head.

'But it is for the church. There is sufficient here to make considerable improvements to the building.' I offered him the bag once more, thinking he must be confused as to my intention.

'I understand well enough, Francesco. But I will not come between a father and his son. I want no involvement in a family feud.'

'Feud?'

'Your father was here looking for you, telling anyone who would listen that you robbed him. He has searched the town and left nobody in any doubt as to his intentions when he finds you.'

'I see.' I lowered the bag of coins and considered this unwelcome news.

The priest stood beside me with his hands clasped in prayer and his head bowed, awaiting my response.

After a long silence, I sighed and placed the bag of coins on the windowsill. 'I raised this money for the church, not for myself. If you change your mind it will still be here.'

The priest nodded but departed without the bag.

Father's voice shook with anger as he stood in the courtyard and confronted the San Damiano priest.

'Where is he? I know he is here somewhere.'

This visit was my father's third attempt to discover my whereabouts in the past few days. On each occasion, his temper had grown worse. I crouched down, scrambled behind the choir stalls, squeezed under a trap door and into the shallow space beneath – an empty tomb I had discovered while replacing some broken flagstones.

'Francesco, where are you? I know that you are hiding in here. Come out and face me now, you snivelling coward.' He stomped into the church, his breath, loud and laboured. 'Francesco, come here, now!' His voice rose to a shrill scream.

I tried to quell my breathing, but my heart pounded so loudly I was sure that he would hear.

His footsteps grew louder as he crossed the floor. One edge of the trapdoor allowed a sliver of light to enter my hiding place, but as his footsteps drew nearer, his shadow caused the light to flicker and diminish until it was totally obscured. He stepped onto the wooden hatch. I prayed it would not disintegrate. Dust showered into my eyes and up my nose. I struggled to check a sneeze. And then, just as I thought he would discover my hiding place, I heard Father stomp his way back to the courtyard.

Clearly the priest had failed to make his escape because I could hear my father: 'Tell him, he stole from me, and I demand justice. He had the audacity to write a note saying he was borrowing against his inheritance. *His* inheritance, I ask you.'

'Signor Bernardone, Francesco is your first-born son. Surely, he is entitled–'

'Entitled! What gives him the right to inherit anything after the way he has disrespected me? If he refuses to see me, I will report him to the court of justice. Do you hear me?'

These confrontations could not go on. Three times now the priest had been subjected to Father's abuse. I needed to take responsibility and confront his anger. After all, I overcame my horror of wearing the beggar's clothes in Rome, and my fear of the lepers; surely, I could find the courage to face my father.

Father was rolling up a bolt of fabric when I arrived. He turned to face me as I entered the shop. Not wishing to be disturbed by a late customer, I locked the door behind me – an act I quickly came to regret. He strode across the room and slapped me hard across my cheek. Instinctively my hand went to my face. His fist punched under my chin, knocking me to the floor. My ears rang like church bells on a Sunday morning. I lay there, dazed, confused and shocked at how angry he was.

'How dare you make me the laughing stock of the town?'

His boot thudded into my stomach. I gasped for breath. He kicked and kicked. I curled into a ball, arms over my head while my father rained blows upon my legs and back.

'Father, I beg you. Have mercy.'

By way of answer, he dragged me across the floor, hauled me through the cellar door and shoved me down the stairs. Dazed by the fall, limbs twisted and bruised, I could do nothing to protect myself as he locked me in chains like a rabid animal.

'You can stay here, imprisoned, like the common thief that you are.' He turned his back on me and stomped away.

The door slammed. The key squeaked and then clunked as it turned in the lock.

I lay there gasping for breath, stunned and confused by the strength of hatred that my father had shown towards me. He was a proud man, and I may have injured his pride, I might have made him the subject of gossip, but did he not love me at all?

Night fell and with it the temperature. I lay in the cellar and shivered. Nobody came near until the next day was well under-way. At the sound of the key turning in the lock, I cringed into the corner, now wet with urine. The door opened, revealing

Mother's outline. I could just make out her shape as she tiptoed down the steps, glancing over her shoulder as she descended.

'Francesco?' she whispered into the darkness. Never had a voice been more joyous to hear.

'Mother? I am over here.'

She reached my side and let out a low moan. The sound pierced my heart with the realisation that I had, yet again, brought so much grief to this good woman.

'Your father will not be gone for long.' She wrapped a blanket around my shoulders and fed me spoonfuls of chicken soup thickened with rice: her answer to all of life's ills. The aroma alone would have soothed me, and the taste was heavenly, but I gleaned the greatest comfort from her feeding me like a child. Once I had eaten, she laid down the bowl and grasped my hands between hers.

'How could you upset your father like this? He is a good man. He works hard for what we have, and you stole from him.'

Her words came as a surprise and pierced my heart.

'But I was doing God's work. I did not intend to make Father angry. I hoped that he would understand from the note that I was only borrowing against my inheritance.'

'You have humiliated him in front of the whole town. You robbed him, Francesco. God would not want you to treat your father with such disrespect. You are my first-born son, and I love you, but what were you thinking? I am so ashamed of you.'

A lump came to my throat. I was unable to swallow and found it difficult to breathe. Tears filled my eyes. 'I am sorry, Mother … I am truly sorry. I will make it up to him. I will find a way.'

'It is too late for that.'

'No, I will–'

'Shhh.' She tilted her head and listened. 'I must away. Fear not, I will return as soon as I can.'

The next day she returned with the key to my chains and released me.

'Leave now my son. You must not return, or he will surely kill you.'

'But what will he do to you when he sees that you have freed me?'

'He is my husband. Leave me to worry about that.' She pulled me to her, kissed my forehead and then pushed me towards the stairs. 'Quick, you must leave this place. It is no longer your home.'

When I reached the door, I turned back to plead with her. 'But, Mother, once he has had time to calm–'

'No, Francesco. Please. Go.'

She pushed the door shut and locked it behind me. My mother had banished me from my home, leaving me alone in the court-yard shivering like a whipped dog.

I did the only thing I could do. I returned to San Damiano and began to work on the repairs. The work proved a welcome distraction from the pain I felt at my eviction.

It was not long before my father turned up at the church. This time, I faced him.

'Father, I know that you are angry. Please forgive me for my thoughtlessness. Here.' I lifted the bag of coins from where it still sat on the sill. 'Your money. I have not spent a jot.'

He snatched the bag from me. 'I want you to leave Assisi.'

'You cannot mean that, Father.'

'Indeed, I do. I never want to see you again.'

'What can I do to make amends? Please, tell me and I will do it.'

'Leave, and never come back. I want nothing more of you.'

His words struck a fiercer blow to my chest than his fists had ever done.

'Then once again I am sorry, Father.' I bowed my head. 'You ask me the one thing that is not in my power to grant you. I have God's work to do here, and I cannot leave. He, at least, has need of me.'

'We shall see about that,' he said.

A few days later, a representative of the town's magistrates visited and summoned me to appear in the town court at the Temple of Minerva. 'You must come to the court and explain why you do not obey your father's wishes.'

'I am a servant of God,' I told the clerk. 'As such, I do not recognise the authority of your court to pass judgement on me.'

He left, but the very next day I received a summons to appear before the Bishop Guido of Assisi in the Piazza of Santa Maria Maggiore; a command that I could not refuse.

Even though it was early morning, a large crowd had gathered in the square. As I approached, the air hummed with a buzz of excitement, like a nest of angry bees. The Bishop sat resplendent on a wooden throne covered in gold leaf and red silk cushions. My father sat on the Bishop's right-hand side on the raised podium erected in front of the Bishop's palace especially for the occasion. I noticed Father Tiberio standing behind the Bishop. He had recently been promoted to the post of Assistant Bishop and was now responsible for, amongst other things, the management of the Cathedral San Rufino. As I drew near, one of the Bishop's guards grasped my arm and led me to a small platform immediately in front of the stage. I looked up at my father; his eyes were cold and full of anger. The crowd at my back "oohed" and "ahhed" as the Bishop outlined my father's case against me.

'By the authority of this court,' he concluded, 'I demand that here, in this public place, you renounce all claims to your birth-right and that you return at once any money or belongings you may have previously acquired from your father.'

The crowd murmured their approval. I stood there, shrinking under the glare of my father's hatred.

'Please, God,' I whispered, 'give me strength.' I turned my back on my father and faced the crowd. 'I hereby renounce all worldly claims,' I proclaimed, 'including any and all inheritance I may once have been considered entitled to.' I removed my cloak and boots and laid them in a pile at my feet. I threw my purse with its few remaining coins on top. 'Until this day,' I told the now silent crowd, 'I have called this man, Pietro Bernardone, my father. But hereafter, I desire nothing else but to serve God, who is my Father in Heaven.'

I continued to remove items of clothing until I stood completely naked. Somebody gasped, and all heads turned to look at my father, who rose to his feet, his face flushed bright red. He shook his head slowly from side to side, stepped down from the podium, and gathered up my belongings. Eyes averted, he negotiated the steps down to the cobbled street and pushed his way through the silent crowd.

I was surprised to feel the Bishop's hand on my shoulder.

'Take this man back to my home and find him an outfit of warm clothes,' he said to Father Tiberio. Then he took off his cloak and draped it over my shoulders. 'Go in peace, my son.'

Father Tiberio escorted me inside the Bishop's palace and summoned the gardener.

'Fetch me your oldest undershirt, tunic and cloak,' he demanded.

The gardener scurried off.

'You know, Francesco, you may think that by receiving the Bishop's blessing today, that you have done well, but you have merely demonstrated that you are unworthy of his faith in you. You have denounced your poor father and caused him considerable humiliation and embarrassment, which he does not deserve. He is a God-fearing man, a good man, always generous to the church, and an excellent father to both you and your brother. I see nothing in this to justify the pride I see on your face.'

His words wounded me deeply. I had not intended to humiliate my father. Before I could respond, the gardener returned with a frayed, but clean and adequate set of garments. I dressed, thanked them both and took my leave.

I strode out of the town gate, dressed in my recently acquired outfit. My family ties and my old life now lay behind me. At the age of twenty-five, I felt born anew. Whatever Father Tiberio might say, my life was no longer my own. Now it belonged to God. I was a Knight of God – the son of a Heavenly Father, rather than the earthly one who had disowned me so easily. I skipped down toward the valley, singing a song I learned from the troubadours. I had no idea where I was going, only that I was on my way.

Snowflakes drifted in the light breeze, the first of winter. Snow covered the ground. Early cyclamen shone through the drifts like jewels. The birds joined in with my song as I danced my way along the path, laughing at my breath, which appeared like clouds of smoke billowing before me. Tiny drops of dew clung to the delicate spider webs, and the bushes sparkled with fragile necklaces of silver droplets.

My peace and sheer joy at the morning's beauty were rudely interrupted by a group of three young men, who jumped from the undergrowth and confronted me.

'Who are you?' the tallest of the three demanded as they gathered menacingly around me.

'I am a knight of God.'

They laughed and pushed me from one to the other until I stumbled. One jumped onto my back, knocked me to the floor and searched for my purse.

'He has nothing.'

'I have nothing except my undershirt, tunic, and cloak.' I continued to smile, although my heart was pounding.

'Then we shall take your tunic and cloak.'

The man stood, and stripped the items from me, then he kicked me so hard that I rolled into the icy stream that ran beside the footpath. The thin layer of ice cracked under my weight, and I fell into the shallow water.

'Some Knight of God – you cannot even fight your way out of a puddle.'

They laughed again and ran off, leaving me battered, bruised and in danger of freezing to death. Dressed only in my thin undershirt, I dragged myself out of the stream and continued on my way. I resumed my singing in an effort to restore my confidence.

The setting sun created crimson streaks across the horizon. The temperature plummeted. Every part of me ached. I had stumbled through the valley all day, frequently stopping to huddle in any shelter that I could find. A pile of fallen leaves, a dilapidated building, anything that would offer the protection I needed to thaw the cold from my bones. None could provide the warmth that my body craved, and I began to fear for my life until I came upon a small monastery and sighed with relief.

A rusty bell hung from an even rustier chain beside the door which contained a small metal grill. I rang the bell and shivered, peering anxiously through the mesh. A candle flame flickered and cast shadow patterns as someone shuffled towards the door.

'Who is it?' enquired a disembodied voice.

'My name is Francesco. I have been attacked by ruffians who have beaten me and stolen my clothes. May I come in and per-form duties for you in return for food and a floor to sleep on for the night?'

The monk allowed me into the building. He gave me some cleaning work to undertake, but he was understandably suspicious of my dishevelled appearance and watched my every move. The smell of hot food in the cooking pot over the open fire inspired me, and I whistled cheerfully in anticipation, as I scrubbed, swept and mopped where directed. My chores complete, he rewarded me with a bowl of soup, a blanket to keep me warm and showed me to my sleeping quarters – in the stable with the animals.

Blowing on my hands, I settled down in the straw and counted my blessings. So, I had a few bruises, but there was much for which I should be grateful. I was no longer hungry, my simple shelter gave me warmth and protection from the snow, and I was beginning my new life in a stable surrounded by animals, just as Jesus began His.

After a good night's sleep, and realising that I was close to Elias's village, I left my warm stable and travelled the short distance, in time to join him for breakfast. We shared a meal of cold ham and boiled eggs while I brought him up-to-date on all my adventures.

'You cannot go around dressed like that Francesco. You will catch your death.'

He scurried off and returned proudly brandishing an old brown tunic, a spare belt, a cloak and a pair of sandals.

'They may not be exactly new,' he sniffed the tunic, 'and the odour could be better, but hopefully they are better than nothing.'

'Thank you, Elias. I am most grateful. I know I want to embrace poverty, but to brave the first snow of winter, dressed only in this thin undershirt, is not something I would wish to repeat.'

Elias smiled. 'What do you intend to do next?'

'Firstly, I need to continue with my unfinished work, rebuilding the church at San Damiano, the quest given to me by God. After that, I am not sure what He has planned for me, but no doubt He will let me know. Whatever it is, I am determined to share my beliefs with others. I want to help them understand how it feels to love and support one another, to bathe in God's grace and live in anticipation of everlasting life.'

'Is that how it is for you, Francesco?'

'Indeed, it is. Come with me, Elias. Join me in my quest. We will have great fun, just as we did as children. But instead of our games of soldiers, we will be God's army, carrying out the Lord's work.'

Elias looked wistful. 'My friend, I may have considered it, but the Bishop of Bologna has offered me a position as his scribe.'

'The Bishop's Palace may well be comfortable, but surely it will not be as rewarding? Come with me, Elias.'

'I'm sorry, Francesco, but you have your dreams, and this is mine.'

We promised to keep in touch, and I made my way back to San Damiano, where the priest seemed pleased to see me, and once again was happy to share his meagre rations of food. By this time, I was running out of spare boulders and tiles for the roof, so I set off on foot for Assisi to acquire additional supplies. With no money to my name, my plan was to offer my services in exchange for materials or to ask for supplies in the name of God, bestowing a blessing in return. I was by no means confident of the reception that I would receive, and I approached the town with trepidation in my heart.

My first stop was the stone merchant, who shook my hand warmly and pointed to a stack of forty tiles, roughly cut but salvageable with a little work.

'I cannot spare as much as I would wish, Francesco, but you may take these if they help you.'

'I will need transport,' I said. 'Willow is mine no more.'

'So I hear,' the stone merchant said, eyeing me sadly.

'I will work for the gift. My building skills are not insignificant. Name the hours you require, and they are yours.'

He grunted. 'I do not doubt your prowess, Francesco, but you have your own work to do, do you not? My boy will deliver the tiles to the church tomorrow.'

'I thank you for your kindness and I invoke God's blessing upon you and your family.' I turned to go and then paused. 'Tell me, why it is you do not send me on my way as a wastrel and scoundrel who abused his father cruelly? That was what I had anticipated.'

He took his time before answering. 'I heard your declaration in the Santa Maria Maggiore,' he said eventually. 'I also witnessed your own father's intolerance. Your quest to rebuild God's church is a noble one. Do not be surprised if you find that many here harbour more kindness towards you than in times past.'

My heart warmed at his words, and they held true as I moved through the town, greeting faces that had once gazed upon me as though upon a mad man. By sunset, I had secured the promise of all the materials that I needed, and I left the town with several cries of "Godspeed" ringing in my ears.

I completed the work at San Damiano within a few months, and we celebrated the completion with a service of blessing. I was exhausted by the physical work but uplifted and elated to discover that the Bishop was in attendance. He approached me after the service ended.

'You have done well, Francesco. What now for you?'

'Excellency,' I kissed his hand. 'I heard the word of God. He directed me to repair His church, but I am not sure what He wants of me now. I hoped for further guidance.'

'The word *church* could be seen to cover more than one,' suggested the Bishop. 'San Pietro Della Spina could also benefit from some work.' He smiled broadly, and my life for the next few months was sorted.

I continued with the rebuilding in the same way as before, collecting stones from the nearby countryside and the town of Assisi. One hot sultry morning, I was pulling a borrowed cart loaded with stones through the town, when I spotted my mother hurrying along on the other side of the street.

'Mother. Stop. It is I, Francesco.' She carried on walking. I abandoned the cart and crossed the street, running until I was directly behind her. 'Mother, please.'

She drew to a halt but kept her back turned to me.

'Would you not look on me, your first-born son?'

Slowly she turned around and raised a tear-filled gaze to meet mine.

'What is this?' I pointed to a bruise on her left cheek, and her hand flew up to cover it.

'Stay away,' she said. 'I cannot speak with you. I beg you, Francesco, if you ever cared for me, you will not come near us.'

'But–'

'I must go.' She spun around and walked away.

It was with an enormous heaviness in my heart that I let her go.

A few days later Angelo appeared at the church just as I was scraping layers of ingrained dirt from the roof of the nave. I stopped at once, climbed down from my perch on a wooden plank and stood before my brother. He now towered over me.

'Good morning, brother,' I said. 'To what do I owe this honour?'

'Honour?' He made as if to spit but then seemed to recall that he was in a house of God. 'How can you even mention that word? How dare you call yourself a man of God when you have treated our parents as you have? Mother is distraught. My father has warned her that if she ever speaks to you again, he will beat her black and blue. Stay away, do you hear. Leave us all in peace. May you rot in your treachery.'

Before I could utter a word in response, he stormed out, leaving behind only his words, which hurt me deeply. I still thought of him as my little brother, despite the fact that he was now so much taller than me.

The San Pietro Della Spina priest appeared beside me, his eyes kind and his voice gentle. 'I am sorry to hear your brother speak to you this way, Francesco.'

'I have lost everything,' I said, with my voice catching in my throat.

'Such as?'

'My mother's love. My father's approval.'

The priest raised his eyebrows at this latter statement.

'I grant you, he gave little enough of it,' I conceded, scrubbing my hands on a rag. 'But then there is my brother's respect. I have lost my friends, my inheritance and my comfortable home.' I threw the rag into the dirt at my feet. 'I have nothing.'

'Nothing?' The priest swept an arm to take in the piles of rubble, the dusty windows and the growing collection of donated roof tiles, all awaiting their transformation. 'You have all this, my son.' He paused, laid a hand on my shoulder and held my gaze. 'You, Francesco, have what most of us can only pray for and are unlikely to have granted. You have heard the Word of God, spoken directly to you.'

I bowed my head. 'Go and repair my Church,' I whispered.

'God loves you.' The priest squeezed my shoulder. 'You have His approval. You have His work to do. Why would you want more?'

CHAPTER SIX
THE EARLY MINISTRY

The next stage of my quest became the restoration of the Porziuncola, the small church located in the valley beneath Assisi. It did not take long for this beautiful and inspiring church to become my spiritual home. I yearned above all to be allowed to spend my days there, living the life of a hermit and dedicating my life to prayer. But for now, my mission was to rebuild it.

The biggest problem was getting the stones back to the church, located some way from the town. The stones were heavy, and I could only manage one, or at most a couple, at a time. I was therefore very pleased when an old friend of mine, Bernardo di Quintavalle, offered to assist me with his horse and trailer.

Bernardo was a rich merchant whom I knew well from the days of my misspent youth. His parents were both dead. He had never married, claiming there was no woman alive who would not bore him to death after a few conversations.

He demolished a dilapidated building on his land and brought trailer-loads of stone to use for the church repairs. Often, he brought his evening meal to share. We sat for hours, enjoying the food and each other's company.

With Bernardo's help, the work on the Porziuncola was soon complete. Exhausted but exhilarated, I stood before the entrance and looked at the facade. The stones, a mellow golden colour, glowed in the final rays of the setting sun. The heavy wooden entrance doors no longer squeaked but opened easily once more on their new pivot hinges, fashioned by the blacksmith; Mario. The stone doorway arched above me. The crumbled blocks had been replaced with stones donated by Bernardo and carved by me to blend seamlessly with the originals. The church was now fully restored to its former glory. I knelt in prayer and thanked God that I, a humble penitent, had been granted the privilege to serve Him in this way.

Bernardo joined me for a celebration supper.

'Thank you for the feast, Bernardo,' I said as I tucked into a slice of ripe melon. The sticky juice dribbled down my chin. 'This is delicious.'

'It is I who should give thanks. It is wonderful to feel useful.' Bernardo paused. 'Please, Francesco, join me at my home for supper on the morrow. I need to discuss something of importance with you.'

'I should be pleased to.'

'It may take some time, so come for the night. I have, as you know, plenty of room.'

Bernardo lived in a beautiful house packed to the beams with extravagant furniture, silver plates, and golden goblets. The next evening, I sat amidst sumptuous surroundings, before a table laden with freshly baked bread, succulent ham and a selection of fruit and cheese, all served with quality wines. My home life had once reeked of such indulgences. I realised now that my poverty had ceased to be a sacrifice. I no longer missed the luxury. The only thing I did miss was the company and conversation, which is why I had valued Bernardo's help and support these past few weeks.

Eventually, my friend grew quiet.

'What is it, Bernardo?'

'How is it that you have such faith, and you were able to give up everything so easily? You live such a hard life, yet you are one of the most joyous people I know.'

I laid down my bread and regarded my friend. 'I am one of the lucky ones,' I told him. 'God chose to speak directly to me. If it were not for this, I might have found my path harder to follow. But, I do believe that I would have found a way eventually.'

'How so?'

'God's signs are everywhere if only we open our eyes and hearts to see them.'

'I am not sure I follow your meaning.'

'Well, as an example, last week when we held Mass to celebrate the completion of the Porziuncola, the priest read from the Bible, thus:

> 'The Kingdom of Heaven is upon you. Heal the sick, raise the dead, cleanse the lepers, cast out devils. You received without cost; give without charge.
> Provide no gold, silver, or copper to fill your purse, no pack for the road, no second coat, no shoes, no stick; the worker earns his keep. Matthew, 10, 9–10.'

Bernardo looked at me with a slight frown and a raised eyebrow.

'Open up your heart and your mind to God's messages, Bernardo. It was as though God spoke to me directly. Through those words, He granted me confirmation that I was doing what he wanted. Those words guided me to give away my shoes and even my belt. Instead, I now use this simple piece of rope.' I touched the cord that hung around my waist. 'God's communications go far beyond words. Do you understand what I am saying?'

'I think so.'

'The very day after that Mass, I began to preach. Not in a formal manner like the priests, but in a way that shared my joy.' I pushed aside my plate and goblet. 'I believe God wants me to reach out to people, to awake their emotions and touch their hearts so that they welcome Jesus into their lives.' I looked across at Bernardo. He was looking uncomfortable as he stared into his wine goblet. 'Bernardo, Jesus is our example. If we follow in His footsteps, we will also enjoy a loving relationship with God, experience His divine love and the promise of eternal life.'

'I know, and I much admire the way you bring the word of God to people. Especially the way in which you point out their sins and shortcomings without causing any offence.'

'To offend is not my intention. I merely offer a clear path for them to follow. I try to encourage them to offer kindness, mercy and compassion to others.'

'I fully comprehend your promises of poverty and chastity, but I struggle to understand your promise of obedience. When I think back to my childhood and remember the difficult times I gave my poor mother ...' Bernardo shook his head at his memories.

'Obedience is not about obeying instructions. It is all about instant and alert listening. It is about opening your ears, heart, and soul to listen, and then making an honest and loving response.'

'Oh, Francesco.' Bernardo sighed deeply. 'I am still unsure of what direction my life should take. I do not especially enjoy or take pleasure from the comfort that comes from my family's wealth. I do not yearn to be married or to have children of my own.' He shook his head slowly. 'I have prayed for guidance, but I have not received such a clear calling as you. No voice, no vision, nothing except these feelings that invade my mind.' He slapped his forehead with the palm of his hand and ran his fingers through his hair. 'My life – as it is now – is incomplete, empty and insufficient. I did think that if I helped you, by bringing you the stones for the rebuilding, then it would be enough to calm my troubled thoughts, but now I realise that I need to do much more.' He reached across the table and clasped my hands. 'Will you help me, Francesco?'

The feeling of responsibility was enormous. I could easily tell my friend to give away all his belongings, and join me in a life of poverty and prayer – but what if he was then unhappy, or if it was not the life that God planned for him?

We agreed to meet again in two days' time, giving us both space in which to pray for guidance. I also suggested that we include our friend Pietro Catanii in the discussion and prayers. Pietro, a priest, was a legal representative to the Bishop, and well-respected in Assisi. Bernardo agreed to go and see him the next morning.

When Bernardo retired to his bed for the night, I maintained a prayerful vigil asking God to help us with Bernardo's decision. I continued to pray my mantra – *My God and my all* – until morning arrived and I took my leave.

Two evenings later I met with Pietro and Bernardo at the Porziuncola. We sat under an olive tree and shared bread, ham, fruit and a bottle of wine for our supper.

Bernardo hardly ate. 'My friends, I know that I have asked much of you both, but my prayers have convinced me that I should give up my home and possessions and join you here, Francesco. I have prayed hard for the past two days, and although I have not been fortunate enough to hear God speak to me directly, I have come to the decision that the life you live makes the best sense for me.'

'I agree,' Pietro said. 'You should be with Francesco, and work alongside him.'

My heart skipped. My prayers had brought me to the same conclusion, but I worried that my interpretation of God's will might have been affected by the considerable comfort I would derive from his company. To have my thoughts confirmed by Pietro in such a supportive way was a relief.

'You think, or even know, that this is the best path for me?' Bernardo asked Pietro.

'Not only for you,' Pietro said, 'but also for me.'

'Pietro,' I touched his sleeve. 'What are you saying?'

'I have given a great deal of thought and prayer, not only to Bernardo's situation, but also to my own. I am a great admirer of our Bishop Guido. He has been kind and so very supportive of me. Due to his dedication and guidance, I am now expected to achieve the position of Bishop myself shortly. However, I do not believe that I would be comfortable in such a role. The politics within the church are difficult to manage at times. Overseeing such complex issues would distract me from the inner peace for which I am constantly searching. I truly believe that I should give up my position and accompany you both on your spiritual journey.'

Immediately we began to make plans. Bernardo intended to sell his home and belongings and distribute the proceeds to the poor of Assisi. Pietro had certain duties which he was required to complete before he could leave his position and take his place with us.

We decided to refer to ourselves as the Friars Minor. We did not want to be monks, even though we shared their vows of poverty, chastity and obedience. After all, monks have a place to live and worship, cut off from the rest of the world: a way of life which we did not want. We wanted to keep our lives simple, lives of humility. We wanted to be nomadic, to mingle with the world and share with others the beliefs that we enjoyed. We rejected the life of monks, and instead we became an order of friars.

I discovered a small abandoned hovel at Rivotorto, which we agreed would make an excellent base, somewhere for us to retire to for prayer and meditation between our preaching sojourns. A stream ran nearby, providing us with a good supply of pure water to drink and bathe. It was also conveniently situated between the Porziuncola, San Damiano and the tranquil grottos and glades of Carceri; an ideal place for us to retreat and pray. Our new life as the Friars Minor was about to begin.

Later that evening we went to St. Nicholas's Church to hear Mass, after which we prayed together. I picked up the Bible that was lying on the altar, opened it at random and read to my colleagues:

> *'If you wish to go the whole way, go, sell your possessions, and give to the poor, and then you will have riches in Heaven; and come, follow me. Matthew, 19, 21.'*

I closed the Bible, opened it again, and my heart surged as I recognised the same meaningful passage which had previously brought me so much comfort:

> *'The Kingdom of Heaven is upon you. Heal the sick, raise the dead, cleanse the lepers, cast out devils. You received without cost; give without charge.*

*'Provide no gold, silver, or copper to fill your purse, no
pack for the road, no second coat, no shoes, no stick; the
worker earns his keep. Matthew 10, 9-10.'*

Again, I closed the Bible, reopened it for the third time in homage to the Holy Trinity and read aloud:

*'And to all, he said, "If anyone wishes to be a follower
of mine, he must leave self behind; day after day he must
take up his cross, and come with me. Whoever cares for
his own safety is lost; but if a man will let himself be lost
for my sake, that man is safe. What will a man gain by
winning the whole world, at the cost of his true self?"
Luke, 9, 23.'*

Tears ran down Bernardo's cheeks as he realised that God was indeed speaking to him directly through these randomly selected passages.

I held the Bible above my head. 'These three passages will become the Rule of our Order, our contract with God, the words that will shape our lives. They are simple words, chosen by God. They will guide us as we serve Him.'

I closed the Bible.

A few days later, I climbed the mountain to Carceri. It was a hot day, and I sought shelter in the cave where I had originally found God. A shaft of sunlight illuminated the cave, and I prayed, wrapped in its marvellous light and warmth. It was as though I were speaking directly to God; I could hear His soft, comforting words of reassurance:

*'Be consoled my son. Rejoice in the Lord and do not be
concerned for your small number for verily you will grow
into a vast fellowship. Do not let your simple message and*

lack of learning make you afraid, because your faith will uphold and sustain you. You have many talents. You will develop wisdom and grow wise with the grace of my blessing. Go forth and bring tidings of peace unto men and preach repentance for the remission of sin.'

My heart was at peace as I walked back down the mountainside to share these revelations with Bernardo and Pietro. I now had the direction I craved; my quest expanded. No longer was I simply required to repair the physical structures of the churches, but also to deliver tidings of peace and to preach repentance for the remission of sin.

We used several places as shelter: the small hovel in Rivotorto, the caves above the town at Carceri and a small building at the Porziuncola. Over the next few months, our numbers gradually increased. Egidio, a farm labourer, decided to join us, soon followed by Philip. After them, Angelo, who had been a knight, and whose sunny disposition and engaging temperament put me constantly in mind of his namesake, my dear brother.

Pietro, Bernardo and I would each take one of the new recruits with us as we toured around the towns, preached, shared our stories and blessed the crowds of people who turned out to see us.

We were extremely grateful to receive a visit from Bishop Guido. He wanted to reassure us that we had his full support and that he recognised the good work we were able to do in reaching the hearts of the people to whom we ministered.

He explained that the Catholic Church was concerned about the damage caused by a few recent cases of corruption and immorality amongst high-ranking members of the clergy. Many people were disillusioned and disappointed. The Church was vulnerable to the preaching of heretics who falsely presented themselves as representing common sense and purity. Bishop Guido told us he was confident that our brotherhood could appeal to these, at risk folk, in a way that the formal Catholic Church could not, and serve as a bridge between the Church and her people. He acknowledged that our style of delivery might be considered by some in the Ministry to be somewhat irregular, but he knew that we always preached obedience to the Catholic Church. More importantly – to us all – he had faith that we would save many lost souls from an eternity spent in Hell.

Every time we returned to Assisi, another brother arrived and joined our happy band. All came from different backgrounds, and each had a very different temperament. Lucido had the urge to roam; he travelled off to preach for months at a time. Masseo was a huge burly figure of a man, practical, with considerable common sense. Leo was a priest and was to become my confessor and spiritual director, and one of my closest friends. He was also an accomplished scribe and therefore became my loyal secretary – writing was not a particular talent of mine. Juniper was a joy, with such a sunny, innocent and loving disposition that everyone he met was captivated by him. Pacifico was a French jongleur, a tumbler, acrobat, and musician. He had previously performed in the court of Frederick in Sicily where he developed the reputation of being a skilled composer. He often entertained us when we sat around the campfire after our evening meal. Then there was Barbaro, whose sometimes acid-tongue I cured via a brief diet composed of ass's dung: a strange and harsh penance perhaps, but an effective one. However, his grumpy disposition was not so easy to remedy, and we simply grew used to his moody presence.

With our numbers now grown to twelve, it was possible for small groups of us to travel further from Assisi and the local towns to deliver our message across Italy. However; our journeys tended to be somewhat random. On one occasion I was travelling along a dusty track with Masseo when we came to a crossing.

'Which direction shall we take?' he asked.

'Whichever God wishes.'

'But how will we know?'

I bade him close his eyes and spin around as quickly as he could, just as he had as a child. I laughed as his large frame wobbled to a halt.

'I am so dizzy. I can hardly stand.'

'Which road are you facing?'

He staggered and struggled to regain his focus. 'The road to Sienna.'

'Then to Sienna, we will go.'

One of the more sombre tasks that the Friars Minor undertook was to give long-term care and support to lepers in the various lazarettos. We lived alongside the patients, and our meals were the scraps left after they had finished.

I was asked to attend one such lazaretto, where the brothers needed my help. One patient's violence and blaspheming had become intolerable. Several brothers wanted to withdraw their care of him and asked for my blessing. I agreed to meet with this man, although I already knew that I could never condone abandoning a sick man to his fate.

'And who do you think you are?' the patient said as I arrived.

'I have come to assist you. What can I do to help you find peace?'

'Peace? How can I find peace when I stink with this wretched disease, and your friars are inept?'

'Inept?'

'They will not wash me. They will not do as I ask. They cannot bear to look at me.'

I took a long look at the man, whose skin was rotting and rancid, and who seemed not to be in possession of his soul. I closed my eyes and prayed for God's guidance; which quickly came.

'Well, then,' I said, removing my cloak and rolling up my sleeves, 'I will care for you myself.'

Masseo looked on with a doubtful expression while I fetched a tub and filled it with warm water, then added fresh herbs and rose petals. I poured jugs of water over each part of the man's body, and gently wiped away the grime. As I did this, I prayed:

*'In the name of Jesus, who called His twelve disciples to
Him and gave them authority to cast out unclean spirits
and to cure every kind of ailment and disease, pity this
unfortunate man, grant him freedom from this affliction
and endow him with humility, patience, and peace.'*

As my hands gently wiped his putrid flesh, I witnessed his skin
healing, and his stinking sores disappear. I continued to wash
him, uttering thanks and praise to God. The man, calmed by the
prayers, watched my progress. His eyes lost their startling glare
as the evil spirit was banished from his soul.

If ever I had doubted that I was the Lord God's instrument,
I would doubt no more. This healing was truly a miracle. My
gratitude to Him for choosing me as His disciple, and for making my path so clear to me, was a thing I could barely contain.
Behind me, I heard Masseo reciting prayers of praise at the sight
he had witnessed.

The man wept. 'You do this for me and yet I am not worthy.
I have been so foul to everyone who tried to care for me; I have
even committed blasphemy. Will I ever be forgiven, or will I
rot in Hell?'

My hands were shaking. I told him, 'God has forgiven you.
You are cured; now go and show your gratitude to God. Care
for others as He has cared for you. And please …' I glanced at
Masseo, including him in my plea, 'say nothing of what occurred
here today. Simply rejoice.'

The man nodded and gripped my hand tightly between his.
'My thoughts will be with you always.'

'And mine with you.'

As I was preparing to leave, Masseo approached me. 'Francesco,
I must speak with you before you go.'

'Then let us do so somewhere private.' I led him out into the
garden.

'You understand what occurred there, do you not? You know
that you have performed a miracle?'

'Not me, Masseo, that was God's work.'

'Just think, Francesco, how many people you could convert if you would only share with them this demonstration of God's supreme power. Have you done this before? Is it something you can choose to do?'

'Please understand, brother. Miracles are a blessing, a manifestation of God's love intended to relieve the suffering of man. They are not a means to demonstrate power, or dazzle innocents into believing. If we are to save souls, pure words and deeds alone must win their hearts.'

'But, Francesco—'

'If people hear us speak, and our words open their hearts so that their soul yearns for His love; if they desire nothing but to commit to His service; if they love their neighbours as they do themselves; if they enjoy the success of others, pity their misfortunes and seek to help those less fortunate than themselves, then they will become sheep of His flock and will be saved for eternity.'

Masseo bowed his head. 'Brother Francesco, your words shame me.'

'I am so sorry, that was not my intention, but there is no easy road on this quest of ours. Come with me. We have much to do.'

CHAPTER SEVEN

OPPOSITION

I entered the Cathedral of San Rufino. The first person who I encountered was the Assistant Bishop, Father Tiberio. My heart pounded in my chest, and my hands felt hot and clammy. I felt like a child once more.

'And to what do we owe this pleasure, Brother Francesco?'

'I wanted to make my confession, for I have sinned.'

'Sit here, Brother Francesco.'

He sat beside me. I realised he must have chosen this seat deliberately because I could see that a pillar blocked the far end of this particular pew. There was no escape.

I made the sign of the cross. 'In the name of the Father, and of the Son, and of the Holy Spirit, my last confession was …' I struggled to remember. 'It has been some time since my last confession.'

'And what does *some time* signify, exactly?'

'Let me see. It must be two months since I last saw my confessor. I was away, and on my return, I discovered that Brother Leo, who usually hears my confessions, is also now away visiting a sick relative in Sienna.'

'Hmm.'

He glared at me and my legs trembled.

'Excuses, Brother Francesco, I expected no less. Now, what is it that you wish to confess?'

'I cured a leper and–'

'You did *what*?'

'I cured a leper. His skin healed, and his affliction disappeared as I washed him.'

'Brother Francesco,' Father Tiberio's voice shook, 'you do not have permission to anoint the sick, and you clearly do not have the temperament to resist the pride that accompanies your success.'

'I recognise that it was not *my* success. I am merely the Lord's instrument, but–'

'And yet your first words to me were: *I cured a leper.*'

I wanted to yell at him; you tricked me into that, but I realised before I did so that it was my fault. 'Forgive me, Father. I was merely trying to explain as I was going on to say–'

'You will not say a thing; for once you will listen. In future, you will refuse the attraction of a healing ministry and concentrate instead solely on encouraging the repentance of sins. And before you dare to contemplate defying me, remember, you must always remain obedient to the Holy Catholic Church.'

Taken aback by his harsh response, I bowed my head and clasped my hands together in a futile attempt to stop them from shaking.

'Do you agree to obedience in the future?' he demanded.

'I do believe in obedience to the Church and her priests. But if God chooses me to be an instrument for–'

'You do not have the authority. Your Order is not even approved. The Church will not tolerate such heretical behaviour.'

'Dear God,' I prayed. 'Please protect me from charges of heresy.'

'Swear to me now that you will never again presume a ministry of healing. No more miracles. Do you swear?'

'I swear it,' I whispered.

I sank to my knees with my head bowed while Father Tiberio granted me absolution and forgiveness. I remembered the first time that he had done this; when he punished me for the accidental damage to my father's fabric. On that occasion, his actions and words had brought me to tears. More recently, following my father's disinheritance, his accusation that I had humiliated my father, had again wounded me deeply. But now, to accuse me unjustly of taking praise from God, and to restrain me through this vow from undertaking God's healing work in the future, was a heavy cross to bear. I left San Rufino with Father Tiberio's words echoing in my head and tears streaming down my cheeks.

In desperate need for some solitude and time to pray, I left the town, climbed the steep pathway to Carceri, and reached a small glade. It was one of my favourite places here on the mountainside – the other being the cave where I had found God, or rather, He found me.

I constructed an altar from logs and a simple cross from fallen branches to complement the atmosphere. It was such a quiet and evocative place, so conducive to prayer and contemplation. I sat on an uprooted tree trunk and breathed deeply. The smell of the damp trees and fallen leaves calmed my troubled thoughts. Everywhere was so green. Even the rocks were covered in a blanket of moss. The sunlight broke through the canopy of tremulous leaves, creating filtered shafts of light that danced before my eyes. I was overwhelmed with gratitude, and fell to my knees in prayer:

Dear Lord Almighty, loving and merciful Saviour.
I thank Thee, my Lord, for the beauty and simplicity of this place.
I thank Thee, my Lord, for Thy continued guidance and divine grace.
Help me to be Your instrument in bringing peace to others,
As You have brought peace to me.
Help me to inflame the desire of others, to love and worship Thee.
To illuminate their path and enable them to discover and experience,
Thy ineffable mercy and eternal love.
Amen.

I looked up at the fading sky. A single bat flitted from a nearby tree, circled above me and then swooped effortlessly, in pursuit of tiny winged insects. Guided by instinct and faith, the tiny creature safely avoided all obstacles as it hunted its prey.

I decided Father Tiberio was, for some unknown reason, determined to place every possible obstacle in my way. I needed to take an example from nature, use my instinct and faith to avoid any difficulties, and continue in my quest. After all, even Father Tiberio had acknowledged that I had the approval to encourage the repentance of sins and the saving of souls. I may have been forced to vow that I would refrain from performing miracles or acts of healing, but there were many other ways in which I could serve God.

Comforted by my surroundings, composed and restored by my renewed determination, I now yearned for some company. Wrapping my cloak around me, I followed the well-worn path beside the stream. I looked forward to joining my brothers for evening prayers at the Rivotorto hovel.

I stared up at the falcon circling high above me. He looked from left to right as he glided effortlessly. His wingtips feathered upwards and stroked the air as he searched for the wind to lift him even higher. Suddenly his focus was upon me, and he dropped like a stone. My heart raced with fear. I spread my wings in a futile attempt to protect my chicks, but they, ignorant of the danger, continued to utter their high-pitched tweets, certain to attract the attention of a hungry bird. Two of my unruly brood broke free from my shelter in search of grass seeds, ignoring my desperate calls for them to return. The Falcon was so close that I could see his talons. Cruel hooks contrasted sharply with the soft speckled down of his underbelly and his smooth, creamy throat. My babies, my chicks, please, God keep them safe.

I woke, soaked with sweat from the terror of my dream. I relived the vision of those terrible talons as the falcon swooped down to clutch my wayward chick. My body shook with the memory of it. But what did it mean? Did my dream contain within it a message from God? Could this dream be a way of telling me that I need to do more to protect my brothers from harm or from the result of what Father Tiberio had referred to as my heretical behaviour? I needed to discuss the dream and my concerns about Father Tiberio with my friend and confessor, Leo. Unfortunately, he had not yet returned.

My thoughts were interrupted as a low moan escaped from Barbaro, who lay beside me. Was he also dreaming of falcons, or were his dreams filled with other demons?

'What is it, Brother Barbaro?'

'Oh, Francesco, I am so sorry to disturb you, but the pains in my gut …' He moaned again and clutched his belly.

'Is it something you have eaten?'

'It cannot be, for I have been fasting as penance.'

'For?'

He sat up, pulled up his cowl and hung his head. 'I am so ashamed, Francesco; I was jealous of Juniper's sunny disposition when my own is so morose and irritable.'

I had to suppress a smile. His words could have sprung from the lips of my younger self, back when I so yearned to be as loved and as lovable as my dear sibling, Angelo.

'Come with me.' I pulled him to his feet and supported him as we climbed over the tightly packed brothers and stumbled to the entrance of the hovel.

'I thank you for your concern,' he said once we arrived outside, 'but I must do my penance and look to my temperament rather than festering in my envy of others.'

Barbaro had a point. He might have suppressed the torments of his tongue, but *sunny* was not a way any man would describe his disposition. I considered his sorry countenance as he again clutched his stomach.

'You have served your penance, my brother, but now you must eat. We will call on my good friend Thomasso.'

'It is very early, Brother Francesco.'

'He is always awake at this time tending his crops and protecting his vegetables from the early morning ravages of the rabbits.'

I guided and continued to support Barbaro as we walked away from the hovel, crossed the stream and entered an orchard of fruit trees.

'Good morning,' I called as we drew near Thomasso's homestead.

'Francesco, how good to see you. And you also, Brother Barbaro. Are you well?'

Barbaro grunted.

'I am afraid that Brother Barbaro has overdone his penance and finds himself close to collapse from acute hunger.'

Thomasso looked at Barbaro and frowned. 'We will soon put that right. Sit down here and rest. I will bring breakfast for us all to share.'

Barbaro sank down on a grassy bank while Thomasso hurried into his house. He returned a few minutes later with a jug of water, a basket containing bunches of grapes and a dish of smoked rabbit. His rosy-cheeked chubby wife and three children followed him. The youngest boy had grown since my last visit and was now walking, although occasionally he bent over and placed his hands on the ground to steady himself. Each time he did so, he stood up, clapped his hands and giggled – a sound so joyous I could not help but join in. His sister hovered beside him, poised to catch her sibling if he tumbled. The older son, who must have now been in his ninth year, walked in front of his mother and carried another basket containing bread, wooden drinking bowls and a large table-cloth, which he proceeded to spread on the ground before us. I blessed the food and the family, and encouraged Barbaro to eat.

'Are you sure, Brother Francesco?' Barbaro looked at the food, and I could see that anguish still tore him apart.

'I am sure that God does not wish you to suffer unnecessarily, and you need to regain your strength. Here, take some rabbit; it looks and smells delicious.' I took a portion and bit into the succulent flesh.

'They eat my vegetables, and we eat them,' laughed Thomasso, pouring us bowls of fresh water. 'The grapes are from our first early crop. You must take some back to the others, Brother Barbaro, when you leave.'

'I will fetch enough smoked rabbit for you all,' his wife declared. 'And some more of those plump and juicy grapes, we have plenty to share.'

'Plump and juicy, just like you, my dear.' Thomasso roared with laughter and winked at his wife.

'Thomasso, behave.' She flushed scarlet. 'These are holy men. And the children – do not say such things before them.' She glanced at Barbaro and me. When she realised we were un-offended by the ribaldry and were indeed laughing ourselves, she smiled coyly at her husband and chased her children back inside.

With Barbaro sufficiently nourished, we thanked Thomasso and returned to the hovel. Barbaro carried the banquet in a basket that we borrowed from Thomasso. As we drew near, he tried to hand the items to me, but I shook my head.

'This is your gift,' I said. 'You must give it.'

My heart filled with joy as I witnessed the delight Barbaro experienced sharing these treasures with his brothers. From that day forth, his disposition was so changed that he threatened to outshine Juniper with his good nature, and I learned a lesson of my own. The past year, when I had been able to share the gift of my calling with my brothers, had brought me more happiness than I could ever remember experiencing before.

Brother Leo was still in Sienna. I was impatient to discuss my concerns with him, but his relative remained seriously ill. It was not appropriate for me to disturb him or his family at this time. I decided instead to spend my time productively by taking my ministry to the region of Giano.

I strolled beside the river, a tributary of the River Tiber. Usually, it was quite small and slow moving, but today the river was swollen with recent rainfall. Water tumbled over rocks, swirled around boulders and created whirlpools. A majestic grey heron flew past slowly, neck tucked in like a scrawny old man. He flapped his huge wings and trailed his long legs behind him. Further along the riverbank, I came across his mate, poised on a small bend in the river. Her blue-grey plumage never moved as she stood motionless, knee-deep in the swirling waters. Her beady black eyes scanned beneath the surface for prey. She began to move stealthily and then, like lightning, struck with her long sharp beak to spear a small silver fish. She carried its wriggling body to the shore and swallowed it whole.

I remembered how, as young children, my father had brought Angelo and me to this area. While we had walked through this dramatic valley, alongside the crystal-clear river, he told us the story of Felice and the dragon. The scenery on our route was stunningly beautiful, but I was overwhelmed with foreboding as Father described the huge monster that could kill a man with its stinking breath. I looked up at the craggy peaks of the mountains towering above us, expecting the beast to fly down and challenge us at any moment.

'Do not be frightened.' Father strode ahead, using his stick to clear our path. 'Felice and his father, Mauro, killed the beast and freed the locals from centuries of his tyranny.'

A loud clap of thunder interrupted his story, and we looked up the valley, towards the dark blue mountains beyond. As so often happens, the weather had changed in the blink of an eye. The sun had disappeared. Ominous black clouds rolled across the sky.

'Come on, boys!' shouted my father as the rain cascaded down and soaked us to the bone. 'Let us take shelter in that small cave over there.'

Angelo whimpered in fright as we entered the inky blackness of the cavern. He never liked thunderstorms, and always hid under his blanket until the rumbling disappeared, refusing to come out again until the sun shone once more.

'It is God shouting, he is angry,' Angelo sobbed, holding his hands over his ears.

'Angelo, stop that noise. Such nonsense, you are a big boy now. Do something useful and help your brother. Gather some of those dry sticks. We shall make a small fire and dry our clothes while we eat our lunch.'

'Will you tell us about the dragon, Father?' I trembled with cold and anticipation.

'All in good time.'

Angelo and I collected dry twigs from under the lee of the rocks. Father fashioned them into a pile and used his flint box and a small pile of dry cotton threads to start a small flame. After a few gentle puffs, he placed it beneath the twigs, which caught. Before long the fire was ablaze and crackling away. Father made us take off our leggings and tunics and spread them on the flat rocks beside the fire. He unpacked the blanket, brought along for us to sit on while we ate our lunch, and wrapped it around our shivering bodies.

We feasted on Mother's seed bread, freshly made that morning, some cheese made from our goat's milk, slices of smoked ham from the joints hung to cure in the kitchen and apples from my father's orchards. Then we settled back, warm and cosy while Father told us the story.

Five hundred years after the birth of our dear Lord Jesus Christ, two pilgrims, Mauro and his son Felice, arrived in the region. They had travelled from the Holy Land to tell everyone who they met about the life of Jesus. They tried to convert the local inhabitants to Christianity, but the people were only concerned with surviving the marauding dragon. They begged Mauro and Felice to free them from the beast. The two men saw this as an exciting challenge, and an opportunity to prove their faith in God.

They set off to the area purported to be the dragon's lair. No one knew the exact location because his toxic breath was sufficient to prevent the locals from straying too close. As they drew near, they could smell the sulphuric odour of dragon-breath. Mauro stuck his walking staff in the ground. Immediately it took root and grew into a fine tree. The two men took this to be a sign from God and set about building a shelter from the loose boulders in the vicinity.

The next morning, they awoke to the smell of dragon's breath, much stronger than before. They rushed to the doorway. The huge creature lumbered towards the newly erected structure. Hurriedly, the two men knocked their way through the back wall, crawled out of the hole and escaped unseen. They climbed to safety and looked back to witness the beast, who convinced they were still inside, engulfed the building in flames. As the beast concentrated on destroying his enemies – or so he thought – Mauro climbed down the rocks and hit the unsuspecting creature a heavy blow with a masonry hammer. The dragon's skull cracked, and the beast dropped to the floor, unconscious. Mauro and Felice then deliberately dislodged an avalanche of rocks that fell onto the dragon and crushed him to death. The dragon's blood flooded into the river, which ran red for three days and three nights.

When he finished his tale, Father pulled us boys closer to him, tucked his cloak around us and told us not to fear.

'I will slay any dragon that dares to look your way. Now sleep and make peaceful dreams, my sons.'

And sleep we did; warmed by the fire and our father's comforting words.

A trout leapt from the water and artfully caught a fly before falling back with a loud splash, rousing me from my happy memories.

Father may have promised to slay any dragon that dared to threaten my wellbeing, and yet, ironically, he had been instrumental in bringing my shortcomings to the attention of the priest, we called the Dragon – Father Tiberio.

As I continued my travels towards the town of Foligno, the thought nagged at me that my father had indeed tried to be a good parent. True, he favoured Angelo and failed to understand me, but perhaps I had been selective in my memories, neglecting to recall those occasions when I had found happiness in my childhood, or that showed my father in a favourable manner.

I decided that rather than taking the direct route home, I would first pay a visit to Bevagna, one of my favourite towns in the region.

The bridge ahead of me spanned the river: the gateway to the town. The bridge bustled with hundreds of people. Laden carts pulled by donkeys, horses, and even an ox lumbered towards the market in the central piazza.

I entered by the south gate, close to the fountain fed by fresh spring water. The women usually brought their washing here early in the morning, filling the air with their raucous laughter as they gossiped. But not today. Today was market day. Instead, the fountain provided refreshment to thirsty animals. I pushed in between a donkey and some goats, cupped my hands beneath the spout and drank deeply.

Trips to Bevagna are always a joy. It's such an interesting town. Unlike any others in the region, it is built on the plain of the river, so all the streets are flat. The old men bring their chairs out into the street and spend hours engaged in long conversations, either with each other, or with any visitor who happened to walk by them. They especially like the excitement of the market and would soon be lining the streets.

The market stalls were still under construction, and the square was alive with the hustle and bustle of traders unloading their trailers. I paused to assist the baker. He was working alone and struggled to lift a heavy plank of wood.

'Let me help you,' I offered. 'The two of us will make light work of this.'

'Thank you, Brother Francesco. How does this day find you?'

'Thanks be to God, it finds me well. And you?'

'Improving. Best not grumble.'

We placed large packing cases at either end and laid the planks across to form a table. The baker covered the planks with a clean linen tablecloth and emptied his baskets of loaves onto the stall, stacking them into neat piles. The smell of freshly baked bread reminded me that I had not yet eaten.

'Choose one for your lunch,' the baker said. 'In thanks for your help this morning.'

I picked a small seeded loaf, gave him a blessing and continued my journey.

A short distance from the town of Bevagna, I noticed a tree, full of small birds. They sang as though their tiny hearts would burst. As I approached, the noise intensified.

'Hush, my little sisters,' I told them. 'It is now my turn to speak.'

The noise abated, and I addressed them and gave them my blessing: a sermon to the birds.

> '*My little brothers and sisters the birds, you, who are noble among all creatures, are especially bound to love and praise God your Creator. He preserved you in the ark of Noah so that you would not perish. He has granted you the freedom of the air and clothed you in feathers. Although you neither sow, reap, nor harvest, he feeds you and provides the rivers and fountains for you to drink, the mountains and the valleys for your refuge, and tall trees for you to build your nests. Your Creator loves you so much and abundantly provides everything that's good for you. Therefore, my little brothers and sisters, beware of the sin of ingratitude, and forever strive to praise God.*'

The birds fluttered down from the tree. Several landed on my outstretched arms, and the remainder gathered on the dusty road before me. They bowed their heads as if my words reminded them of their indifference to the love of God and the need for them to repent. Their song joined with mine as we praised God for His unconditional love.

I crumbled some of the seed bread and threw it among them. A flurry of hungry birds pounced on the crumbs, pecking each other in their efforts to reach the food first. 'There is enough for each of you. Stay calm and you will all enjoy your meal.' The birds seemed to understand my words, and soon settled down to share the crumbs. They danced around my feet and chirruped their thanks. Few things could match the joy I derived from sharing my time and communing with God's simple creatures.

But then I remembered my words: *Beware the sin of ingratitude.* It was if they came back to haunt me. My stomach sank to my knees as realisation dawned. Perhaps Father Tiberio was right to chastise me. I fully recognised that I was merely God's instrument in curing the leper, but did I truly acknowledge that fact sufficiently at the time? My earlier doubts had caused me to visit the Cathedral to make my confession, but then because I was upset with Father Tiberio's response, I had wallowed in my self-pity instead of repenting my sin of ingratitude.

Father Tiberio had also chastised me for ingratitude towards my father, and I realised now his words were possibly well founded. When had I ever shown gratitude to my father? A word of thanks now and then, but what he had really expected, and deserved, was my full commitment to the family business.

I knew now what Brother Leo would say to me when I finally caught up with him. I had indeed been guilty of the sin of ingratitude. I sighed deeply, sank to my knees and prayed for forgiveness.

CHAPTER EIGHT
ROME AND APPROVAL

I had forgotten that the street leading up towards San Rufino Cathedral was so steep. I became so intent on my breathing that I failed to notice the man who walked towards me until he spoke.

'Brother Francesco, how good to see you,' said Bishop Guido.

'Your Excellency.' I knelt before him and kissed his hand.

'I hear wonderful things about the number of pagans you have converted to Christianity.'

Still struggling to catch my breath I murmured an acknowledgement of thanks.

He bid me stand and held my gaze.

'However, Brother Francesco, I am concerned for you and your brothers. The way you live in such poverty seems to be unnecessarily harsh. I hear one of your brothers fainted in the Piazza from lack of food last week, and that this was not the first time it has happened.'

'Your Excellency, by being wed to my Lady Poverty and having nothing, we have no worries, no cares. We are indeed care-free.'

'My dear boy, this may be the life that you covet, but what of your brothers?'

'Ownership of property or possessions requires arms to defend them. We do not need those items. They will only distract us from God's will.'

The Bishop frowned and shook his head. 'And what of your Rule? Is it any more structured yet? Does it give you and the

Friars Minor clear guidance on how you should live your lives and go about your ministry? If you were to adopt the Benedictine Rule, the Pope would surely look more favourably on you and your brothers.'

'Your Excellency, our Rule remains those three simple passages from the Bible, given to us by God. Our Rule demands nothing more than complete poverty as we serve Him as His humble servants.'

'Hmm.' He looked at me and rubbed his chin. 'I also understand from Father Tiberio that you are calling yourselves the Order of the Friars Minor. He also reminded me that the Pope has made a declaration – no groups should claim to be an Order until he approves them? You could be storing up troubles by ignoring his decree.'

I bowed my head. 'Our lack of official approval has been troubling us for some time. Accusations of heresy are easy to make and nigh-on impossible to disprove.' I remembered only too well, my childhood experience with Dimitri and his family. 'I promise you that I will discuss your comments with my brothers and give prayer and thought to how we should respond.'

'But *will* you respond, Francesco?' There was no mistaking the exasperation in the Bishop's tone. 'Or will you continue to do things your way, against the advice of those who care about you?'

'Your Excellency, please believe that we do appreciate your patronage. We will give this matter serious thought.'

He blessed me as we parted.

It was a warm evening, and as I walked the sun sank below the mountains, crimson streaks tinged the sky, and unadulterated joy swelled my heart. A joy that dispersed immediately upon my arriving back at the Rivotorto hovel, I was surprised to see that all eleven of my brothers were gathered together, whispering and wringing their hands.

'Francesco, thank goodness you have returned,' Pietro said. 'We have heard the most distressing news. Lucido has just returned from his travels and … you tell him, Lucido. It's your news.'

'Welcome back, Brother Lucido,' I said. 'We have missed your company these past few weeks. Let us all sit down together and hear this news of yours.'

The news was indeed distressing. Lucido had been satisfying his roaming urge for some weeks and was travelling back from the north of Italy, through an area known as Piedmont. He had met a group of people who called themselves the Poor Men of Lyons. The Pope had previously declared the group disobedient, and excommunicated them, but had stopped short of declaring them heretics.

Lucido had listened to the preaching of Pietro Waldo – their elderly leader. He was impressed with part of his message: the need to adopt genuine poverty and to live a life of adherence to the Gospels. However, he was concerned with the second part of his message. Waldo claimed that purgatory did not exist; it was the invention of the *Antichrist*, the name he gave to the Catholic Church.

As Lucido was leaving the area, he witnessed a dreadful scene. Three of the ministers, or *barbas* as they were known, were seized and tried as heretics. They were found guilty and handed over to the secular authorities for punishment. These arrests had happened before, and usually the punishment, as with my old friend Dimitri, was banishment. On this occasion, the authorities decided to take a tougher stance. The three men were condemned to death and sentenced to be burnt at the stake in the town square. Lucido arrived just as the sentence was being carried out, and was unfortunate enough to witness the scene.

'Their screams were unbearable, and the smell of burning flesh will haunt me for the rest of my life. I wanted to walk away, but it was as if my legs were frozen to the ground. I could not move.'

Lucido had been so distressed by the experience that he cut short his trip and returned to find comfort with us.

'You do not think it could happen to us, do you?' The look of terror on his face wrenched my heart.

We comforted him as best we could. We always knew that in serving God, it was possible we could be tested, even martyred, but to witness such appalling deaths would take anyone some time to get over.

Leo and Pietro, as our ordained priests, delivered a service for the dead. We spent the rest of the day in prayer, asking God to grant peace of mind to Lucido, and forgiveness to the tortured souls of the three Poor Men of Lyons.

Juniper and Pacifico entertained us that evening as we shared our evening meal around the campfire, but neither Juniper's beautiful singing voice and sunny temperament nor Pacifico's musical talents could lighten our sombre mood.

Masseo pushed aside his bowl. 'It is no use wallowing in self-pity, waiting for someone to point the finger and denounce us as heretics. I vote that we do something positive.'

'Bless you, Brother Masseo,' I said. 'As practical as ever,'

'So, what do you suggest, Francesco?' snapped Barbaro, reverting to his grumpy disposition.

I thought back to the dream when I was trying to protect my young chicks from the Falcon. Perchance the dream is a warning. Perhaps I was required to do more to protect my brothers. Bishop Guido had been right to chastise me. 'I believe we should take the Bishop's advice.'

'Do you think Bishop Guido knew of the fate of the Poor Men of Lyons when he spoke with you, Francesco?' Pacifico asked.

'It is certainly possible. Clearly, he intended to ensure that we do not succumb to the charge of heresy. What say you, Masseo?'

'To what?'

'To taking action. Perhaps the time has come for us to visit Rome and submit the Rule of our Order to the Pope.'

We arrived in Rome and approached Saint John Lateran's Archbasilica, the ecclesiastical seat of Pope Innocent III, and the cathedral church of the Diocese of Rome. I was surprised to see Bishop Guido of Assisi leaving the building. I could feel the blood rush to my cheeks when I realised I should have informed him of our intentions to visit the Pope before we left for Rome. I thought he would be angry, but he welcomed me warmly, and kindly offered to introduce us to Cardinal Giovanni di San Paolo, the Bishop of Sabina, who was responsible for recommending the approval of new Orders.

Guido escorted us across the vestibule. Numerous candles on tall golden candelabras supplemented the light from the windows.

We approached a richly gilded throne and knelt before Cardinal Giovanni, who watched our approach, unsmiling, unmoving, unmistakably unimpressed as we shuffled forward in our ragged tunics and bare feet.

'Your Eminence.' Guido kissed his hand. 'May I introduce Francesco Bernardone of Assisi and the Friars Minor? They seek recognition of their newly formed Order and their Rule.'

'Do they have your support, Bishop Guido?'

'My Lordship, they do. Brother Francesco and his brothers have been very successful in converting hundreds of pagans into devout Christians. You will find that they are totally committed to the Roman Catholic Church.'

'The fact that they come so highly regarded by you, Bishop Guido, is sufficient recognition to warm my heart.' He smiled, and it was as if a ray of sunlight illuminated the room.

He interrogated us, firstly as a group and then as individuals. He asked searching questions about our beliefs, intentions, and faith. He examined the Rule, which had been carefully prepared by Leo. He gave us his blessing and then directed us to pray throughout the evening before returning to see him again the next day.

Jacoba of Settesoli, an old family friend, opened the door.

'Brother Francesco, my dear boy, how lovely to see you again. You are looking well. A bit thin, perhaps. You need a bit of feeding up. How are things with the family?'

'Difficult. We are still estranged.'

'Your poor dear mother, I must write to her. Come in, what brings you to Rome?'

'My brothers and I are here to visit the Pope. Would it be possible to use your stables as a place of rest for the night?'

'The stables? I think not. You will enjoy the comfort of my hall. Since my husband died and the children have grown and flown, I rarely use it. It will be wonderful to have the excuse to entertain. Come in and refresh yourselves while I arrange your supper and raid the wine cellar.'

We spent the evening in her sumptuous home, well-fed on plump roasted chickens, freshly baked bread, olives, and fruit, all washed down with the finest wines. Jacoba also made some of my favourite biscuits, Mostaccioli, baked with almonds, sugar, and honey: an exquisite taste approaching something made by angels. After supper, Jacoba joined us in prayer. We gave thanks for the hospitality and prayed for a successful outcome with Cardinal Giovanni the following day.

On our return to the cathedral the next morning, we were again received by Cardinal Giovanni. The smile had vanished. He looked stern as we gathered before him. Perhaps his night had not been as comfortable as ours. He looked down from his throne and scrutinised our straggly group. We shrank under his ponderous gaze.

'I am happy to tell you that I do not believe there is any heresy in your beliefs.'

He leaned back in his chair, and I felt a weight lift from my shoulders. I looked across at Bernardo and Leo, who were both smiling.

Our relief was short-lived.

'However.' The Cardinal continued, 'In my opinion, the life that you wish to lead is far too harsh. Your answers have convinced me that you will all individually be able to embrace such poverty, but I am concerned for others in the future.' He stroked his chin and frowned. 'I believe your faith is best served if you were to join another Order, rather than struggle to establish one of your own.'

My heart sank like a stone to the river bed. I felt totally crushed by the weight of this disappointment, but I was not about to abandon our hopes and dreams at the first attempt. We did not need the Pope's approval of the Rule because it was given to us by God, but the Pope's approval of our Order was important for us.

'Your Eminence, I respect your opinion, but is it possible to have an audience with the Pope?'

'And I respect your determination, Brother Francesco, but the Pope is a busy man.'

'But is it possible?'

He tilted his head as he considered my request. 'Very well. I am seeing the Pope shortly to take his confession. I will put your request to him. Return to see me this afternoon and I will give you his response.'

Cardinal Giovanni, smiling once more, greeted us at the entrance, with the news of his successful entreaties. We were to be granted an audience. He led us into the nave of the cathedral. He walked so slowly; I feared that we would never arrive. My eyes raced ahead, drawn to the red marble throne occupied by the Pope.

Pope Innocent III was only forty-nine but had already been Pope for eleven years. During this time, he had developed a reputation as a highly intelligent, powerful and influential leader, with an ability to assert absolute spiritual authority. I remembered how the people of Assisi had much to thank him for when he banished the evil Duke Conrad.

He sat in his pristine white robe, draped with a red silk cloak. He was not wearing his mitre, and his bare head revealed auburn hair complemented by a full beard. He did not look up as we approached but continued talking to a group of Cardinals.

As we drew close to the throne, I could not help but stare in awe at the magnificent apse, decorated with a mosaic of Christ. I tore my gaze from the image and realised that the Pope was now watching us.

'Cardinal Giovanni, what do we have here?'

'Your Holiness.' Giovanni knelt and kissed the Pontiff's ring. 'I bring you Brother Francesco Bernardone of Assisi and the Friars Minor. They come to seek your approval for their Order and are highly recommended by Bishop Guido.'

We knelt at the Pope's feet, bowed our heads and clasped our hands together in a prayerful manner.

'I remember now. These are the brothers who have won the hearts and souls of so many, and who desire to live in complete poverty, are they not?'

I was excited to hear that he remembered who we were, but my excitement soon turned to disappointment as he continued.

'You would aid your case, Brother Francesco, if you would consider taking guidance from, or even joining a Benedictine Order. The life you propose for your Order is too severe.'

'Holy Father, you would not tell our Lord Jesus Christ that the life He chose was too severe. We simply want to live by His example. *Please* reconsider. I beg of you.'

The Pope looked taken aback at what he could have interpreted as impertinence but agreed to pray for guidance overnight and asked us to return the next day.

After another pleasant evening of fine dining and convivial conversation with Jacoba, followed by a vigil of prayer, we were welcomed back into the Pope's presence.

'If I may, Your Holiness, I wish to tell you and the Cardinals a story?' I begged.

'Speak freely, Brother Francesco.'

I drew a deep breath and began. 'There was once a poor woman who lived in the wilderness. One day, the King was passing. He saw her, and he fell so in love that he desired to have sons by her.'

Several of the Cardinals fidgeted with embarrassment at the thought that I was about to tell the Pope a lewd story, but I continued unabashed.

'The King wed her, and sons were born, just as he hoped. But she enjoyed the wilderness, the simplicity, and quietness of the countryside and remained there to bring up her children. When they grew up to be young men, she sent them to the King, saying, "Do not be afraid, you are the King's offspring. He will recognise you and provide you with food." When the King saw them, he was overwhelmed with their beauty and asked, "Who is your mother?" They replied, "A poor woman who lives in the wilderness." The King embraced them with much joy and said, "Fear not, if I feed strangers at my table, shall I not feed you, my true sons?"'

I looked up from my story. The Cardinals were looking at me confused, but the Pope waved his hand gracefully, palm upwards, to indicate I should continue.

'Your Holiness, God is that King, and I am that poor woman embracing poverty in the wilderness. Every soul I present to the King, Our Lord, will be His child in His own likeness.'

The Pope pondered for a moment, while I trembled, nervous of his response.

'Last night, Brother Francesco, I did as I promised and prayed for guidance. I dreamt that I walked on the terraces of our ancient temple of St. John Lateran, but the walls were all crumbling and in danger of collapse. The domes and turrets also bent over, like trees on an exposed hillside.' He gently placed his hand on my shoulder. 'I looked again and saw you lean against the walls. Your action prevented the walls from falling. I believe that this dream came from God.' He gave my shoulder a gentle squeeze. 'It showed me that you have an important role in rebuilding the Holy Roman Catholic Church. I believe your role is to preach the repentance of sins, to harvest human hearts and souls, and to bring them into the Catholic faith. I will give my verbal support to your Order, and when you grow in number, return and I will reconsider my position concerning your Rule.'

I knelt before him and kissed his ring, overwhelmed with relief and gratitude.

'I will give you permission to continue with your ministry on the condition that you accept official recognition as the responsible superior. Your appointment as Minister General is necessary so that the ecclesiastical authorities are able to communicate with you and your Order. Bishop Guido will conduct the service to appoint you this afternoon, and you will all be tonsured before you leave today to symbolise that you are now under the spiritual authority of the Roman Catholic Church.'

'Your Holiness, I once heard the word of God, who asked me to go and repair his church. I thought at first that He wanted me to restore the fallen boulders, but your dream has confirmed my belief; there is much more to be achieved.'

The organ music surged as we entered the Cathedral for the service. The congregation and choir joined voices and melded together into something very powerful that resonated deep within me. I overheard several people commenting that they had never heard the choir sing so perfectly. God had called these people together to witness my appointment as Minister General. The service was truly a celebration, while at the same time being a very spiritual and overwhelming experience.

After the ceremony, Bishop Guido gave me his blessing, but then explained that he had to leave due to a previously arranged meeting. The Assistant Bishop of Assisi, Father Tiberio, was in attendance and agreed to continue with the tonsuring ceremony. As we knelt before him, he skillfully shaved our heads leaving a ring of hair – a physical demonstration of our acceptance by, and allegiance to, the Catholic Church.

'Brother Francesco, you may think that you have the Pope's approval now,' whispered Father Tiberio, 'but remember he only gave his *verbal* endorsement for your Order, and he has not approved your Rule. You are only allowed to preach repentance, no more of this mystical mayhem or miracles. If I hear of any such things I will be reporting you to the Bishop, or indeed the Pope himself if needs be.'

Even Father Tiberio's harsh words could not dampen my spirits on this occasion. The Pope's dream clarified my quest. I had originally misunderstood the word of God. Our quest, confirmed by the Pope, was to preach salvation and harvest souls on behalf of the Holy Roman Catholic Church.

We left Rome filled with joy, tinged with only a few misgivings. Father Tiberio was correct in that the Pope had only given us his verbal support, but he had also given us the authority to preach, and we no longer ran the risk of being charged as heretics. The Pope's authority allowed us, with the agreement of the local priests, to conduct our services within the churches and cathedrals of the towns that we visited, as well as continuing with the services conducted in the open air. However, with the badge of our tonsured hair, along with my formal recognition as Minister General and spiritual leader, it could be argued that we were no longer such free spirits.

We quickly threw off these minor concerns as we began our journey back to our beloved Assisi. We sang and danced, joyous as troubadours of God.

So intent was I on our return to Assisi that I forgot how treacherous the route could become in midsummer, with scorched terrain and dry roads. Each weary footstep created clouds of dust, which billowed over us causing us to cough, choke and splutter. Tears coursed down our cheeks.

At first, we would race towards each stream that we came upon, but they offered no relief; they were all completely dry. The shrivelled vegetation provided no nourishment. Even the olive trees hung listless in the heat and offered little shade.

We came upon a fallen donkey, flat on his back, legs stiff, stomach swollen and split by putrid gasses. A cloud of black flies crawled over the creature's gaping wounds. I stopped and stared, gagging at the stench. Before much longer the corpse would become a mass of maggots, tumbling over each other as they reduced the carcass to bones. Then the relentless sun and wind would take their turn until nothing remained except more dust. My eleven loyal brothers, stood before me, shrunken, parched, each and everyone exhausted. Was this how it would end for us, with our work barely begun?

Masseo's huge burly frame towered above me; he tugged at my sleeve and pulled me onwards.

'Look,' Masseo pointed towards the mountains.

Ahead the land shimmered. Water and trees danced before our eyes.

'They are strange trees Masseo. Unlike any I have ever seen before.'

'But they will give us shade, and there is water.' He pointed again. 'Come on brothers. We are saved. Not far to go.'

But as we looked at the trees floating before us, they disappeared, taking with them our hopes.

We stumbled towards the foothills and our skin blistered with the searing intensity. Juniper screamed in terror. Thrashing around on the floor, he mumbled and clawed at his skin. Blood droplets appeared across his throat resembling a necklace of ruby red beads.

'Quick Bernardo, grab him before he does himself more damage.'

Bernardo and I dragged Juniper to his feet and draped his arms over our shoulders.

'Come Juniper, we must get you out of this sun,' I said.

'Save me …' Juniper screamed. 'Save me from this bat.'

'There is no bat.' I said, trying my best to calm him.

'Yes, yes, a giant bat. It claws my neck and sucks my blood.' Juniper struggled in a frantic effort to remove the beast who he believed was attacking his flesh.

Bernardo and I hauled him a short way, but then Bernardo fell to the ground, taking Juniper and me with him.

I tried to stand but got no further than my knees. Kneeling in the heat and dust, I prayed for our salvation.

A single black cloud appeared from behind the mountain and totally obscured the sun. The temperature plummeted, cool air drifted over my skin – sheer bliss. Under the cloud's protection, we were able to resume our journey.

We eventually arrived at the grottos that lie close to the town of Orte. We fell to our knees and gave thanks for our deliverance.

The thudding of feet aroused me from my prayers. A young man approached at speed from the direction of Orte. Clouds of dust billowed around him as he raced across to the entrance of the cave where we knelt. He stood beside us and gasped for air. His chest heaved with the strain of his hectic journey. He untied a sack from his back and produced a large loaf of bread, which he presented to me.

'This is for you and the brothers. It is a gift from my father.'

'I thank you, and your father, for providing us this day with our daily bread.' I placed the bread on a stone before me. 'Let us give thanks.' I led the brothers in the Lord's Prayer.

As the prayer ended, I turned around, intent on asking the young man who his father was and how he had known that we were here. But the young man had disappeared. I checked back in the direction from which he had come, but there was no dust cloud to indicate his whereabouts.

We were totally exhausted and agreed to rest and enjoy the peace and tranquillity of the caves for a couple of weeks until we fully recovered. The caves offered shelter, a chance to gather our strength and recuperate. The damp walls produced sufficient moisture to quench our thirst and cool our burns, and the vegetation that continued to thrive in the moist conditions provided some sustenance.

Juniper quickly resumed his perpetual smiling countenance, and even Barbaro stopped moaning.

Each day, two or three brothers would travel into the town to preach or to work in return for sufficient food for us to share. The rest of us enjoyed the time to reflect quietly, pray, give thanks for our rescue and share our plans for the future.

As the brothers walked through the town, they would ask about the young man and his father who had provided us with bread. No one could identify him from their descriptions. His whereabouts, and how his father had acquired knowledge of our predicament, remained a mystery to my brothers. To me, however; the explanation was clear. My arrogance had placed my brothers at risk; my Father in Heaven had saved us.

The Pope had challenged us to extend our ministry and deliver souls to the Catholic Church, and in saving us, my Lord had demonstrated His endorsement of our quest.

PART THREE

CHAPTER NINE
PEACEMAKER

The townsfolk of Assisi were greatly excited by our news of the Pope's recognition. Everywhere I went, people came up to me and asked when they could hear me speak in public. Several approached Bishop Guido and he graciously granted permission for me to preach in the town's Church of San Giorgio. Word spread. More people from the town, and then from the villages around, expressed an interest in hearing the former *mad* son of Pietro Bernardone preach.

When the day of my inaugural service arrived, the crowd was so large that the Mayor asked if the Cathedral of San Rufino could instead be the venue. Father Tiberio, as Assistant Bishop, was responsible for the Cathedral and refused the request, but the Bishop overruled his objections and granted permission.

I waited by the fountain and watched as the congregation streamed into the cathedral. Bishop Guido had advised me to let them settle before I made my entrance. It was a warm day, and I was nervous of preaching before the townsfolk. I vividly remembered how, after my disastrous attempt to join the crusade with Giovanni, they had ridiculed me on my return to the town, a broken and troubled young man. Those times might be behind me now, but I was still unsure of the reaction that I would receive.

The water spilled from the gargoyles and splashed into the shallow basin of the fountain. My hands felt clammy, so I plunged them into the cool refreshing water, instantly feeling calmer. I smiled at the antics of the pigeons as they bathed under the water spouts and drank from the trough. Two male birds fanned their tails and uttered throaty coos to attract their mates. I remembered how the dove had called to me on the day as I knelt beside the lake, the day that I was called to His service, the day that I began my journey to become His instrument of peace, not only in Assisi, but also across the wider world.

But first, I must begin with Assisi.

As I crossed the threshold and entered the cool interior, I prayed to St. Rufino for his blessing and guidance. The familiar smell of incense soothed my nerves. I saw my loyal brothers standing at the rear of the congregation. Juniper smiled and gave me a cheerful little wave of encouragement. Bernardo winked, and Pietro clasped his hands together in prayerful support. I turned to face the congregation. 'Good morning, good people. I thank you for your good wishes and for welcoming me here today.'

In the usual tradition, the crowd cheered and applauded.

Encouraged, I told them of our trip to Rome and our delight at being received by the Pope. I told them how joyful we were that he had given us his blessing to continue with our Order and our ministry.

They cheered and applauded again.

I told them about our desire to live, following the example that was given to us by our Lord Jesus Christ, living in poverty, and the joy and freedom that this brought to the Friars Minor.

More cheers. Not one voice called me mad, or a fool.

'How do we discover the inner peace we all crave?' I asked.

I looked around the congregation who by now had become more subdued.

'We need to love our neighbours as we do ourselves. We need to help and support each other, and in return we will find peace, contentment and God's blessing. Repent the things you have done and said to each other, and God will also forgive you. Return to others those things that you have taken, and you will find much greater rewards in Heaven. The more you give, the more you will receive. We must dedicate our lives to our Lord Jesus Christ. In return, we have His promise that we will enjoy His abounding love, peace of mind, and everlasting life.

I prayed for them as individuals, as families, and as a town. I told them how saddened I was to see that our beloved town was still ripped apart by conflict and bitter squabbles. I reminded them of the bloody war and the battle which took place on the plains between Assisi and Perugia. I shared my sadness with them at how several of my friends, their sons, had died that day, and how those of us who survived had rotted in prison for a year while our health deteriorated. I explained my pleasure in the fact that the riots that followed had now settled down, but I was concerned, as they must be, that there were still bitter disputes and considerable anger amongst the people of Assisi and the surrounding villages. We, the common people, had been promised more liberty and involvement in the administration of the town, but as yet, this had not transpired. These issues, I told them, needed to be addressed before Assisi could be at peace.

I put my hands together. 'Let us pray.'

Most of the congregation knelt and assumed a prayerful position, although a few of the older and more infirm ones simply bowed their heads.

'Lord, make me an instrument of your peace,
Where there is hatred, let me sow love;
Where there is injury, pardon;
Where there is doubt, faith;
Where there is despair, hope;
Where there is darkness, light;
Where there is sadness, joy.
O Divine Master,
Grant that I may not so much seek to be consoled, as to console;
To be understood, as to understand;
To be loved, as to love.
For it is in giving that we receive.
It is in pardoning that we are pardoned;
And it is in dying that we are born to Eternal Life.
Amen.

The congregation stood in shocked silence. This message of peace was so unlike the prescribed church service that they normally experienced; and was not what they had expected. My breath failed to come as I awaited their response. Slowly, one by one, they began to applaud. Neighbour turned to neighbour and shook hands or hugged each other. They began to talk amongst themselves.

'He is right,' cried one. 'This has been going on for more than five years. It must be sorted, once and for all.'

Cries of agreement reverberated throughout the congregation.

I was more than happy to offer my support in the various meetings that followed, and to act as arbitrator. Within a few weeks, on November the ninth in the year of Our Lord twelve hundred and ten, an agreement was signed. The nobles gave up their feudal right for an annual payment; a fair taxation system was negotiated; the villagers acquired equal rights with the town folk, and exiles were given the freedom to return without fear of retaliation. The agreement restored peace to the town of Assisi.

Peace also continued throughout the winter at Rivotorto, but as the winter turned to spring, a local peasant arrived one morning, herding an ass. We were kneeling in prayer at the entrance to the building. The animal was reluctant to pass through the centre of our group for fear of trampling us, but the peasant pushed him on into the shelter, beating him with a stick.

'Go on, go on in. We will be comfortable in here. We have as much right as these fellows to make this our home.'

My brothers and I looked at each other and then at the peasant as he disappeared into the hovel.

'Well,' I said, 'a home is a possession as much as any other. If somebody else wants use of this place that has sheltered us so well, then so be it.'

And just like that, we were homeless.

What a joy. Being made homeless was the best thing that could have happened. The Abbot of the Benedictines of Mt. Subasio heard of our plight and approached me with the excellent news that we could have the use of the Porziuncola in perpetuity.

The rent was a basketful of fish from the river once a year. The Porziuncola was the answer to my prayers – the chapel which I had so lovingly restored and where I had experienced a direct link to God.

The new location also gave us space and capacity to undertake the Pope's bidding; grow our numbers, recruit new brothers and increase our endeavours to save numerous souls.

Our immediate task was to set about working on the grounds of the chapel, building small willow huts for each of us to sleep in, with a suitably large one to accommodate Masseo. We planted more trees and a hedge around the compound to create and enhance our tranquil sylvan home. Egidio used his farming expertise and created a wonderful vegetable garden.

We also built some workshops, so that as we recruited brothers with skills, such as carpentry or leather work, they could offer their services to the locals in exchange for food. The one concession to the Rule relating to poverty was that those brothers with a trade could retain possession of the instruments required to carry out their work.

Often, as we preached in the villages and towns, people approached who wished to join us but were unable to, as they had wives, children, or responsibilities that made it impossible for them to do so. I began to realise that there might be a need for a new Order in the future, with a Rule similar to our own, but for families. For now, with so much to achieve, I put it from my mind.

I arrived back in the town of Bevagna. My purpose today was not to visit the town itself but to pass through on my way to the Annunziata. The dozen or so Benedictine monks who lived there had invited me to take a short retreat with them. I was looking forward to renewing my friendship with Abbot Antonio, my old friend from the *Societas Iuvenum* youth group.

Leaving the town behind me, I walked until the sun was high and the temperature uncomfortable, forcing me to look around for somewhere to sit and seek some shelter. Turning a corner, I found the perfect place. Before me lay a small lake. The smooth surface reflected the sky, and trees – a mirror image. A spring fed into the lake and supplied clear fresh water. I sank to the grass under the shade of a weeping willow tree, dangled my feet in the cool water and gave thanks to God for this heavenly spot.

When the temperature cooled sufficiently, I resumed my journey. The view from the far side of the lake filled me with joy. Assisi, in the distant hazy sunshine, clung to the mountainside and glowed with a pale rosy tint under the sun's rays, the perfect picture of serenity.

But serenity was no longer apparent when I arrived at the convent. Abbot Antonio, always the more thoughtful member of our youth group, looked not only serious but gravely ill. He thanked and dismissed the young novice who brought me to his room, waited for him to leave and then turned to face me.

'Brother Francesco. How wonderful to see you, and looking so well. How long since we last met?' He embraced me warmly.

'Too long, my friend. I am grateful for your kind invitation.'

'Come and sit down. Let me offer you some wine to refresh you after your journey and that steep climb.'

He walked over to his desk, picked up a silver jug and poured wine into two goblets.

'Thank you, I will take a little. Could you mix it with water? Strong wine makes my head spin these days.'

'Goodness, Francesco, where is that young man who drank us all under the table?'

'Long gone, and best forgotten. What of you, Antonio? An Abbot at such an early age. Congratulations – you have done well.'

'Have I?' He passed me a goblet of wine. 'Brother Francesco, I beg your forgiveness. I know I invited you here for a retreat, but I also need your advice on an urgent issue.'

'As God's humble servant, if there is anything I can do, you know I will, gladly.'

Antonio leaned forward and lowered his voice to a whisper. 'It is Brother Bartholomew. He is creating mayhem.' He wrung his hands. 'I have tried to speak to him, but it makes no difference. He undermines me at every opportunity, questions my authority and openly defies me.' Antonio pushed back his chair and paced the room.

'I am not sure that I know him, do I?'

He moved over to the window and flung the shutters wide. 'See, over there on the far side of the vegetable plot. There. Do you see him?'

I looked over Antonio's shoulder. A tall, lean monk, with black hair speckled with grey, a bushy black beard, and a pointed nose, hoed the soil with considerable vigour. He paused briefly to mop his forehead with his sleeve.

'No, I do not believe that we have met. Do you know why he behaves this way?'

'He is older than I and more experienced. Everyone expected the Bishop to recommend him as Abbot Paulo's replacement last year, but the Bishop took us all by surprise and recommended me. There was a vote, and I was elected.'

'Why did the Bishop endorse you, do you know?'

'He told me that, in his opinion, the convent had become too comfortable, and the monks lax and lazy. And he was correct. The place was dirty. The monks employed too many staff, so they lived very well without any need for work. Abbot Paulo claimed that this gave the monks more time to pray, but in my opinion, idle hands make idle monks. There needs to be a balance.'

'Do you think that Brother Bartholomew intended to continue in the same way as Abbot Paulo?'

'He certainly appears to resent the changes that I have made. I have adopted the Rule of Benedict himself so that only those monks who work hard are allowed red meat in their diet. The monks are now eager to work. They do their own cleaning, cooking and laundry, and grow vegetables. We milk the cows, make cheese and sell the excess, along with any surplus vegetables. We also keep honey bees, vines, and pigs.'

'So I can smell.'

Antonio laughed and closed the shutters. 'We are now completely self-sufficient. We no longer depend upon the generosity of the local population and handouts from the Bishop. And yet ...'

My old friend looked gaunt with worry, and I was determined to help in any way possible.

'I will carefully watch while I stay,' I promised, 'and I will pray for guidance. By God's grace, we may solve this thorny problem.'

Antonio thanked me profusely and showed me to my cell.

The next morning, I was walking towards the chapel when I spotted the young novice who had been my escort the day before. He sat in the cloisters, head bowed and covered by his cowl. I went to pass by but then I noticed that his shoulders shook with emotion. I sat beside him. He was stroking a wet lump of fur. A dead kitten.

'What has happened here?'

'I was training him to catch mice.' The young novice choked back a sob. 'Brother Bartholomew drowned him.'

'No, that cannot be; surely he would not take an innocent life? What reason did he give for such an act?'

'He said that it was a lesson to me. I put the love for my pet before my love for God, and now the kitten is dead in punishment for my sins.'

The feelings that surged through me at this news were far from Christian. I swallowed, prayed for calm and focused on bringing some consolation to the young man. We wrapped the animal in some sackcloth and buried him under a rose bush. We said a few words in prayer for his innocent soul, and then I left the grieving novice and went in search of Bartholomew.

I found him on his knees, weeding around the base of a garden bench.

'Brother Bartholomew, what is the meaning of this abomination?' I fought to keep my voice steady. 'How could you sacrifice a poor creature, simply to teach a young novice a lesson?'

He looked up, startled by my anger.

'What are you saying? Do you believe that I would kill a small kitten? What monster do you take me for?'

'I have spoken to the novice.'

Bartholomew stood. He was much taller than I. He looked down his long nose and frowned, clearly shaken by the confrontation.

'If there is another explanation,' I said, 'please, share it with me.'

He stared at me, then at the sky, then at his feet. 'I did not kill the kitten, Brother Francesco. I found him floating in the garden pond this morning. He must have taken a drink and toppled in.'

'Then I am much relieved. But why did you imply that his death was the fault of the young novice?'

'The boy will make an excellent monk if he does not get distracted by his popularity or his tender personality. I was trying to teach him a lesson.'

'His heart is broken. Do you truly believe this to be an effective lesson?' I put my hand on Bartholomew's shoulders. 'I do not think you need me to tell you that a gentle rebuke would have been sufficient to remind him that his love for God must come first.'

Bartholomew slumped onto the bench. 'Forgive me, Brother Francesco. My intention was honest, but I see that the execution may have been wrong.'

I sat beside him. 'And is this the same intention you show towards Abbot Antonio?'

'I do not understand.'

'Do you not? Then sit awhile with me in silence and perhaps the answer will come.'

I sat beside Bartholomew and watched his face as realisation slowly dawned.

'Truly,' he said, 'I believe that Abbot Antonio is doing an excellent job of turning the Abbey around. He is yet young, and has much to learn, but I do not doubt that he will become an outstanding Abbot. Does he think that I believe otherwise?'

I maintained my silence, and after a short while, he spoke again.

'My criticisms were intended to challenge him, to make him question his judgement and decisions and thus to learn from them.' He dropped his head into his hands. 'I have only criticised, have I not? I have undermined his confidence. How could he know my true intentions when I failed to communicate them?' He fell to his knees and covered his head with his cowl. 'Brother Francesco, please forgive me. I see now how wrong I was. I will speak to Abbot Antonio at once, and the other brothers.'

'And to the young novice?'

'I will tell him what happened and beg his forgiveness. Is there anything else I can do? I welcome your advice, Brother Francesco.'

I thought for a moment. 'Well,' I smiled, 'every monastery needs a well-trained cat to keep it free from mice.'

By the time my retreat ended a few days later, peace and tranquillity was restored, and a new kitten instated. I had also come to realise how hardworking the monks were, both physically and spiritually. However, my stay also confirmed my belief that the nomadic life of a friar, living in poverty and following in the footsteps of Jesus, was the right one for me. Everyone had learned important lessons.

Approaching the village of Gubbio, I came upon a group of excited and angry people gathered on the village green. I say *green*, but in fact, it was not green at all – more like an area of mud in the middle of the village covered with piles of discarded refuse, broken pots, animal bones, entrails, rotting food and even human excrement. The place stank. Flies swarmed around the heads of those gathered there.

'What has happened here?' I asked.

'Yesterday a wolf attacked and killed a young child who was playing out on the green,' a man told me.

'My baby was such a good boy. We loved him so much, and now he's gone.' The dead child's mother turned to her husband, who took her into his arms as she sobbed uncontrollably.

'The wolf is evil,' a woman cried.

'For two years he has terrorised our village,' said another.

'He has slaughtered our chickens and goats,' a young man said shaking his fist.

'And now a child. That poor boy,' an elderly man shook his head. He looked across to the parents. 'His poor mother.'

I approached the young couple and placed my hands on their shoulders. 'No words I can say will take away your pain. Take comfort from your love for each other. God is with you, and will help you through this dreadful time.' I turned to the man who had first spoken to me. 'Tell me where I can find this animal. I will see what I can do.'

He looked at me with fear in his eyes. 'You must not approach him. He will surely kill you.'

'Fear not, for God is with me. Fetch me a sack and a couple of chickens.'

I headed in the direction indicated, and before long I came upon the beast, sheltered in a glade.

His yellow eyes followed my every move. I knelt, quiet and still, and prayed for his troubled soul. He snarled, drooled and thrashed his tail against the grass. I continued to pray. After some time, he matched my stillness. I prayed for a while longer and then reached into the sack and removed one of the chickens.

'Eat this, brother wolf, and be happy that God has provided for you.'

I stood and threw the chicken towards him. He gulped it down and then walked towards me with his head bowed. I held his gaze, and he lay at my feet.

'Come with me and you shall have more,' I said.

The villagers were still gathered on the green. As we drew near they huddled together, pitchforks raised. I turned and held my hands out above the wolf. He lay down at my feet and lowered his head. I removed the second chicken from the sack and gave it to him. He took it gently and proceeded to eat.

'Tomorrow,' I told the townsfolk, 'you must put food out for him at this spot, at this time. He will no longer trouble you, your children, or your animals.'

'How do you know?' somebody called out.

'Trust in God. This wolf is now your brother.' I pointed to the green. 'You must also remove this rubbish. Dig a pit in the woods and bury it to reduce the odour that attracts wild animals and flies, and to reduce the spread of disease. Plant this area with grasses and wildflowers, so your children can play safely and enjoy the space. Go and live your lives in peace, give love and support to each other.'

I patted the wolf's head, and he paused his eating to lick my hand.

'It's a miracle,' somebody shouted.

'No miracle,' I assured them hastily. 'I love all God's creatures, and they respond. If you love this wolf and give him food, he will respond to your kindness with gentleness.'

I returned to Gubbio often on my travels. The village green had been transformed into a children's grassy play area, covered in wildflowers. My friend the wolf was also transformed. The children gathered around him without any sense of fear. They patted him and draped daisy chains around his neck. No rumours of a miracle reached Father Tiberio, and for that I was thankful.

The farmer's wife emerged from the cowshed carrying two pails of creamy milk.

'Brother Francesco, how are you and the brothers?' she called.

'We are well, thanks to God and this wonderful weather we are enjoying.'

'Are you sure? You look troubled.'

'I am off to visit my old friend, Enricho, who was always so generous to my brother and me. I hear that he has fallen gravely ill.'

'Wait there,' the farmer's wife bade me. 'I have something for you.'

She returned moments later with a basket holding two containers. 'I want to share our bountiful harvest with you and your friend. The bees were especially generous this year.'

I gladly accepted the two pots of honey, promised to return the basket next time I was in the vicinity and gave her and the bees a blessing. My heart lifted a little at the prospect of being able to share the gift with Enricho.

I reached his home and knocked on the front door.

'Come in, the door is open,' a feeble voice called from within.

I entered the dimly lit room. A blazing log fire provided the only light. I was shocked to see how thin and frail Enricho looked. He shivered, although the room was warm, and he sat wrapped in several blankets. A mattress lay beside his chair, festooned with cushions and more blankets. It was obvious that Enricho could no longer mount the stairs to his sleeping quarters.

'Enricho, my dear friend, is there anything that I can do for you?'

His gaunt face stretched into a smile as I approached. 'Your company means a great deal to me, I want for nothing else.'

I reached into my basket. 'I have brought you a pot of honey, heaven's nectar. It will soothe your throat.' I placed it on the table beside his chair, happy to give him a present for a change. 'Have you eaten?'

Enricho nodded. 'Thanks to my neighbour, God bless him. He comes in every evening and brings me a bowl of soup and some freshly baked bread. He also lights my fire to keep me warm through the cool evening and night.'

I sat beside him and patted his hand. 'Do you know, Enricho, I often think of those happy times when we enjoyed our meals together, and you brought us the carved animals for our ark. Do you remember the camels?'

'Indeed, I do. They were happy times.' A tear welled up and rolled down his cheek. 'I see your mother often. She brings me any items that I need from the shops or the market. She speaks of you all the time and tells me how she always knew that your destiny was to become famous across the world as a man of God.'

My own eyes became teary as I thought of how I missed my dear mother. 'What of my father, does he visit you?'

'He is not a well man, Francesco – close to death, I hear. While you are so near to your old home, could you not go and see him, make your peace?'

I remembered with sadness the last time I met my mother. How she had begged me to stay away, her eyes full of fear. I also thought about the way my brother, Angelo, had threatened me. I held Enricho's parchment-thin hand in mine.

'It is strange, is it not, my old friend? As God's instrument, I may have brought peace to numerous individuals, the town of Assisi, to an abbey of troubled monks, and even more recently, to a village under threat from a marauding wolf, but I fear that peace in the Bernardone household proves to be beyond me.'

He clutched my hand. 'You know, Francesco, I told your father once that you were capable of becoming a great leader, and now here you are with an Order of your own. He was so frightened of what might become of you, but he need not have worried.'

The memory of that night took me by surprise with its intensity. 'What is it, Francesco?'

'It shames me to say it, Enricho, but after all these years I must confess I eavesdropped on that conversation. Not by design, but ...'

Enricho's eyes widened. 'And did you hear what was said?'

'I did.' I looked him in the eye. 'My father's words hurt me deeply, but you should know that the generosity of your words has meant so much to me over all these years. Even more than that beautiful ark, or any of the animals you carved for us.'

'Francesco, I am sorry that you were a witness to your father's despair, but his drive and ambition and your differences have made you the man you are today. Never forget that. And never doubt him. He only ever wanted the best for you.'

'But he never loved me.'

'Oh yes he did. Do you know why you are called Francesco when in fact you were christened Giovanni?'

'I never thought about it.'

'When you were a baby, your father was so proud of you. He used to call you his little French man. The name, Francesco was created from his love. How many children can say that they have a name created especially for them?'

'I never knew.' I could feel the tears burning behind my eyes. Had I misjudged my father so badly?

I gave Enricho my thanks and a blessing, and then, with a sudden rush of emotion, reached over and kissed his thin, pale cheek. I knew that this was the last time we would meet in this world, and the knowledge filled me with sadness.

CHAPTER TEN

THE GROWTH OF THE FRIARS MINOR

My steps quickened as I drew closer to the Porziuncola. I enjoyed my spells away preaching, but after a few weeks, thoughts of returning to this sanctuary of peace, meeting with the brothers and sharing news, always lifted my spirits. I was surprised to find Sylvesto, a local priest, kneeling beside the church entrance, his head bowed in prayer, his hands clenched tightly together.

I remembered the last time that I had seen him; a week after the sale of Bernardo's home and processions. Bernardo and I were distributing the proceeds, in small bags of coins, to the poor families of Assisi.

I clearly remembered Sylvesto's words that day. 'You robbed me,' he had cried as he stood before us and shook his fists. 'How could you do this? You stand here and give away your money and yet you paid me so little for the stones that you needed for the Porziuncola.'

Bernardo had grabbed a purse of coins from the pile and thrust it at Sylvesto. 'I'm sorry, but I thought I paid you a fair price. Are you satisfied now, or do you want more?'

Several people in the crowd commented on Sylvesto's greed. He hung his head, flushed with embarrassment, and sidled away. I had not thought about the incident again until now.

'Good morning, Sylvesto, what brings you to see us today?'

He rose to greet me. 'Oh Brother Francesco, please say that you can forgive me for my greed. I have not spent a day without thoughts of our last meeting. I have carried the heavy burden of my guilt since then and have prayed constantly. I am so ashamed. Please, I beg you; say that you can find forgiveness in your heart.'

'I have already forgiven you,' I said.

'Brother Francesco, my shame brought me here to see you today and also my dream. Last night I dreamt that a giant dragon terrorised the town of Assisi. He flew above the town breathing fire, scorching the Basilica of San Rufino, and the townsfolk who gathered there for sanctuary.'

An image of Father Tiberio sprang to mind, and how, in my youth, we had always referred to him as the Dragon. His words and punishment had most certainly scorched me on the day that I accidentally damaged my father's cloth, and on the several occasions we had crossed swords since then.

Falling back to his knees, Sylvesto looked up at me; his eyes sparkled with unshed tears. 'Then you appeared, Brother Francesco, wielding your sword and carrying a shield emblazoned with the cross of our Lord. The cross was made of gold and it flashed in the sunlight and dazzled the dragon so that you were able to approach him without the beast realising. You thrust your sword into his throat.' Sylvesto mimed the plunge of a non-existent sword. 'Wounded, he collapsed at your feet, whereupon you climbed onto his back and drove your sword into his neck. The foul and loathsome dragon was slain.'

Sylvesto raised his arms in praise. 'I sincerely believe that my vision came from God and that you and the Friars Minor will not only save Assisi from the fire of damnation but also that you will become famous. Your humble message will spread around the world, saving souls wherever it is received.'

'You sound like my mother, Sylvesto. She was always telling me she had a vision of how famous I would become one day. It is not fame I desire, but our quest is indeed to save souls and deliver them to the Holy Catholic Church – a quest confirmed by the Pope himself.'

Sylvesto continued to kneel before me, reached for my hand and kissed it. 'Brother Francesco, I beg that you allow me to come and be of service to you and the other brothers. I am not one for missionary adventures, I could not preach to large crowds, but I do have a calling from God to offer contemplation and spiritual counsel. May I join you and the brothers in your mission, offering my humble service in this way?'

I smiled warmly. 'Another priest will be a useful addition to the Friars Minor, and a spiritual counsellor will be of great value to us all. Welcome, Brother Sylvesto.'

Sylvesto joined us that day. He made his home in one of the caves at Carceri.

It was essential that we not only increased our capacity by recruiting more brothers, but also by increasing the physical area and geography of our preaching. To make this possible, we established several hermitages to accommodate the brothers as they ventured out on long journeys to evangelise. I was preaching in the area of one such hermitage, called Monte-Casale. I knew Angelo was in residence at the time and decided to pay him a visit. He was pleased to see me and – as was the custom – offered to wash my feet, but I could see that he was troubled.

'What is it, Brother Angelo? You do not seem as carefree as normal.' I touched his arm and made him look at me. 'Are you disturbed or ill?'

He shook his head. 'I have done wrong, Brother Francesco.'

'Then you must tell me.'

Angelo bowed his head. 'Just before you arrived, three well-known robbers came and knocked at the door. I told them there was nothing to steal. They asked for some food. I scolded them and said that they should be ashamed. I am humiliated to say this, but I slammed the door in their faces.'

I was shocked and unable to disguise my anger at this uncharacteristic and ungenerous behaviour.

'Brother Angelo, whatever happened to your knightly training and sense of chivalry?'

He hung his head in shame, fell to his knees and pulled his cowl over his head.

'Brother Angelo, I beg you in humble obedience to go after these men and take this wine and bread.' I thrust the sack that I was carrying into his hands. 'When you find them, kneel down and beg their forgiveness for your harsh words, and then ask them, in the name of our Lord Jesus Christ, to refrain from their evil ways. Tell them that God will pardon and provide for them. Invite them to return and take supper with us.'

Angelo chased after the three robbers and did as I asked. So taken aback were they that they accepted his invitation and joined us for the evening. That night, the five of us shared food, kindness and no measly portion of laughter. After that, the three men often returned to the hermitage. In time, they gave up their evil ways and became brothers dedicated to carrying out God's work.

Our numbers continued to increase. Rufino, the cousin of Chiara di Offreduccio, also joined us at this time. He was so devout that he prayed in his sleep, but he was very shy. I decided that he should, for his sake, overcome this affliction, and so one day I asked him to preach in a nearby village, divested of his clothes. I watched him walk away with his head down, looking completely dejected. Filled with remorse, I relented and chased after him. He stood naked on the village green surrounded by a crowd of jeering onlookers.

'He must be so devout he has gone mad,' one man in the crowd cried.

I was ashamed that my attempt to help Rufino had resulted in him being the subject of this humiliation. I took off my garments and stood beside him.

'The Lord Jesus Christ was born naked in a stable and died unrobed on a cross of crucifixion, to save our souls. He has given us His promise that if we give up everything and follow Him, we will be rewarded in Heaven and shall enjoy everlasting life.'

At this point, my wise and loyal friend Leo arrived. He had witnessed me running off after Rufino and followed. He picked up our garments; handed them to us and we both dressed. From that day, Rufino was no longer shy when he preached – or maybe he was so scared that I would ask him to preach naked again that he forced himself to appear less inhibited. I also learned an important lesson that day. I had tried to help Rufino overcome his shyness, but my over-zealous demands could be construed as unkindness. They could have resulted in Rufino rejecting our way of life and walking away from the Friars Minor.

When we arrived in the small towns and villages, the local priests now accepted that we had the Pope's approval to preach. They allowed us access to their churches, albeit sometimes reluctantly. However, I was often surprised at how dirty and uncared for the churches were. It did not seem right to me that worship should take place within such squalor. It was my usual practice to arrive sometime before the service. On this particular day, I began by washing the altar cloth in fresh water from the nearby stream and hanging it out to dry in the fresh air. I then took a fresh cloth and dusted down the altar and lectern, before applying a thin film of a mixture I made from melting together beeswax and olive oil. I rubbed the surfaces with a soft cloth until they shone with a burnished glow. Next, I turned my attention to the floor. I fashioned a broom from some heather and a stick and began to sweep the church.

One of the locals arrived and introduced himself.

'My name is Giovanni, and I have hoped to meet you for some time. I hear good things about you and the Friars Minor. I also heard a story of how you cured a leper. Is that true?'

'I believe the Lord Jesus was able to help him. I was merely his instrument.'

'Let me help you with this sweeping.'

Giovanni made himself a broom and proceeded to copy my actions. When we had finished the floor, I recovered the altar cloth and spread it out across the gleaming wood. I lit some candles and then arranged several pots with the wild flowers I had collected on my journey that morning. Placing the candles and flowers on the altar and window ledges, I stood back to admire our hard work. The church looked remarkable, its beauty enhanced by the delicate fragrance of the flowers. What an improvement. Now it was a suitable and an appropriate place for worship.

Giovanni stayed for the service and approached me again later.

'May I join you, Brother Francesco? I have thought of doing so for some time. Today has confirmed my earlier ambition. This life is definitely the one I have yearned for.'

Of course, I was happy for him to join our growing community. Giovanni tried to learn very quickly, and he did this by mimicking everything that I did. If I paused to blow my nose, he did, too. If I bent down to pick something up off the floor, he did the same. The other brothers laughed at him at first, but eventually they came to recognise his actions as a demonstration of his extreme obedience and willingness to learn. He imitated me in the same way that we attempted to follow the example of our Lord Jesus Christ. I called him Brother St. Giovanni, and he became a valued member of the Friars Minor.

I pulled up my cowl to protect my ears from the cold night air, thrust my hands deep into my pockets and strode through the town. After three weeks away preaching in Sienna and the surrounding areas, I was looking forward to arriving at the Porziuncola.

In front of me, a shadowy figure knelt by the roadside. Was it a beggar, a thief or a frail old man who had collapsed from the cold? I drew closer and gasped as I recognised the figure of Brother Celano crouched by an open window. He was another new addition to the Order; with us for only a few months. I approached him slowly so that I did not distract him, but he was so engrossed that I need not have bothered. He was peering over the windowsill and into the kitchen of a small house. As I drew closer I could see over his shoulder and into the room beyond. In shocked silence I watched as a young maid washed her hair in a bowl of water that stood on the kitchen table. Her young breasts swelled over the bodice of her dress and it was this image that transfixed Brother Celano, turning him into a statue.

Reaching over, I gently placed my hand on his shoulder. He leapt up and gasped as he recognised me, his face flushed scarlet.

'Let us leave this place, Brother Celano.' I gently steered him down the steep road until we reached the west gate of the town.

By this time Celano had recovered his breath. 'Brother Francesco, I am so ashamed of my behaviour. Please forgive me.' He fell at my feet, grasped my hand and kissed it.

'Get up, brother. It is not me to whom you should apologise, but to our Lord God, to whom you have promised complete obedience and chastity.'

'I will never approach the maid. I have not broken my vows.'

'In thoughts, you have indeed broken them. Celibacy means complete abstinence, in thoughts as well as deeds. We will return to our brothers, and as we walk, we will do so in silence and contemplation while we both reflect on what should be done.'

We trudged back to the Porziuncola, both of us deep in thought and prayer. My own were of the previous winter when the snow had lain heavy on the ground. I remembered how I had woken one morning from a dream. It was an exciting dream. A young and beautiful woman was walking towards me with her arms out-stretched. She was entirely naked, and I woke just as she was about to take me in her arms. I was embarrassed by the dream, and by my reaction to it. I hurried outside into the frozen morning air, stripped myself bare and threw myself down into a bank of snow. The chill of the snow quickly cooled my ardour, but I continued to roll on the ground as penance for my thoughts, unsolicited though they were.

The brothers were pleased to see us and insisted that we should sit while they washed our feet.

'What news, Francesco?

'I have been received well. Many have pledged allegiance to our Lord after they heard the word of the gospels. Several new brothers will be joining us.' I paused and looked at Celano, 'and some may be leaving.'

Celano flushed scarlet as the brothers turned and stared at him.

'I am sorry, brothers,' he mumbled. 'I have let you all down. I am not worthy to remain here with you.'

I put my hand on Celano's shoulder. 'That is not my meaning, Brother Celano. For some time now, I have thought that there should be an Order for those who are married, or those who find celibacy difficult or even impossible.'

'Oh ho,' Brother Barbaro said, grinning at Celano.

'I confess,' Celano stuttered. 'I am unable to commit to a life of celibacy.'

'The more I travel amongst people,' I said, 'the more convinced I become that a new Order is needed. Celibacy in such an Order will mean discipline and faithfulness within marriage. The Order of Tertiaries will be established for those who want to commit to our principles, but within a family setting. What say you, Brother Celano?'

Celano looked as though he might faint with gratitude. 'I say that I, a humble penitent, will embrace this new Order, Brother Francesco. I thank you for this chance to continue to serve God.'

'Go in peace, Celano.' I gave his shoulder a gentle squeeze. 'We cannot all be celibate, or there would be no more children, and the world would come to an end.'

I laughed, and the others joined me. Each, in turn, clapped Celano on his back and wished him well.

'Go forth, Celano. Find you a good woman.'

'Yes, get married, settle down and have children.'

'May God be with you.'

'Good luck, Celano.'

Celano returned a few months later and proudly introduced us to his young bride, and to their families and friends. I recognised her from the night she had washed her hair and ignited Celano's passion.

'Brother Francesco, will you do us the great honour and bless our marriage? It will truly make the occasion very special for us both.'

I was happy to bless their union, and we all celebrated the occasion with a wedding banquet provided by the bride's family. Celano's problem with the vow of celibacy was yet another important lesson for me: not every brother would find it easy to live by our Rule or vows, and some tolerance would be required. After all, losing Celano from the Order did not mean he was lost to God. Sometimes, I realised, it is important to know when to stand back and let go.

Not all our recruits were human. My love of animals and their affinity with me had become widely known. A young man came across a baby hare, injured in a trap. He took pity on the creature and brought him to me. The hare's leg was damaged. I bathed it in clean water and bound it tightly to ensure that the bone would repair and that the wound would heal. I kept him by my side as his health improved. He would sit on my lap, gazing up at me with his huge bright eyes while I gently stroked his soft fur. After a few weeks, I was able to remove the bindings from his leg, and we were both relieved to find he was able to move without any problems. He leapt into the air, ran in a circle, returned to my side and nudged my ankle with his nose. I picked him up, took him to the edge of the woods and carefully placed him on the ground. Much as I enjoyed his companionship, it was time for me to put the lesson I had learned from Celano into practice, stand back and let him go.

'Off you go now, brother hare. Go and find your family, and may the Lord give you peace, good health, and a long and contented life.'

I turned back, intending to pray and give thanks for the hare's restored health. However, as I reached my cell, I discovered the hare had followed me. I picked him up and took him back to the edge of the woods, but it was no good; every time I put him down and turned to leave him, he followed me.

Over the next few months the hare grew, and on occasions he went for a run into the woods, but he always returned in the evening. He came to me one night, and I sat stroking him until he jumped from my lap and lolloped over to the entrance of my cell. He turned to look at me, and it was as though he wanted me to follow. I walked over to the doorway. He continued to lollop into the centre of the compound, and then turned again, encouraging me to follow. As we arrived at the edges of the woods, there was a rustling in the undergrowth and out jumped a female hare followed by two small leverets.

'Oh, how clever you are,' I exclaimed. 'No wonder you are proud. You have a wonderful family of your own now. Well done, go in peace and live a happy life.'

He continued to return, sometimes with a new brood, but often just to spend an evening on my lap. What a delight his friendship brought to me. What joy I shared with all these animals. Their unconditional love, acceptance and approval reminded me of the love our Lord God in Heaven bestowed upon us, His humble servants. It stood in stark contrast to the approval and love that I had struggled to earn from my father.

Recruits to the Friars Minor, both animal, and human, came to us in all sorts of ways. I was walking into Assisi when a young man overtook me, carrying a cage containing two white doves.

'Where are you taking those?' I asked.

'To market, I hope to sell them.'

'But they're such beautiful birds. What if they fall into the hands of someone who will treat them badly?'

'Oh, I had not thought of that.' The young man looked at me, then at the birds, and then back at me.

'Or even eat them,' I added.

'You are right.' He thrust the cage at me. 'Here, you can have them. I know you will care for them well.'

He accompanied me back to the Porziuncola and sat with me while I made a woven basket lined with soft grasses.

Carefully, I lifted each dove from the cage. 'There you go, my little sisters, you shall be happy here in this comfortable nest.' I could feel their tiny hearts fluttering as I placed them in their new home and handed the empty cage back to the youth.

'May I come and visit them?' he asked.

I looked at him. He was obviously a kind and caring person. He would make a fine brother. I thought about asking him to join us, but since the episode with Rufino, I had learned to curb my enthusiastic demands. 'You are welcome anytime,' I told him. 'Go in peace.'

The young man returned many times, until after several visits – without any pressure from me – he made the decision to stay and join us as a brother. The doves also remained. They raised chicks and grew in number, and from that time, there was always a cloud of doves at the Porziuncola; symbols of peace and love.

The growth in our numbers was certainly something to celebrate. It increased our capacity to extend our preaching and save more souls. However, one recruit unintentionally became the cause of a major upset. Ginepro, the newest recruit to our Order, was a simple fellow, always full of fun and good cheer. Everyone adored him, even though he was the clumsiest and most ungainly young man I had ever met.

Angelo was feeling unwell, and Ginepro volunteered to care for him. Angelo, having been used to employing the services of a page in his past, was clearly in his element. Despite his illness, he obviously enjoyed the experience as Ginepro fussed and ministered to his every need.

'What can I fetch for you, Angelo that will restore your appetite?' Ginepro asked. 'You must eat to get your strength back.'

'I know,' Angelo sighed. 'But the thought of food turns my stomach. I remember when I was a child, and I was ill like this, my mother always brought me a pig's trotter and boiled it for me. I was always better for eating a pig's trotter.'

'Then I will fetch you one.'

Ginepro bounded off in search of the yearned-for food. He returned an hour later, proudly brandishing a pig's trotter, which he placed into the soup pot.

'There you are, Brother Angelo.' He proceeded to light the fire beneath the pot. 'It will soon be ready, and you will start to get better.'

Shortly afterwards a large man with a bulbous nose and angry red complexion ran into the yard, shaking his stick.

'Where is that thief? Where have you hidden him?' he demanded.

'Thief?' I asked, astonished. 'I do not know whom you mean.'

'There he is.' The man pointed at Ginepro. 'He stole the foot from my best sow and left her lying in her pen close to death.'

It seemed that in his haste to help Angelo, Ginepro had not thought of the consequences. He had chopped the foot off the first pig he found.

'What can be done to save her?' I asked horrified at the idea of the poor creature lying butchered in its bed.

'I have put her out of her misery – what other choice was there? In stealing the foot, he condemned the pig to death.'

It took us some time and a lot of persuasions to calm the farmer, but eventually he accepted that Ginepro's intentions were honourable, even if his actions were hugely misguided.

'Well, you may as well have the rest of her now,' the farmer grumbled, but I noticed that he was looking at Angelo's wan figure as he spoke.

Later that evening the farmer, escorted by his family, brought us the pig's carcass, and joined us as we roasted the pig on a spit and enjoyed the unexpected bounty.

CHAPTER ELEVEN
CHIARA, THE CHILDREN'S CRUSADE AND THE FIRST ATTEMPT TO VISIT THE HOLY LAND

It was early spring in what many believed to be a magical or a significant year, the year of Our Lord twelve hundred and twelve – one, two, one, two. It was my thirtieth year and one that certainly became a special one for me. It began with a visit from Brother Rufino. He wanted to introduce me to his cousin who craved an audience to discuss the matter of her faith. I agreed to meet her that evening on the condition that she brought along a female chaperone and that Rufino also remained with us.

He returned that evening, accompanied by the chaperone and a slim, beautiful young woman with long blonde hair and the fairest skin: unusual and so extraordinary. Her lips were sensitive; her eyes were dark, shaped like almonds, and framed with long dark lashes. Eyes that men dream about: modest, but with a hint of mystery. I judged that she must be around eighteen years of age.

I had seen her before on three occasions. Once as a young girl leaving town following the deposition of Duke Conrad from Assisi, and twice accompanied by this same chaperone, her aunt, as they visited us in the prison at Perugia. It was Chiara, daughter of Count Favarone di Offreduccio.

Rufino introduced us, and she sat demurely, head bowed. She spoke to me with such reverence in her gentle voice.

'I have seen you in town, but have never been given the opportunity to talk with you.' She lifted her hand to the side of her mouth and spoke in a loud whisper. 'My chaperone is a dragon.'

I glanced across at her aunt and caught a glimpse of laughter in the old woman's eyes.

'My mother found your visit a great comfort,' I said.

'But not you?'

'Yes ... err ... I mean, of course.' I blushed.

She laughed. 'It was nothing, but I was relieved to hear that you were free and that you eventually recovered your health. I was in the square on the day you disowned your earthly father and swore your faith to God. I was only a young girl, but it made a huge impression on me.'

This time, it was her turn to blush, and I guessed it was from the memory of seeing me naked that day.

'I was also in the congregation in the Cathedral of San Rufino, where you preached so movingly.'

'God inspired my words that day, and San Rufino himself.'

'His namesake, my cousin, Rufino, speaks highly of you. He tells me how happy he is since he joined the Friars Minor.'

'Your cousin is a real blessing to us. He is a very popular and devout young man.'

'For some time now, I have wanted to talk to you about my faith.' She looked up and gazed into my eyes, her expression earnest. 'I have yearned to serve God as you do. It is my ambition to follow your example, break away from my rich and futile life and become a servant to poverty, the sick and the poor.'

Her passion made my breath catch. I could sense that she was desperately sincere.

'Let us pray together for guidance,' I suggested.

We knelt, facing each other, our hands clasped before us in prayer. I opened my eyes to look at her and was overwhelmed by her beauty. Here was an intelligent, kind, devout and gentle woman whom I could love and cherish: a wonderful mother to my children. How I longed to have children. We could live our lives together, worship God, read the Bible and share in our prayers and love of our Lord Jesus Christ. Surely this was a better life? Serving God in this way, taking comfort from each other? If only I could take her into my arms, kiss her tenderly and experience the warmth of her body held tightly against mine.

God help me, what was I thinking? Chiara had come to me in faith, risking her reputation by coming to me under cover of night without her parents' knowledge or approval. She had put her trust in me to advise and guide her on her future life. Already I had failed her by succumbing to improper thoughts. How could I contemplate abandoning my vow of chastity, my brothers and the life that we shared together in service to God? These thoughts must be the work of Satan. I closed my eyes and prayed for the strength I needed to resist temptation.

'Dear Lord,' I prayed aloud. 'Help us to understand how we can serve You. Into Thy hands, we commit ourselves, body and soul. Do with us as Thy will.'

'Amen,' she whispered.

I spent several hours in discussion with her, talking about her faith and her ability to cope with a life of poverty after such a sheltered and affluent upbringing. It was obvious from her answers that she was the most devout and committed person, fully aware of the harshness that her new life would bring. Her father was also about to force her to marry a distant cousin, an older man for whom she held no feelings, and it was this commitment that had forced her decision to become a bride of Christ instead.

A nun usually serves as a novice for some months or even years, before taking her vows, but it was clear from our discussion that Chiara's dedication and devotion were absolute, and the usual practice was not necessary.

It was not possible for Chiara to live alongside the Friars Minor at the Porziuncola – this would invite scandalous criticism – but she was happy to stay with some Benedictine nuns until we were able to find a suitable home. An appropriate dwelling for what was sure to become the Second Order, for women who wanted to live by an adaptation of our Rule.

She agreed that they should return home for now, but while family celebrations took place on Palm Sunday, Chiara, and her aunt were to be collected by Rufino and, under the cover of darkness, brought to the Porziuncola for her to take her vows.

Waking early the next morning, I entered the garden. When we had first arrived at the Porziuncola, Egidio had created this area for growing vegetables, but I insisted that one corner was made available for growing roses. My justification was that the rosehips could be used to make syrup that would soothe the sore throat of any brother unfortunate enough to suffer from such a malady. In truth, I loved to walk amongst the flowers and breathe in their heady scent.

A recent addition to the centre of the garden was a small dish on a wooden plinth. I kept it constantly filled with water for the birds to drink. I laughed for joy as I watched a small finch bathing. He flattened his body and allowed the water to flow over his back. As he stood, large droplets of water glistened on his greenish feathers, until he shook himself, scattering them in a fine mist. But I was not here to be entertained; I was here to pray for forgiveness concerning my thoughts of the previous evening.

I knelt in prayer and begged pardon for my improper thoughts. I prayed. Forgive me, Father, for I have sinned. I remained on my knees for some time. I decided that I must do penance for my wicked feelings. Looking up from my prayers, I saw the bed of roses before me. The bushes were covered in sweetly fragranced pink blooms, but also in evil thorns. At times, as I removed the dead flowers to encourage more vigorous growth and enhance the yield of rosehips, I snagged my skin on these thorns. I knew from experience that they could inflict considerable pain. I removed my tunic and threw myself into the rose bushes, asking God for his forgiveness as I did so. I waited for the pain, but it did not come. How could this be? I stared at the roses. The thorns were gone. God, in his mercy, had saved me from my painful penance and granted me pardon from my sins. From that day, the bushes remained thorn-less.

The Friars Minor lined the pathway to the small church. Each one carried a burning torch to welcome Chiara and to light her path. Tonight, the Porziuncola looked more beautiful than ever before. I had applied my beeswax and olive oil mixture to the wooden surfaces and polished them until they shone. We had gathered wild flowers, filled a bowl with them and placed it on the altar between the two wooden candlesticks. The light from the candles and rushlights that adorned the walls reflected in the burnished wood. The air smelled of floral scent and incense. The brothers were all in attendance, together with four Benedictine nuns and Chiara's aunt. The small church was packed, warm, and filled with divine love.

Leo led the service, and then I asked Chiara to denounce her old life. She took off her affluent clothing and knelt before me, dressed only in her simple white slip, while I cut off her hair as a symbol of her humility and lack of vanity. The nuns dressed her in a cloak and cowl, and I tied a white cord around her waist. We prayed through the night and gave thanks for Chiara as she committed to her new life of poverty, penance and seclusion.

After the early morning Mass, I accompanied Chiara and the nuns to their convent, while Rufino escorted their aunt Bianca back to the family home.

The Benedictine nuns lived at San Paolo, a small convent situated a short distance from Assisi, at the conjunction of two streams and surrounded by marshland. The pathway leading from the village of Bastia was lined with cypress trees, their tops lost in the heavy morning mist. No wonder the place was called *Isola Romanica*; it floated before us like an island shrouded in fluffy white clouds. I left her at the door of the convent, knowing full well that she would be safe.

How wrong could I be? The following day Chiara's father, Favarone, traced her to the convent. Chiara told me later how terrified she was as he battered on the door, shouted abuse and demanded her return to the family home. Chiara believed that she could calm him and so she opened the door. She removed her cowl to reveal her shaven head, and told him that she had vowed to serve God, believing that he would respect her decision. He ignored her resolve, grabbed her arm and tried to pull her from the building. She struggled free and raced into the chapel, chased by her father. Clinging to the altar and claiming sanctuary, she told him that she was prepared to die rather than return to her futile life. At this point, her father realised that she was lost to him forever, and left.

Shortly afterwards, Bishop Guido announced his intention to visit Chiara. The brothers all joined me in prayer while they spent several hours discussing Chiara's future and plans. She told me how they had discussed her faith, and how she intended to follow a life of poverty and develop her Order to provide support to the ill. At the end of the meeting, he announced that he was satisfied with Chiara's dedication and that he was convinced of her ability to establish the Order. He also said that he was pleased to discover that she had no intentions of following the nomadic life which we, the Friars Minor, embraced. Although Chiara confessed to me some time later that she secretly yearned to join us on our pilgrimages, but recognised that this would be unacceptable to the Church.

We were overwhelmed when the Bishop announced that Chiara and her sister Caterina – who had joined her and took the name Agnes on taking her vows – could have the dwelling that adjoined San Damiano as their convent. Our prayers were answered. Chiara's happiness was complete when another sister, Beatrice joined her, closely followed by Chiara's mother, Ortolana, and eleven other like-minded young women from the town. The Poor Sisters, as they became known, were officially recognised as the Second Order. They spent their days caring for the ill, baking bread and creating magnificent altar cloths which they gave us to present as gifts whenever we visited a new church.

We built a small terrace for them and planted it with rose bushes and fragrant flowers. From here they could sit for their evening prayers and look across to the Porziuncola in the distance, knowing that we shared our spiritual thoughts and prayers across the valley.

I recalled a tune from my youth, one which I had learnt from the troubadours, and hummed it softly while I smeared the wooden altar with my mixture of beeswax and olive oil. On this occasion, I also added a small quantity of lavender essence. I rubbed the wood with a soft cloth until it shone like wet stones on a riverbed. I stood back to admire my hard work, but my thoughts were interrupted by a loud knock on the church door.

'Elias, my old friend, how good to see you. Come in, sit here and let me look at you.'

'Francesco,' Elias laughed, 'slow down. It is so dark in here after the bright sunlight I am at risk of tripping.'

I led Elias towards a pew, pushed him into it and sat beside him. 'How are you, my friend? How's your Aunt? And the job, do you still enjoy it, and what of–'

'Stop! One question at a time, please Francesco, you will make my head spin.' Elias laughed again. 'Now, in order: I am well, thank you; Aunt is good and sends her love, and the job was excellent.'

'Was?'

'I left last week.'

'But whatever brought on that decision? I thought the role as the Bishop's scribe was your dream?'

Elias frowned and looked directly into my eyes. 'True, I did love it, but I have listened to reports on the numerous souls that you have saved, and I began to feel that I should do more. I recently visited the small hermitage in Bologna and spoke directly with Leo and Angelo about your ministry.'

'They never said.'

'I asked them not to, but I did as they suggested and prayed at length for guidance. Gradually, I came to realise that the time is now right to accept your offer and join you here.'

I looked at him in stunned silence.

'If you will still have me?'

'I cannot believe it.' I clapped Elias on the shoulder, grasped his hand and shook it vigorously.

'Is that a yes then?'

'Brother Elias, welcome to the Friars Minor. Our forty-fifth recruit I do believe.'

Elias looked around the church. 'This is an amazing transformation. I remember it was virtually derelict when I left for Bologna, what was it, five, almost six years ago?'

'Is it that long? It seems like it was only yesterday when I last visited you.'

'I remember, you arrived in the snow half naked, and I gave you my old tunic.'

'And I am still wearing it, look.' I stood and twirled around. 'It has a few more patches now, but it still serves me well.' I took his hands in mine and pulled him to his feet. 'Oh Elias, you were with me on that first day in Carceri when we discovered the cave, and I found God, and now you will be by my side helping others to find Him. You have made me so happy.' I threw my arms around him and gave him a hug.

Elias's eyes filled with tears. He coughed. 'It is the smell of lavender. It always gets to me.'

I was deadheading roses – one of my favourite pastimes – when I heard footsteps. My heart leapt when I looked up and saw my mother approaching, but my joy was quickly marred as I saw how pallid and frail she looked.

'Mother, how good it is to see you. Come and sit with me.' I swept aside a stray branch of small pink roses which had clambered over the seat, and their sweet fragrance wafted over us. My mother slowly lowered herself onto the bench, shuffled her feet on the cobblestones and stifled a sob.

'What is it, Mother,' I gently squeezed her hand. 'What ails you?'

She looked into my eyes and raised her free hand to stroke my cheek. 'My darling boy, I have sad news.' She wiped a tear from her eye. 'Your Father … he passed over yesterday.'

Father, oh no my father – dead! Enricho had begged me to go and see him months ago. Now it was too late.

I placed my arm around her shoulders, hugged her close and waited while her sobs subsided. 'I am so sorry Mother. What can I do to help?'

She lifted her head from my shoulder and looked at me. Tears continued to stream down her pale cheeks. 'Will you pray for your father's soul? He was a good man, a God-fearing man, but occasionally he could be … difficult.'

I remembered the time when I saw her last, when she had tried to hide the bruising to her face. 'Did he beat you often?' I asked gently.

'Only when I deserved it, if I disobeyed him – or if he thought I had. Otherwise, he was a good husband. He looked after me.'

My suspicions were confirmed. My father was responsible for that bruising; he had beaten my mother. I could feel the pressure build in my temples, but for now, Mother needed my comfort.

'Of course, I will pray for him,' I assured her. 'Will Angelo continue to look after you? Financially, I mean.'

'Angelo has been wonderful. He has achieved great things with the textile business. The shop is even more prosperous than before. I will be well provided for.'

'What of the funeral – has everything been arranged?'

'Angelo has arranged it all, but promise me that you will stay away.'

'But–'

'No, Francesco, you must honour my wishes. Your brother will never forgive you, and I do not want any ugly scenes at your father's funeral. I came to tell you of your father's death today, not only because I did not want you finding out from someone in the town, but also to beg you not to attend the service.'

'But surely Angelo could find it in his heart–'

She shook her head. 'I'm sorry; your brother's heart has not healed as well as I would hope. And … and it is not just Angelo. Father Tiberio has honoured your father by offering to take the service in the cathedral. He said he will stop the ceremony if you attend and have you physically removed. I could not live with the humiliation, Francesco. Please, I beg of you, stay away.'

'Whatever you wish, Mother.'

'I shall continue to come and visit you whenever I can.'

'I am sorry, Mother. I have let you down.'

'Nonsense, I am proud of you. Look at the way you have established the Friars Minor. I was in the crowds the day you preached in San Rufino. I did not tell your father I was coming, although secretly I suspected that he knew. I was so very proud of you as you preached that day. You spoke so movingly, and the whole town joined you in prayers for peace. You have achieved so much, and you have made me very happy.'

'Mother, I have achieved nothing in comparison with others. Have you heard about the children in France that joined the Children's Crusade?' Mother shook her head.

'No? Then let me tell you about this inspirational story.'

I told Mother the story of Éloise and the children, who gave up everything to join the Children's Crusade. * *page 242*

My mother patted my arm; tears streamed down her cheeks. 'I am sure that Éloise's mother, had she lived, would have been proud of her, just as I am proud of you.'

'But, Mother, there is so much I still want to do. If young children can sacrifice so much, surely I can do more?'

'And you will, Francesco, you will. I saw it in the vision on the day you were born. One day you will be famous across the world as a man of God?' She stood and brushed the creases from her skirt. 'I must go now before Angelo realises where I am. God bless you, my son.'

'Mother, please—'

'I am sorry, but I must go.'

She walked away, leaving me to grieve for the loss of my father. I wanted to follow her, but I bit my lip and returned to deadheading the roses. One particular branch appeared determined to defy my endeavours. I hacked and chopped away at it until it finally came away. Resilience, I need to take my example from Éloise and cultivate my resilience.

Sharing the story of Éloise with my mother had reignited my determination to proceed at once to the Holy Land. It was late September when leaving Bernardo and Pietro in charge at the Porziuncola; I arrived in the busy port of Ancona. I was fortunate to find a captain willing to give me passage to the Holy Land. The price demanded was that, when we arrived, I would help him to load up the boat with spices. The crew consisted of: the captain; a giant bearded man called Paolo, and a young crewman whose name nobody saw fit to share with me.

'Be warned, it will be a rough trip. Weather is bad, and boat's empty so it will get tossed about. This shall be our last trip for spices this year. I shall not risk another 'til the spring.'

The captain untied the mooring ropes and the boat moved away from the quay. There was no going back.

Never having undertaken a long sea journey before, and with no experience of what might happen on such a voyage, I trembled with trepidation.

The sea grew rougher throughout the night as an enormous storm broke. Dawn arrived, and dark grey waves towered above us, each one topped with a white crest. It was impossible to stand on the deck without losing our balance. We tied ourselves to the mast with a strong rope, which prevented us from being washed overboard, but the relentless pounding continued. The deck was awash with water that foamed around our feet. Barrels broke free. The rigging snapped loose and debris crashed around us. We clung on.

All day long the storm raged. The thunder crashed with increasing intensity. The skies, dark as night, were split by lightning that forked and flashed across the sky. Each episode lit up our surroundings, until it gradually faded away, leaving us in darkness once more. Those brief moments of light were the worst, for they exposed each gigantic wave as it advanced towards the boat, all undeniably capable of taking us under to our watery graves. The relentless battering made the timbers of the boat creak, and grind.

An enormous fork of lightning struck the mast, which splintered and broke off halfway down. The rigging prevented the fallen mast from breaking loose, and it dragged to one side, the weight of it threatening to pull the whole boat over.

'Quick, cut the ropes,' shouted the captain as he struggled to stand.

He chopped desperately at the rigging. The young crewman and I rushed to assist him. The mast broke free and washed overboard. We watched with horror as Paolo, who had been slow in releasing his ropes, disappeared over the side. The boat righted only moments before another torrent of water hit us. We scanned the seas for any sign of Paulo, but there was nothing we could do except pray that the mast would float him to safety.

Our nightmare continued for hours. I lost all sense of time. I prayed for deliverance. There were still things I wanted to do in the Holy Land. I was not yet ready to die.

I must have dropped off with exhaustion. I woke to a loud splintering noise and the boat shuddering to a halt. I looked down at ominous jagged rocks that gnawed at the hull like blackened and broken teeth. The next wave threw the boat forward and freed us from their lethal embrace.

'We're taking on water,' shouted the captain over the continuous noise of the storm.

'But I cannot swim,' wailed the young crewman.

'Tie yourself to one of these barrels.' The captain tossed us some rope. 'They will help keep us afloat and take us to shore. It cannot be far now. I can see rocks.'

My ears suffered from another heart-stopping crash as we landed on yet a further outcrop of rocks. This time, the boat held firm and started to disintegrate with each wave that hit. I clung onto my barrel as a giant wave approached.

Water poured across the deck and swept me overboard like some inconsequential piece of flotsam. I plunged into the deep cold water, bubbles churning around and above me as the world that I knew vanished. The barrel landed on my chest, forcing me deeper under the angry waves. My lungs ached. I struggled to free myself from the barrel but could not. And then I burst to the surface and bobbed up and down, gasping, choking and clinging to my rope.

I searched through the flotsam, desperately seeking any sign of my companions, but the mass of driftwood obscured my view. I was unable to see anyone. A wave broke over me and left me spluttering. Each time I recovered, another came, pushing me below the surface and forcing water into my lungs. I struggled to stay afloat, but the barrel was throwing me around, and my strength was exhausted. This was it; I was drowning. May God forgive me for my sins.

I thought back over my life and remembered how arrogant and proud I had been as a youth, how demanding. I even stole from my father. How little I had respected the care he lavished upon me. I remembered my pride in establishing the Friars Minor, gaining the Pope's approval and bringing peace to Assisi, without sufficient acknowledgement that my achievements were My Lord's, and I was merely an instrument. I remembered how strongly I believed that I alone could bring peace to the Holy Land. I remembered how I abandoned my brothers, without a second thought, to achieve my ambitions. *My* ambitions! I should instead be seeking God's guidance on *His* ambitions. God forgive me. My life had been a failure, and now it was ending.

My limbs ached. My head throbbed. I thrashed my arms, but instead of water hit soft blankets and a comfortable mattress. I thanked God for my deliverance and ran my hands over my body. Cuts, a few bruises, but miraculously nothing was broken.

A young woman rushed into the room carrying a small baby. She spoke rapidly in a language I could not understand.

'Parla italiano?' I asked.

She shook her head and frowned.

I tried again. 'Parlez-vous français?'

This time her face lit up with a smile, and she replied that yes, she did speak a little. Haltingly, she told me that two days ago her husband and father-in-law, both fishermen, had gone to check on their small boats, which they had hauled high up onto the beach to avoid them being washed away by the storm. They had found me unconscious on the sand and brought me back to their home in this small village on the coast of Slovonia.

'Et mes amis?'

'Oui, oui.' She nodded vigorously.

The captain and the young crewman were safe and now lodged with other families in the village.

'Et mon autre ami? Paolo?'

The woman smiled sadly and shook her head. Nobody knew anything about him. I prayed that he had washed ashore somewhere.

The woman told me that the family was happy for me to stay until I recovered sufficiently to travel. I explained that I was a friar from the Order of the Friars Minor on my way to the Holy Land. She did not know of us, but it transpired that she had learnt her French from a young boy – also shipwrecked – on his journey to the Holy Land as part of the Children's Crusade. The other children had drowned, but he had been rescued and made his home with a childless couple in the town, who looked upon this young boy as a miracle; the answer to their prayers.

I was deeply saddened to receive confirmation that rumours of the children's shipwreck were true. The children were my inspiration. I had hoped to reach the Holy Land – as had they. Most of them did not survive – despite their faith. So why had I been saved?

It was two weeks before I recovered sufficiently to continue my journey. As I was leaving, the woman presented me with a large sack containing three loaves of bread, a mound of dried fish and dozens of biscuits.

'Pour votre santé et bon voyage,' she said.

I thanked my rescuers for their generous hospitality, gave them my blessing and made my way to the nearby town in search of passage to the Holy Land, or failing that back home. Finding anyone who would take me was not an easy task, as I quickly discovered. Few boats were prepared to risk the long trips during the poor weather. The captains who did set sail could choose their crew from well-qualified sailors. They were not interested in someone like me, with experience of only one trip, and still recuperating from a shipwreck. I found one boat that was return-ing to Ancona, but the captain flatly refused to take me on as a member of his crew.

'I have enough hungry mouths to feed,' he shouted.

I tried to tell him that I had food aplenty, but he wanted to hear nothing of it and stormed off. I was bitterly disappointed. If only I could get back to Ancona, I could return to Assisi and spend my time usefully, until the better weather made it possible for me to try again.

I noticed, as I was standing on the quayside, that the captain had given his crew a few coins, and they were making their way to the nearby tavern to enjoy a last drink before they set sail. The captain stood on the prow as he leaned over and spoke to someone on the quay. Driven by desperation, I jumped on board the poop-deck, found an empty wooden crate lashed to the deck, worked a couple of the planks loose and squeezed inside. My plan, in asmuch as I had conceived of one, was to remain hidden throughout the journey and then figure out how to make my escape once we reached Ancona.

Three days into the voyage, two large swarthy crewmen prised open the crate. They hauled me out of my haven and threw me onto the deck, adding fresh bruises to my already battered body. Having assessed that I was unarmed, they proceeded to pull and drag me, one gripping my legs and the other my arms, and then tossed me like a landed fish at the feet of the captain. He loomed over me, purple with rage.

'What in God's name … have I not got enough problems? The wind has blown us back, making our trip longer than planned. One of my stupid men left a large crate of biscuits on the quayside, which means we have run out of food. And now we have a stowaway. I should throw you overboard and leave you to swim home.'

'Please, let me try to make amends,' I begged.

I untied my sack, which by now contained two and a half loaves, twelve dried fish and about thirty biscuits. The captain's face lit up.

'You are all welcome to share everything I have, and if you find me an iron nail, which I can fashion into a hook, and some thin twine, I could tie the fish heads onto the hook and catch a few more.'

I spent the next few days fishing to replenish our food supply. The winds eased, and we eventually made our way back to Ancona, the captain and I now the best of friends.

CHAPTER TWELVE
REFLECTIONS

The winter drew to an end, and I chose the time of Lent as an op-portunity to take a retreat. I persuaded Alfredo, a fisherman I knew from Lake Trasimeno near Perugia, to take me in his boat to a small uninhabited island in the centre of the lake called Isola Maggiore.

'What have you got for food?' he enquired as he rowed me across the water.

'Oh, I have plenty. I have these two loaves of bread.' I showed him my sack.

'There is no food on the island. How long do you plan to stay?'

'Will you collect me on Holy Thursday?'

'But that is forty days. You will starve. Here, take this at least.' He pulled up his keep net from the rear of the boat and offered me a large fish.

'Thank you.' I lifted the creature in both hands. 'Bless you, brother tench. Have a long and happy life.' I placed the fish back into the water and watched as he swam away to safety.

'That was for you to eat.'

'I know, and I thank you for the gift, but I do not need food – just peace and quiet, to pray and to give thanks for my deliverance. The absence of food makes my conversations with God so much more meaningful, more spiritual.' The boat scraped along the sandy shallows. 'Thank you again,' I said as I stepped from the boat. 'I will see you on Holy Thursday. Please be sure to tell no one where I am. I crave solitude.'

I clambered ashore and waved to Alfredo as he pulled away, leaving me totally at peace with only a few birds to keep me company. There were no buildings on the island, so I made a small shelter from branches and reeds.

I sat by the lakeside that evening. The blackbirds entertained me with their fluty warbled evening chorus, each one, it seemed, trying to outdo the other. It brought me such joy. A young rabbit appeared from the brambles at my side. At first, he was cautious as he watched me, but as I remained seated he crept closer.

'Here you are.' I reached over to pick some clover and held it out to him.

He edged forward and nibbled at the leaves. Then he hopped closer and sprawled at my feet, his front legs stretched before him and his hind legs both angled to one side. The pale downy fur of his belly tickled my toes. His triangular pink nose, whiskers and ears twitched, as he sniffed and sounded out the surroundings, alert for any danger that might threaten. I reached down to stroke him, and he looked up at me with big trusting brown eyes framed with long black eyelashes. He licked my toes, and I gently stroked his soft underbelly. We looked out over the lake and drew comfort from each other's presence.

The swallows swooped low and darted gracefully just above the water in search of flying insects. Their forked tails streamed out behind them as they flew with incredible agility, their little beaks were wide open to gather the flies and to sing their characteristic wit, wit, call as they fed.

Several of these birds were repairing their distinctive round nests for the forthcoming season and gathered before me on the shoreline. They collected mud in their tiny beaks and mixed it with chopped strands of grass or straw. As they worked on their task, they called to me in their soft, husky voices, twittering a series of thin, strained, drawn-out rattling sounds, giving the impression of a squeaky door on rusty hinges. What amazing creatures they are. They return to their own individual nests each summer, like human souls returning to God.

The lake stretched away before me, framed by the mountains on the far distant shore. A fish jumped out of the water to catch a fly and fell back, creating a spray of water and an expanding series of circular waves that gradually diminished until the surface returned to its silky smoothness once more.

Father had brought Angelo and me here to camp one summer. We built a shelter and made a campfire. We caught fish, cooked them over the fire and ate them with huge excitement, knowing we had landed them ourselves, with only a *little* help from Father.

'Tell us a bedtime story,' I begged.

'That is your mother's job.'

'But she is not here. Please, Father.'

'Very well, but get under your blankets. I am not carrying you to bed. You are too heavy now for such things.'

We snuggled under our blankets and gazed into the campfire while Father told us of the bloody battle that had happened on this lakeside fourteen hundred years before.

Gaius Flaminius was a young and handsome commander of the Roman army returning home from battle. Thirty thousand soldiers, many injured, most dejected and battle-weary, slowly stumbled their way towards Rome, closely followed by their greatest enemy, the mighty Hannibal, and his Carthaginian army.

Flaminius arrived at Lake Trasimeno and entered a narrow gorge, not realising that Hannibal's troops were hiding in the surrounding hills. As Flaminius and his men rode into the ambush, Hannibal blew his horn: the signal to attack. His infantry and cavalry forces charged down behind the Romans and cut off any means of escape. A few Roman troops managed to break through and scramble into the woods to safety, but twenty-five thousand men remained trapped in the gorge.

The only means of escape was the lake. Many tried to swim to safety but, weighed down by their armour; they either drowned or were caught and massacred.

With his back to the lake, Flaminius wielded his sword and mounted a tenacious defence, but it was all in vain. He was slaughtered alongside his men and died on the shoreline. The water was stained red with the blood of the defeated army.

An owl hooted and disturbed the memories of that evening I had shared with my father and Angelo. I had forgotten how happy I was as we camped beside the lakeside all those years ago. My father and I may have fought our battles; he may have beaten, slapped and spanked me on numerous occasions – usually unjustly – but he also provided us with happy times.

My friendly rabbit licked my toes one last time and then departed, the swallows had already retired for the night, and it was time for me to do the same.

That night I dreamt again, but this time, I battled beside Flaminius, my back to the lake. The scene before me was terrible; the beach littered with bodies. I could smell the blood. I could hear the agonising screams of dying men. Harsh cries, desperate with mortal fear. I glanced at Flaminius; his face was white with terror, but at the same time he laughed as he lunged forward and plunged his sword into his opponent. Too late, he turned to face another, but this time, his attacker had the advantage, and a look of surprise replaced his smile. He looked down at his tunic, stained with his life blood. His legs gave way, and he dropped into the shallow water. I fell to my knees beside him. 'Flaminius.' I screamed. But when I looked into his eyes I realised this was not Flaminius; it was Sergio. I was not at Lake Trasimeno, but the battleground at Collestrada. My head swirled.

I woke with my head still ringing with the noise of battle; my heart was pounding, my body soaked in sweat. Another futile battle: more pointless deaths, and for what? Retribution? Pure greed? How many men must die defending their land or faith in these wars of senseless carnage?

I spent the next forty days in quiet contemplation and prayer. I did not need food, but for humility's sake, I did break one of the loaves and took a small piece each day. The rabbit visited me daily but preferred clover. When Alfred returned on Holy Thursday, I was able to give him the remainder of the loaves as fishing bait.

'But you look so well – how have you survived on less than half a loaf of bread?'

I smiled. 'Row us back quickly. I am so alive today, more than I have ever been, and anxious to resume my ministry.'

Brother Leo and I had extended our ministry into the area of Urbino. As we approached the grand chateau of Montefeltro, the air reverberated with loud music, singing, excited voices and laughter.

'Sounds like a good party,' I said.

'It is a very long time since I last enjoyed such revelry.' Leo stared across at the happy gathering, a look of hope and even a hint of envy in his eyes.

'Shall we go and see if they need any help?' I suggested.

Leo's face broke into a broad smile which gave me my answer.

A large crowd, dressed in brightly coloured clothes and draped in jewellery, gathered in the courtyard. I approached one young man and asked him about the celebration.

'It is for the investiture of the Duke's son, Manaldo. Come with me. I will introduce you.'

The Duke smiled as we approached. 'Brother Francesco, and Brother Leo, I heard you were in the area. Today is a very special one. My first-born son, Manaldo will be knighted.'

Manaldo's eyes shone with excitement as he stood proudly at his father's side, smiling and trembling slightly.

'I am so proud of him,' the Duke patted his son's shoulder. 'We would be pleased if you will join us today, perhaps you could be persuaded to say a few words and lead us in prayer after the service?'

I was happy to agree.

Leo and I stood in the shade of a tree and watched as everyone bustled around the courtyard, meeting and greeting friends and relatives they may not have seen for many months, or even years.

'I never told you this Leo, but as a child, I longed to be a knight.'

'I had no idea.'

I smiled. 'Every child has their dream, but for mine to come true I would have needed to become a page. At the age of seven, I would have been taught how to handle a sword, ride, and hunt with hawks and falcons.'

'You know all of these things.'

'But I would also have learnt the finer things in life. How to butcher deer, serve at banquets, how to play music, sing, and dance.'

'Well, you know how to ride, play the lute and sing. Can you dance?'

'Like a war-horse.'

Leo laughed.

'It gets worse, at the age of fourteen, you become a squire and train alongside a knight: care for his horses, armour, and dogs; and practice the art of fighting, jousting and horse-riding. The only shortcut is to gain your knighthood on the battlefield for an act of bravery. That was my plan when I attempted to join Gaultier's army.'

'I think God had other plans for you, Francesco.' Leo patted my shoulder. 'Look at Manaldo. He is just a boy, so young and excited, and very pale. I hope he does not pass out. I cannot imagine he got much sleep last night, do you?'

'He would not have had the chance. Like all young knights before him, Manaldo will have kept vigil in the church last night, to demonstrate the fact that he will always remain watchful and renounce evil.'

The music stopped, the crowd followed the Duke and Manaldo into the castle, and the service began.

A local priest celebrated Mass, and then the Duke received his son into the chivalric brotherhood by dubbing him with a sword and striking him on the shoulder with a tender blow known as an accolade.

The Duke presented his son with a gift – a sword and a suit of armour – then invited me to give the blessing.

'Manaldo,' I said, as he knelt down before me and I placed my hand on his shoulder, 'today, you have become a knight. You have justified all the love and faith your family has invested in you, and you have made them very proud. You have also become a man, a servant to God's holy will. Our Father, loving and merciful Saviour, grant Manaldo humility, strength, and faith as he goes forth to serve Thee with good deeds. Glory be to Thy name, through Jesus Christ our Lord, *Amen.*'

Manaldo looked up at me, his eyes bright with unshed tears.

'You may now take your place by your father's side,' I whispered.

The Duke looked up from his prayers as Manaldo knelt beside him, nodded encouragement and patted him gently on his shoulder.

'Let us pray.' I led them in the words of the Lord's Prayer.

One of the guests at the ceremony, Count Orlando de Cattani approached me.

'I found your words very moving, Francesco. I wonder if it I could speak with you about my troubled soul.' He looked anxiously over his shoulder to where his family stood patiently waiting for him to return.

'Gladly I will, but for now, go and enjoy the celebrations with your family and friends. We will talk later after the banquet.'

The banqueting hall looked magnificent. The pale-yellow walls were beautifully decorated with pictures of birds, bees and flowers. The servants, squires, and pages brought tables and benches into the hall and positioned them to form a horseshoe. The boys placed white linen tablecloths over the tables and dressed the benches with brightly coloured silk cushions. Two young men positioned strips of red velvet to form a crusader cross on the top table, and then positioned the Duke's chair centrally, under the red silk drapes hanging from iron hoops high above.

Further hoops hung from the ceiling. A pulley was used to lower each one allowing the page boys access to the hundred spikes holding candles, which they lit, before hoisting them back high above the crowd.

The Duke sat with his close family and special guests at the top table. I felt highly honoured when he invited me to join them. The minstrels began to play and a young squire, the Duke's son, carried a tray of steaming bowls into the hall. He knelt before his father, who smiled and took a small sample from each dish.

The Duke nodded his approval; a signal for the dozen or so page boys, who immediately entered the hall carrying trays of food, and proceeded to serve the guests.

I took a piece of bread and some chicken baked in a clay pot with various herbs. It was simple fare and more suited to my constitution in comparison with some of the rich and highly spiced alternatives on offer. Squires circulated with jugs of wine. They smiled broadly as they served the guests, no doubt anticipating the day of their own ceremony. The Duke's minstrels joined with a group of troubadours and jongleurs. Together they played their instruments, sang and performed acrobatics as the guests cheered loudly.

Count Orlando approached me again later that evening.

'Brother Francesco, your words this evening have stirred my soul. I am deeply troubled by the disservice and injustices I have committed in my life.'

'Sit here beside me, and tell me what troubles you.' I patted the chair beside me, and he sat, sighing deeply.

'Brother Francesco, your words reminded me of how badly I have treated my dear parents, and the pain I brought to them. They only ever wanted the best for me and yet I did not honour them as we are told to do in the Ten Commandments. I was a spirited youth and I defied them constantly.' He sighed deeply and twisted his hands together. 'As they got older, I never visited them, and when I heard of my father's death, my first thoughts were of my inheritance and my joy at becoming a Count. If only I could go to them and thank them for their patience – for everything they did for me – but alas, they are both now dead and will never know the depth of my sadness.'

I pondered on his dilemma, aware of how it resonated with my own guilt over the way I had treated my parents. I recognised now that they had only wanted the best for me. Instead of giving them respect, I had rebelled against them, had stolen my father's goods without a second thought, taking without ever giving anything back and never attempting to make peace with my father. Whatever I thought of my father's pride and ambition, he had not deserved the way I treated him, and now, as with Orlando, it was too late for me to make my peace.

'My dear Count, it saddens me to say this, but I believe many, if not most of us, fail to respect the love and sacrifice our parents make to give us the best start in life. Even Jesus, when told that his mother and brothers were outside asking to see him, replied: "Who is my mother?" Mark, 3, 34.'

I placed my hand on his shoulder. 'Go in peace. God has heard your sorrow. He will grant you forgiveness.'

'Thank you, Brother Francesco, but I must do more to appease my sins. I own a mountain in Tuscany. It rises to over two thousand and five hundred cubits above the valley of Casentino. It is a beautiful and isolated place, an ideal retreat for you and your brothers. I am happy to give it to you, for the salvation of my soul.'

I accepted the use of his mountain in perpetuity, and Alvernia became another retreat for the Friars Minor. I was eager to visit this secluded spot, but with much to do, and many souls to save before returning to the Porziuncola, I delayed my visit until the following year.

Our numbers continued to grow, and it was apparent that if we were to expand our missionary work and save as many souls as possible, we should travel across Italy and even further afield, evangelising and bringing the gospels to everyone possible. However, we also wanted to find a way to keep in touch with each other and share our experiences, thoughts, and prayers. I began to realise what Bishop Guido meant about the need for some structured organisation.

My brothers also declared a need to draw strength from my council and directions. We agreed to meet twice a year at the Porziuncola; the first meeting was to be on Whitsunday and the second on September the twenty-ninth for Michaelmas. We named them chapter meetings because they would begin with us reading a chapter from the Gospels.

Our ministry was well received wherever we travelled, and by Whitsunday in the year of Our Lord twelve hundred and thirteen, our numbers had grown, from the twelve who visited the Pope in Rome, to three hundred brothers. As we grew in numbers, so we grew in ambition.

Elias, Bernardo, Masseo and I decided that it was time to take our evangelising much further. Our intention was to travel to Spain, take a sea journey across to Morocco, and meet with the caliph, Muhammad al-Nasir. The hope was that after suffering the recent humiliation of defeat and numerous casualties, he would be totally dejected and ripe to embrace Christianity.

Several days into our trek, I deemed it fitting to remind the brothers that we should walk in a quiet and prayerful manner.

'Let us not indulge in idle chatter, but instead, as we walk, let us reflect on our crusade of taking the gospels to the Moroccan infidels. What say you?'

Only silence greeted my question. When I looked around to ascertain why, I realised that I was alone. I turned and retraced my steps until eventually I found my brothers some way back. Elias was sitting on the roadside, his eyes streaming and his chest wheezing from inhaling grass pollen. Masseo was leaning on a rock, and Bernardo was sprawled across the grass, snoring.

'What is this? We have a long way to go, brothers. Come on, keep up.'

Bernardo yawned and sat up. 'We find it impossible to keep up with you, Brother Francesco.'

'You walk too fast,' complained Masseo, clutching his fulsome girth.

'Slow down, or we will all be exhausted,' pleaded Elias.

Of course, they were right. Before we reached the coast of Spain, I suffered a relapse and was taken ill, coughing up blood. I collapsed, too weak to stand. The brothers cut down two strong saplings to make poles, tied blankets across them to create a litter, and with Masseo at the front and Bernardo and Elias on either side at the rear, they carried me back to the Porziuncola where I spent the next year in convalescence.

The enforced periods of quiet reflection, necessitated by my ill health, caused me to think deeply about my future. I was disappointed that I had failed in my endeavours to reach both the Holy Land and Morocco. I could not help but wonder if this was God's way of telling me to change direction. Was my evangelising serving God in the best way possible, or would it be better for me to retreat to a cloistered, prayerful and contemplative life? A life to which I was so often drawn.

I decided that I required help with such a major decision, so I asked Brother Masseo to go and see my beloved Chiara and our counsellor, Brother Sylvestro, and ask them both to pray for direction.

Masseo returned two days later. I made him sit down while I washed his feet. I was anxious for news but knew I should bestow this simple courtesy on him first. My task completed, I sprang to my feet, anxious to receive any advice he might have gathered.

'What news do you have for me, Masseo?'

'Calm yourself, Francesco. I went to see them both and put your quandary to them. I told them you were in prayerful retreat and asked them to join you in your prayers for guidance. I returned firstly to Brother Sylvestro. He had spoken with God who told him: "He did not call you for your salvation alone. He called you because your work saves so many souls." I then returned to Sister Chiara, who said God had spoken to her and said the same thing. She told me to urge you to continue with the missionary work.'

I sighed with relief. 'Thank you, Brother Masseo, you have helped me to find peace in the sure and certain knowledge that I am serving God as he wishes me to do.'

I retired to my cell to pray and give thanks for the clear guidance. My trips to the Holy Land and Morocco may have failed, but this was obviously because the trips had been at my instigation, not His. I must learn to be more patient and less arrogant. Although we were successful in saving thousands of souls in Italy, so far, we had failed in taking our message further. I should have listened more closely to His wishes, and trust that when the time was right, He would let me know.

The next morning Brother Masseo approached me.

'Brother Francesco, I did not want to discuss this last night as I could see how important the messages were to you, but our beloved Sister Chiara also asked me to confer with you on another matter. She has remained within the confines of San Damiano since she and her sisters were granted the building as their convent. However, she craves to visit the Porziuncola, where she took her vows, and begs that she be allowed to take supper with you.'

'But Bishop Guido will never sanction such a visit. Surely he will resist Sister Chiara leaving the confines of San Damiano?'

'Could we not ask for his approval? She is sorely missing her sister Agnes since she took up her role as Abbess of Monticelli in Florence. Granting Chiara her desire to share supper with you will give her much consolation.'

I looked at Masseo. He was a giant of a man, but a gentle one with a huge heart to match. I was ashamed that he had realised Chiara's distress when I had been completely oblivious to it. I should have known that she would miss Agnes.

'I will happily agree to Sister Chiara's request if the Bishop gives his blessing.'

Masseo visited the Bishop, who surprisingly gave his blessing on the condition that we were both chaperoned.

It was a joyous occasion. I welcomed Chiara and Sister Beatrice. We celebrated Mass and then retreated to the rose garden to enjoy our evening meal. Chiara had baked loaves of bread, each one decorated with a cross. As the bread was broken and blessed, it was as though God was with us, sharing our table. His divine grace wrapped us in His warm, comforting embrace. I thought that my heart would burst; tears streamed down my cheeks, and my throat choked with emotion as we gave thanks to God.

Our peace and prayers were interrupted when a crowd of a dozen or so men came running into the garden, panting for breath, their faces red with exertion.

'What is the meaning of this?' I asked them.

'Brother Francesco, where is the fire?' gasped the first to recover.

'Fire?' I looked around us, and into the quiet darkness surrounding the Porziuncola.

'We saw it from the town. It looked as though the whole friary, and the woods surrounding it, were ablaze. We raced down here to quench the flames before you were all devoured and …' An air of bafflement descended on the speaker as he too, noted the peaceful stillness of our surroundings.

'Fear not,' I told him. 'The flames you bear witness to here today are the celestial fires of our divine love. The only thing that burns is our passion for our Lord Jesus Christ.' I laughed at the expression of wonder on the faces of our unexpected group of visitors. 'But we are grateful for your neighbourly concern, and would be honoured if you would join us.'

Later that evening, I watched Chiara leave. 'I will visit soon,' I called as she reached the bend in the road and turned to wave.

Bishop Guido entered the Porziuncola. 'Brother Francesco, I bring sad news.'

'If you have travelled here in person to deliver it, then it must be bad. Tell me, is it about my mother?'

'Cardinal Giovanni di San Paolo has passed over.'

'I am sorry to hear it, though he may well be himself rejoicing. He was kind to us in Rome when he negotiated our audience with the Pope.'

'He was a tremendous diplomat and very supportive of you and the Friars Minor. I believe he always held a soft spot for your Order.'

'Do we know who is to replace him?'

'Cardinal Hugolino of Ostia. He is a completely different kettle of fish. A strict disciplinarian. Woe betides any of us who steps out of line. The rumour is that he may become the next pope.'

Bishop Guido took some refreshments with us and returned to Assisi, leaving me to ponder on what these changes might mean to the Friars Minor.

Father Tiberio heard of Chiara's visit to the Porziuncola from one of our *rescuers*. He quickly ascertained that the Bishop had authorised her visit – a decision with which he disagreed. He went straight to the Pope to protest and found a sympathetic ear. The Pope decreed that Chiara's convent should become an enclosed religious Order with strict separation from the affairs of the external world. No one could visit without prior approval from the Pope; an approval only granted in exceptional circumstances.

No more visits and discussions with my beloved Chiara? How should I bear it? I replayed over and over my memory of our last farewell, her hand raised in friendship, and my words: "I will visit soon."

But even more bad news followed. My good friend Bishop Guido, equally outraged by Father Tiberio's actions, had confronted him. A fearful row followed. The Bishop's aging heart could not withstand such an onslaught. My dear friend had collapsed and died.

Elias sat with me while I prayed for strength and Christian thoughts. The latter proved quite a challenge as far as Father Tiberio was concerned.

'Brother Francesco, please know that your brothers would bear every part of your pain if only we could.'

'I would not give it to you.' I smiled at Elias, comforted as always by his presence.

'Is there anything we can do to aid you?'

I shook my head. 'This news has more than just a personal significance, Elias. Our Order has lost two of its strongest supporters. Our position in the Church may yet prove uncertain.'

Elias shrugged. 'We have God's work to keep us busy. No time for such concerns.'

I patted my friend's shoulder and nodded.

With a heavy heart, I left Bishop Guido's funeral service and headed off in the direction of Cannara to rendezvous with Masseo and Leo.

The whole village came out to hear us preach. Although I arrived with a heavy heart, an extraordinary turnout such as this deserved an exceptional response. We preached and sang extracts from the Gospel, and then invited the inhabitants to give penance for their sins. Each family came to us, and not only committed themselves to God but also begged to join the Order. We were overwhelmed by their response and I finally made the decision to proceed with the necessary arrangements to establish the Third Order of Tertiaries.

It was necessary to seek ratification for the establishment of the Third Order, from a senior cleric of the Church. The new Bishop of Assisi was appointed but was yet to take up his post. His name was also Guido, but those who had met him said that this was where the similarity to my old friend ended. Rumour was that Cardinal Hugolino had appointed the new Bishop Guido because of his reputation for being a strong administrator and a strict disciplinarian. He was also known for his taciturn nature. Unlike his predecessor, it was unlikely that he would venture out of the palace to visit us.

With no incumbent yet in the Bishop's palace, I decided that this was a good opportunity to meet for the first time with Cardinal Hugolino and to request his authority to establish the Third Order. I heard that he was on one of his regular visits to Perugia and hastened over to crave an audience.

As I arrived, one of the clerics was leaving the building. 'Good day, Brother Francesco. How do you fare on this fine bright morning?' he asked.

'By God's grace I am well, but I have urgent business with the Cardinal. Is he available for conference?'

'Cardinal Hugolino has been hearing great things about you and the Friars Minor. He knows that Cardinal Giovanni and Bishop Guido held you in high esteem, as do we. Go through – he may not be expecting you, but I am sure he will always find time for you, Brother Francesco.'

As I approached the open doorway, I heard voices.

'Bishop Guido always described him as "a dear boy", but from what I hear, Brother Francesco is far too soft-hearted and could not punish a rabbit.'

'He does not understand the meaning of the words *organisation* and *discipline*. He is a dangerous fantasist.'

I knew that second voice. I hung back out of sight.

'It sounds as if he could learn a thing or two from my cousin, Innocence III. Now there is a man who rules with a sword – never afraid to dish out severe punishment or even death to unrepentant heretics.'

'I wish you luck teaching Brother Francesco anything,' laughed the Assistant Bishop of Assisi, Father Tiberio.

'Brother Francesco will have his uses,' Cardinal Hugolino said. 'True, he is a dreamer, and his brothers are an undisciplined rabble. They need to be knocked into shape, sharpened up – and I am the man to do it.'

'Is he worth all that effort?'

'These pagan peasants are drawn to him while the Church, for many, remains unpopular. We cannot seem to get through to them, and that leaves the way open for the heretics. But in Brother Francesco and his army of brothers, people see the humble, self-sacrificing side of Christianity. From what I hear, he is truly committed to the Church and will help us to regain our reputation. His Friars will convert thousands away from paganism and heresy and into the arms of the Catholic Church. So yes, there is *definitely* a role for him and the brothers.'

'I do not doubt his commitment, but he has a few things to learn about obedience. Do you *really* believe that he can help you to achieve this?'

'I do.' Hugolino chuckled. 'I might even promote some of these humble friars into high positions within the church and teach one or two of our pompous bishops a thing or two.'

Cardinal Hugolino and Father Tiberio burst into laughter, and I took the opportunity of their distraction to beat a hasty retreat.

Whereas my childhood eavesdropping had deflated my self-confidence considerably, hearing Hugolino declare that he believed the Friars Minor to be capable of ensuring the Church's continued existence had the exact opposite effect.

A few hours later, after I watched Father Tiberio slide out of a side door and slither away, I returned to Hugolino's office, greeted him formally and accepted his words of welcome as genuine and heartfelt.

I explained the purpose of my visit, and how I wished to obtain his approval to establish the Third Order. I explained how we sought to establish the Tertiaries for people who wanted to commit to our principles, but from within a marriage and family life. Cardinal Hugolino was very happy to accept the concept, subject to a suitable Rule being presented and approved by the Pope.

I left the building, inspired by our meeting. Now I was able to fulfil my promise to Celano and his young bride and the people of Cannara. And as for Hugolino, whatever else this man might turn out to be, he believed in our capability, and for now, that would have to be enough.

CHAPTER THIRTEEN
FESTIVAL OF MATS

The Whitsunday chapter meeting the following year, organisationally, was an important one. The Pope urged us to increase our endeavours to save souls on behalf of the Catholic Church.

'The Pope honours you greatly, Francesco,' Cardinal Hugolino said when he joined us to discuss how we might best achieve the Pope's request. 'I believe that you should show faith in the Pope's judgement by bringing the Friars Minor into line with the Benedictine monks and adapting their Rule.'

'Our Rule was given to us by God. I believe that no authority exists that supersedes His.'

'Hmm, we will see. As for your ministry, the Pope wishes you to expand your remit over many more provinces: not only in Italy but also France, Spain, Hungary, and Germany.'

'What of his entreaty for us to revive our endeavours with the Crusades?'

'You must make another attempt to reach the Holy Land and convert the Infidels.' Hugolino laughed. 'But before you go rushing off and throwing yourself onto the first boat going that way, I must insist that for now you remain in Italy and instil some principles of organisation into your Order.'

'But a leader must lead from the front. I thought perhaps that I should lead the mission into France as I know the language.'

'I will not sanction you leaving Italy until the Friars Minor becomes established on a firmer footing.'

I could see that he was adamant. 'In that case, I believe Brother Pacifico and our more recent recruit, Brother Agnello, should go to France.'

'And who should be the Provincial Minister for the Holy Land?'

'I believe it should be my old friend, Elias.'

Hugolino also counselled me on the dangers of too much zeal without sufficient enlightenment.

'You should not send the brothers into situations they are not fully prepared for, Brother Francesco. You could be putting their lives at risk.'

'But we are fully prepared to die for our cause. Some of us crave martyrdom.'

'Yes, I know your intentions are good, but you must be careful. God does not wish for you to throw your lives away carelessly. Martyrdom is a risk we need to accept if it is God's will. It is not something that we should seek.'

How right he was; in Spain, the brothers were forced to take refuge and flee to Portugal after being falsely accused of spreading heresy. In Germany and Hungary, the brothers did not understand the language and found it impossible to communicate with those they wanted to convert to Christianity. Attacked, beaten and chased they were eventually forced to return home.

These setbacks were disappointing. However, my spirits were restored by the time I met with Brother Dominic in Rome. Dominic was a Spanish brother who had established a small Order; I heard that they currently numbered seven. He was also going through the process of gaining approval for his Rule, and therefore, he also came under the protection of Hugolino. He was leaving the building as I arrived; tall and dark, with a strong Roman nose and a beguiling smile that made his dark eyes twinkle. He wore a black habit, and I was able to recognise him from Hugolino's description.

'Brother Dominic, I presume?'

'Brother Francesco.' He shook my hand. 'I have heard all about your wonderful successes from the Cardinal. Converting pagans, expanding the Order – well done, and God bless you.'

'I believe your success at conversion in Spain is greater than ours.'

'Perhaps.' He shrugged his shoulders. 'We have the advantage there, with the language. I wonder … will you consider giving me the cord from your waist, as a talisman?'

'Gladly.'

I removed the cord and handed it to him.

'You know, Francesco, I would dearly love to see our two Orders united.'

'I know that Cardinal Hugolino has similar ambitions, but we are different, you and I. Our Order is all about living in complete poverty and the simplicity of lay preaching, whereas yours relies on learning and the formal preaching of the clergy. You enjoy and thrive on the structured services that suit your temperament. I think you would quickly become exasperated with the uninhibited spontaneity that we enjoy. Also, I swore never again to receive something for nothing, so your mendicant Order does not sit comfortably with the Friars Minor or me. We prefer to labour in return for our food.'

We wished each other well and went our separate ways.

Cardinal Hugolino was in conference with the Pope when I arrived at his quarters. I was shown to a visitor's cell and offered refreshments. Later that day I was summoned to appear before Hugolino. It passed through my mind that Brother Dominic might have orchestrated the content of this meeting. Was I to be encouraged once more to combine our Order with another?

'Your Eminence.' I bowed my head. I knelt before Hugolino and kissed his hand.

'Brother Francesco, I apologise for not being available when you arrived. Thank you for attending so promptly.' He wore a grave expression. 'I have a matter of concern to share with you. Please be seated.'

'Have I displeased Your Lordship?'

'Brother Francesco, there have been rumblings of discontent in the Curia. A few prejudices have circulated, and I am anxious to prevent these from spreading and getting out of hand.'

He paused, and my heart raced as I realised that I might yet stand accused of heresy.

'I want you to prepare a sermon for presentation to his Holiness the Pope and the College of Cardinals.'

Although the thought of preaching in front of the Pope would normally have left me daunted, I was so relieved that Hugolino was clearly trying to offer me his full support that I enthusiastically agreed.

'You may learn your speech by heart and recite it to me by way of practice.'

Hugolino's advice appeared to be excellent, and I returned, with my speech, to see him the next day. He listened kindly, made suggestions for a couple of slight amendments and invited me to return the following day to present my address.

The next morning, I looked down at the rows of Cardinals, all prim, and proper in their silk and ermine gowns. They turned to each other and whispered behind their hands as I shuffled forward in my scruffy, torn and tattered tunic. Convinced that they were talking about my appearance; I glanced across at Hugolino for encouragement. He appeared pale and tremulous and gave every appearance that he was even more apprehensive than I, his humble protégé.

The silence was unbearable. I opened my mouth to speak but found I could remember nothing of the prepared words. I closed my eyes, shutting out the staring faces of the Cardinals and the frowning countenance of the Pope. I prayed for guidance and a feeling of calm invaded my senses; I spoke from my heart.

As the service ended, Hugolino rushed to my side. 'Brother Francesco, whatever happened to the speech we practised?'

'I'm sorry to say that I forgot it,' I said, anxious that he may well be displeased with me. 'But tell me, was my talk well received?'

'It was a wonderful speech – simple, heartfelt and eloquent. Some even say it was not you who spoke but the Holy Spirit. I do believe the rumbles of dissent will be banished.'

I breathed a sigh of relief.

Hugolino invited me to join him and take some refreshments. He seemed agitated and distracted, lacking his normal self-assurance.

'What is it, Your Grace?'

'Your speech made me think about my position.'

'In what way?'

'How can I put this? It is difficult to explain. God has called me to this life within the Church. I live in these palaces, dressed in these fine gowns, and yet I am not at ease with these trappings. When I see the joy you celebrate by accepting poverty, living the Gospels and following in the footsteps of Jesus Christ, I must admit I would dearly love to give up all of this and join the Friars Minor.'

I reflected on this surprising admission for a few moments.

'Your Grace, your endorsement is more than I could ever expect. However, I believe that God has brought you to this role for a reason. You are a brother to us, a faithful protector of our Order, and as such, we rely on you to guide us. I will pray for you in the hope that you will receive God's reassurance that you should remain in your present role, for I believe it is extremely important to us, and to God.'

Hugolino smiled and patted my back, and I reflected on how, despite our first encounter when he appeared to favour my antagonist, Father Tiberio, I had grown to appreciate his support. He did appear to hold my best interests at heart.

Whitsunday marked the end of our carefree approach. The Pope demonstrated his support and issued a written decree, making it clear that the Order of the Friars Minor enjoyed his support and should be treated favourably, with consideration and kindness. However; the Pope also delivered a crushing blow: in future, he ordered, all assemblies or chapter meetings were to be more formal, and presided over by a senior priest.

I felt considerable sadness and some confusion with these changes. Hugolino said that the Curia were now happy with the Friars Minor. He implied that they were satisfied there was no rebellion or heresy, and confident that we would always give our full support to the Holy Catholic Church. Why then were all these changes necessary? A more structured format would detract from the spontaneity and cheerfulness that our congregations appreciate.

We gathered together for our first chapter meeting of the year. I was determined to enjoy the service as much as possible, despite the new restrictions. Brothers and sisters arrived from all over Italy. People from Assisi and many other towns journeyed there to join us. Everyone sang and danced in the bright, warm sunshine as they made their way out of the town, down the mountainside and across the valley towards the Porziuncola.

I caught sight of Cardinal Hugolino, who was with us to take Mass. I made my way through the crowds, pausing to shake hands with an old school friend and to bless a small child, and eventually reached his side. He held out his hand, and I knelt to kiss it.

'We are pleased to have you with us here today, Your Eminence.'

'Francesco let me introduce you to Brother Dominic and a few of the brothers from his Order. He was travelling to Rome with me, and I invited him to attend the service with us here today.'

'Brother Francesco, how good to meet with you again.' Dominic stepped forward and held out his hand to shake mine. 'I am on my way to Rome for one of my regular visits to the Pope. He always speaks so well of you, Brother Francesco.'

'The Pope always speaks very warmly of you, Brother Dominic,' Cardinal Hugolino said. 'I believe he gives you more regular audiences than any other brother.'

Dominic tilted his head modestly and smiled at me. His dark eyes shone as they reflected the light from the bright sunshine. He was taller than I remembered, his tunic black and in better condition than my own. He no longer wore the cord he had requested from me; instead, a new white cord encircled his waist. His superior countenance made me a little uncomfortable in his presence.

'I have wanted to hear you preach for many years, Brother Francesco. I hear wondrous things about the numerous pagans you have converted to Christianity. Just look around us today. There must be five thousand people here.'

'At least,' I said.

'How ever are you going to feed everyone?' Dominic's lips smiled, but there was no mistaking the thinly veiled criticism that lay behind his question.

I forced a smile of my own and replied, 'I have told everyone that they should not be concerned about food or drink. Our Lord will care for them. They only need to concentrate on prayer and their praise of Our Father in Heaven.'

Dominic turned away and surveyed the crowd. Cardinal Hugolino had by now made his way to the front, where he was preparing to open the prayers for the day. I was anxious to find out if the rumours about the approval of Dominic's Rule were true.

'Brother Dominic.' I waited until he turned back to face me. 'I understand that the Pope has given approval to your Order's Rule.'

'He has indeed given us his full support.' His eyes glinted with unmistakable pride.

'I hoped that the Pope would grant our Rule at the Lateran Council last November,' I said, aware that I was experiencing something akin to jealousy. 'But even until now he has withheld his endorsement.'

'I was advised that we should adapt our Rule to one based on that of St. Augustine, which I agreed to do.'

I smiled – a genuine smile of relief. He had won the Pope's written approval only by compromising his beliefs. My jealousy receded, and I was able to offer him my genuine best wishes.

'Perhaps if you took St. Benedict's Rule and adapted it,' he offered, 'you may also gain his agreement?'

'Hugolino has indicated as much, but God chose our Rule. We should not be asked to change it. Please excuse me – I am needed. I hope to see you again at the end of the service. Go in peace, brother.'

Dominic was correct; the crowd did amount to around five thousand people. The service was about to begin, and they settled down on their brightly coloured mats. The grassy area surrounding the Porziuncola assumed the quality of a richly patterned patchwork quilt. Cardinal Hugolino took Mass and then invited me to take the dismissal.

I spoke to the crowd. 'Good morning, good people. Mass has ended. We have made our promises to God, and He has promised us great things in return. If we observe the things that we have promised, then we can be assured that God will also keep His promises to us. Our lives are brief, but the life that comes next is everlasting. Take comfort from each other, offer help wherever it is required, love your neighbours, brothers and sisters, live in peace and forgiveness, observe purity and chastity and continue to practice holy poverty. Always remember to give obedience and reverence to the Holy Catholic Church. Go in peace and glorify the Lord through your life.'

Five thousand people responded as one: *'Thanks be to God.'*

Brother Dominic approached me once more. 'Forgive me, Brother Francesco; I thought you were somewhat rash when you said you had not made any provisions for the crowds, but I now see that your faith was justified.'

He waved a hand at the crowd. Many carried large baskets of food to share. People from the town had brought baked bread and cakes enough for everyone, and they walked among the crowds distributing them. A local farmer had brought a large sack of walnuts and another a sack of apples, carefully stored over the winter. They stood at the front of the multitude and handed out the food to the children. Another farmer had brought pork sausages, flavoured with fennel, chilli, salt and pepper. He cooked them over an open fire. They smelt wonderful, and a queue of children stood before him, licking their lips in anticipation while they waited for the next batch to be ready. No one would go hungry today.

I smiled. 'I have faith in the kindness of people.'

Dominic nodded. 'I will take away important lessons from today. Thank you for allowing me to share this with you.'

Meeting with Dominic and hearing that his Rule was now approved, if only through compromise, gave me courage. I decided to crave an audience with the Pope and try once more to gain approval for our Rule.

It was July before I could free up the time to make my journey. However, our meeting was not to be, because, on my arrival in Perugia, I was met with the news that Pope Innocent III had died the previous day.

The Pope had been carried to the cathedral in an open coffin and left in the Chapel of Rest overnight in readiness for the funeral which was to take place later that day. I was shocked to hear that during the night, thieves had broken into the cathedral and stolen the Pope's garments and possessions.

The brother who was telling me this with tears in his eyes, slowly shook his head. 'No beggar would be treated in such a miserable and wretched way as this, our beloved Pope.'

It gave me little comfort to reflect on Pope Innocent III's words when he warned us about making life too hard for ourselves by giving away all our possessions.

As I made my way towards the cathedral for the funeral, I met Cardinal Hugolino, and he told me how he was at the Pope's bedside as he died. His position in the Church was sufficient to award him this honour, but I also remembered that the Pope was his cousin.

'The Pope told me that he was heartened by your success, and with the numerous men and women who renounced their wealth and followed you.'

'Thank you, my Lordship. It is a comfort to hear your words. I have on occasions believed the Pope found me troublesome.'

'No, no, Brother Francesco. The Friars Minor and you are held in high esteem by us all. You have such a way with words. After people hear you preach just once, they follow you, and their troubled souls are saved. Your numerous conversions multiply as new recruits also evangelise and spread the words of the Gospels. Thanks be to God.'

Although widely anticipated, Cardinal Hugolino failed to become the next pope. The position went instead to Cardinal Cencio Savelli, who at his inauguration chose the papal name Honorius III. He was reported to be yet another strong administrator, and also someone committed to the Holy War to recover Jerusalem from the Infidels.

A few days after the inauguration of Honorius III, I was at prayer in my beloved Porziuncola when a bright light flooded through the building. I turned to see from where it had come. The rear wall of the church had melted away. I could see the pathway leading up towards the town as it nestled into the mountainside. The colours of the trees and grass were much brighter than usual, and I knew that this was to be a *showing*. I was to receive a vision of some kind.

Crowds of people walked towards me. Some were young men and women dressed in fine clothes, others were old and crippled and leaned heavily on sticks; still others were village folk and farm workers, and even a few children skipped towards me. As they drew close, I heard the voice of my Lord Jesus Christ.

'Francesco, these people are here to beg for forgiveness. I grant you the Indulgence of the Porziuncola. From this day forth, anyone who prays for forgiveness in this place will be absolved from their sins and their prayers will be answered. Go and see your Holy Vicar to have this indulgence confirmed.'

As He finished speaking, the light was extinguished, and the ghostly crowds faded away. I stayed on my knees all night giving thanks for this colourful vision.

I left for Perugia the next morning. I knew that the newly appointed Pope Honorius III was visiting, and I wasted no time requesting an audience, which he granted. I told him of my vision and begged him to convert the Indulgence in perpetuity.

'You ask for too much, Francesco. Indulgences are only granted on rare occasions, usually as a reward for victories in the Crusades.'

'But Holiness, my Lord Jesus Christ has already granted the Indulgence. He merely wanted you to ratify it. I beg of you to grant this request.'

'I will grant it, but it can only be on one day of the year. Which will it be?'

My heart sank. God had granted the Indulgence; why should Pope Honorius want to restrict things in this way? I decided that there was little to be achieved by arguing, and much at risk. If the Pope refused, people might lose their opportunity to enjoy an everlasting life. Or if they did pray, and their sins were forgiven in a tangible way, such as being cured of their afflictions, I could be accused of defying Father Tiberio and performing miracles. I sighed deeply.

'Let it be from the afternoon of August the first until sundown on August the second in recognition of the anniversary of the Porziuncola's dedication. It will also serve to celebrate the day of *St. Peter in Chains*, to recognise the day the Angel of the Lord released Peter from Herod's prison and led him to freedom. It will be a symbol to those who pray that they will also be freed from their chains: the chains of their sins.'

'So be it. Do you need this in writing, or is the word of your Pope sufficient?'

I considered my options and decided that this was yet another test.

'My Lord, our Lady is the parchment, Christ is the notary, and the angels will be our witnesses.'

Pope Honorius III's obvious admiration for the Crusaders re-ignited my ambitions to visit the Holy Land and restore peace. I was reflecting upon the practicalities of this as I scrubbed the floor. My thoughts were interrupted as a young boy ran into the Porziuncola and raced to my side, gasping for breath.

'Francesco, you must come at once. Your mother is asking for you.'

'Mother?' My heart thudded. 'What is it, is she ill?'

'Come quickly. I am to take you to her.'

I dropped the rag I was using and sped after him.

By the time we reached the road leading up to the town, I was forced to reduce my pace to a brisk walk. I arrived at the family home and stumbled through the front door, hopelessly out of breath.

Gasping for air, I leaned on the cutting bench and wondered why I felt disorientated. The last time I had been here was that distressing day when my mother released me from the cellar and begged me to leave. I looked up and was amazed at the transformation. I had heard Angelo had become very successful but had been unaware that he had taken over Dimitri's old shop, knocked through, and doubled the size of our original space.

The young boy called up the stairs.

'Mother, he is here.'

A woman, younger than my mother, came down the stairs. It was her best friend, Maria, who lived a few doors down the road.

'Francesco, my dear boy.' She walked over and embraced me warmly. 'Thank goodness, you are here. Your mother is ill and desperate to see you.'

'And what of Angelo.'

'Away on a buying trip, although he is due back soon. Father Tiberio has sent for him.'

'What ails my mother?'

'She has not been well since your father died, but two days ago, shortly after Angelo left, she developed a fever. The doctor says she is very ill. She may not survive the night.'

My heart hammered in my chest at her words. 'I must go to her.'

'I shall return shortly, but while you are here, Francesco, I must go home and feed my family.'

'Take your time, Maria. I will stay with her tonight.'

I climbed the stairs, full of dread, and entered my mother's room. The only light came from a candle on the bedside table. Her favourite goblet, a bowl of water and a lavender compress sat beside it. The smell of lavender filled the air. Mother resembled a corpse; she was so pale, so still, hardly breathing. Only a slight rise and fall of the patchwork bed throw persuaded me that she was still alive. I knelt beside her bed, head bowed.

'Mother do not leave me, please, I love you ...' Grief swelled my throat, and my voice broke.

'Francesco,' her voice was so faint I could hardly hear. I moved closer and knelt beside her. She raised her hand and rested it lightly on my shoulder.

'Oh, Mother, I am so sorry. I have been such a wretched son.'

'No,' she paused; tears ran down her cheeks and soaked into her pillow. She stroked my arm and sighed deeply. 'Banished from your father's funeral–' her voice faltered as she choked back sobs. Her hand dropped from my arm.

I kissed the salty tears from her cheeks, took her hand and cradled it between my own. 'Hush, Mother, please do not cry. It was not your fault.'

'I should have stood up to them.'

'Please, Mother do not blame yourself.' I squeezed her hand and her sobs subsided. I thought she had drifted off to sleep, but a few moments later I heard her whisper.

'Please forgive me?'

'There is nothing to forgive. You have always been a wonderful mother – kind – supportive – understanding. No one could ever ask for more. I do not deserve you.'

'You do not understand.' She turned towards me and stroked my cheek. 'You give my life meaning. My vision …' Her voice faded, and she slumped back.

'Here, Mother, take some water.' I reached for the water, supported her head, and held the goblet to her lips. She took a couple of sips. 'You must sleep now, get some rest. I shall be here by your side.'

I prayed, as my mind drifted through the years remembering all the good times we had shared. Maria returned, I asked her to refresh the bowl of water, and told her to return to her family until the morning. I bathed my mother's forehead and thought about the times she had done the same for me. The cool water must have refreshed her because she opened her eyes and smiled.

'Remember when you did this for me, Mother? When I returned to Assisi as a failed knight? I always yearned to become a knight, join the crusades and end the bloody wars.'

'And you will. Remember … one day you will be famous around the world.'

I smiled at the memory of her vision and continued to apply the lavender compress. 'Hush now mother, conserve your strength. You must sleep.'

Her breathing steadied, and she slipped into a deep sleep.

In the early hours of the morning, I noticed that her breathing had changed. It became shallow, and her breath rattled in her chest. My mother was dying – four simple words, easy to say, but impossible to comprehend. I held her hand and prayed. As dawn crept into the room, my mother's soul left her frail body. Her loss pierced my heart. The physical pain of it was like no other I had ever experienced. Even though I knew that she would now be with God, at rest and happy, I felt empty. I was an orphan.

There was a noisy tread on the stairs.

'Angelo.'

'Get out!' Angelo snarled.

'Angelo, I am sorry. You are too late; she is gone.'

Angelo paused, then roared like a wild beast, yanked me to my feet, pulled me over towards the stairs and pushed me down. I landed in a heap at the bottom.

'Never, ever come near us again. Do you hear?'

I got to my feet and stumbled into the shop.

Father Tiberio stood by the door. He glared at me. 'What gives you the right to be here?'

'She was my mother.'

'Was?'

'She has passed over.'

'This is all your doing, Francesco. She was too young to die. You were the burden she carried. You caused her death. Mark my words: her blood is on your hands.'

I staggered from the shop. His words stung like salt rubbed into the raw wounds of my grief.

I retreated to the tranquil glade in Carceri and considered my position. The gulf between Angelo and I was clearly irreparable. He and Father Tiberio would no doubt banish me from my dear mother's funeral. I did not want to be around to see that happen.

The Order I had established was successful and growing. However; changes were being introduced by Hugolino and Rome, which resulted in an even more structured approach to our ministry. This imposition of control did not sit comfortably with me, but I realised that if I continually challenged the situation, I would be in danger of undermining Hugolino, and putting myself, the Friars Minor, and everything I held dear at risk.

It was time for me to step back and let go; allow the new structures to flourish. So long as they did not contravene the simple Rule given by God, then some administrative changes might yet prove to be a good thing. Younger brothers were joining us all the time, with new ideas and innovative notions. I should not crush their spirits with my stubbornness and old habits.

I remembered my dream when, as a small hen, I struggled to spread my wings over my chicks to protect them from the Falcon. At the time, I was confused by its meaning, thinking perhaps it could be a warning; that I needed to do all that I could to protect my brothers from harm. Hugolino, with his larger wings bestowed upon him by his position in the Curia, was able to protect my brother chicks far better than I. It was no longer necessary for me to be constantly present.

I was only thirty-seven years old, but I did not enjoy good health, and it was essential, while I was able, to renew my efforts to reach the Holy Land. My Mother's last words to me were the further encouragement I needed. My success, the fulfilment of her vision, would give her life meaning and be a fitting tribute to her memory. I remained convinced that I could explain the simple words of the Gospel to the Saracens, convert them to Christianity, end the bloody wars, or become a martyr in the process. Death held no fear for me.

But first, I would need to discuss the possibility with our protector, Hugolino. Perhaps I would be able to persuade him that the time was right for me to make another attempt at restoring peace to the Holy Land.

I established that he was currently visiting Perugia, left immediately and requested an audience. It seemed that the time was indeed right. The Pope had issued a Bull asking everyone to support the efforts in the Holy Land. In the past, Hugolino had discouraged me from ministry work away from Italy, but this time, when I broached the subject, he encouraged me to renew my efforts to join the Crusaders.

PART FOUR

CHAPTER FOURTEEN
TRIP TO THE HOLY LAND

A large group of us set out for Ancona, leaving Brothers Matteo of Narni and Gregorio of Naples in charge at the Porziuncola. Unfortunately, it was midsummer and a busy time and we could only find a boat willing to take twelve of us. I found it impossible to choose, so I approached a young boy who stood on the quayside, asked him to cover his eyes and point out which eleven should accompany me to the Holy Land.

On arrival in Acre, we met up with Elias and enjoyed a few days of recuperation while we shared our news and prayed for the successful outcome of our mission.

Elias explained how the Crusaders had been able to develop a stronghold close to Damietta in Egypt, from where they now laid siege. The Sultan, not wishing to be constrained within the confines of the city, had retreated and re-established his camp at Fariskur, a short distance up the Nile. The situation appeared to be desperate, but I hoped that God would guide me to serve as His instrument, to act as arbitrator, and to negotiate peace to bring this senseless carnage to an end.

Some of the brothers remained in Acre, but Pietro, Elias and a more recent recruit, Illuminato, came with me as I hastened to Egypt and the Christian camp, a short way upstream from the mouth of the Nile.

The camp was full of rowdy, drunken Crusaders. It reminded me of the time when I had set off with Giovanni to join the crusade in Sicily. But here the men were not just talking about their vile deeds; they were dragging women, kicking and screaming, from their homes and carrying them back to their tents to practise their lustful immorality.

Traders packed the camp selling items purported to be holy relics. Soldiers were buying them because supposedly the items brought about miracles without the need for religious faith. The soldiers believed that ownership of these false items would protect them from injuries on the battleground, or would cure their wounds if they succumbed to a Saracen sword. The misguided customers soon discovered that their battle scars continued to fester and rot and that the *holy relics* provided no such miraculous cures.

On the night we arrived, exhausted from our journey, appalled by what we had witnessed and too tired to eat, I fell into a deep sleep and dreamt of a huge battle in which the Crusaders suffered an appalling defeat.

'Brother Illuminato,' I said when I woke, 'what should I do? Do I tell them what will happen? If so, they will no doubt say I am a madman. But if I do not, hundreds of men will die, and my conscience will be much troubled.'

Illuminato laughed and slapped me on the back. 'What does it matter? It will not be the first time you are called a madman.' He pulled me to my feet. 'We should go and seek out the commander. Tell him of your dream.'

Commander Giovanni de Brienne was the sibling of Gaultier de Brienne, the hero from my youth with whom, alongside my friend Giovanni, I had hoped to gain my spurs. Gaultier had died several years earlier, but his brother was in robust health and welcomed me warmly. I told him of the vision and begged him to refrain from his planned assault on the Saracens. I pleaded with him to reconsider, telling him that to attack would be to violate God's will. My attempts to convince him were futile. He completely ignored my pleas and the next day, on August the twenty-ninth in the year of our Lord twelve hundred and nineteen, the Crusaders launched an attack, which inevitably resulted in a bloody battle. Six thousand men lay slaughtered.

A catastrophic battleground lay carpeted with corpses. They rotted in the blistering heat, creating a putrid stench and attracting clouds of bloated flies. I was appalled. Why had Gaultier ignore the message from God? Could I have done more to prevent this senseless carnage? I prayed that both sides would see that the fighting had to stop.

Eventually, my prayers were answered, and a four-week cease-fire was agreed; hopefully, this would provide sufficient time to restore order, dig mass graves and bury the dead. The pause in fighting, though brief, also presented us with the opportunity to visit the Sultan, Malek al-Kamil, to negotiate with him and try to discover a route to peace. I wanted to leave immediately. However; in holy obedience, I needed first to seek permission from the Papal Legate, Cardinal Pelagius of Albano, the represent-ative of the Catholic Church in Egypt, and therefore the person responsible for reflecting on the will of God for such a mission.

At first, he was reluctant, fearing for our lives, but eventually, after much prayer and persuasion, he conceded and gave us his blessing.

Under the protection of the ceasefire, Brother Illuminato and I made our way from the Crusaders' garrison. My stomach lurched with revulsion as we left the town. We walked along a road, littered with bodies; many beheaded. The scene brought back memories of the day that I had lain in the mud on the Collestrada battlefield and watched Sergio's life blood drain from him; my heart grieved for the senseless loss of so many young lives.

We chanted from Psalm twenty-three, to sustain us as we walked:

'Even though I walk through the valley of the shadow of death
I will fear no evil: for Thou art with me; Thy rod and Thy staff they comfort me.'

The psalm lifted my spirits, and I laughed.

'What is it, Francesco? Why so amused?'

'I was reminded of Jesus' words that aptly describe our mission today.'

'Which ones?'

> 'I am sending you like lambs among wolves. Carry no purse or pack, and travel barefoot. Exchange no greetings on the road. When you get to the house, let your first words be "Peace to this house".
> Luke, 10, 3–6.'

We arrived at the gate of a large compound.

'Peace to this house,' I cried. 'Let us in. We have come to see the Sultan, Malek al-Kamil.'

The guards let us in, beat us soundly, dragged us before the Sultan, and threw us to the ground at his feet.

My gaze travelled around the interior of the Sultan's tent, lined with the highest quality silk. The Sultan sat on a richly carved and gilded throne, covered with brightly coloured tapestries and cushions. Despite our precarious situation, I could not suppress a smile as I reflected on how excited my father would have been to see such fabrics.

Sultan Malek al-Kamil looked down at us with piercing black eyes. His skin was the colour and texture of leather, his face framed by long dark hair. Two young boys stood beside him. Both were fair-skinned, tall and blond; one had blue eyes, the other green. They wore white linen tunics with golden chains at their waists.

I struggled to my knees, bowed my head and adopted a sombre expression.

'We come in peace,' I told him.

The Sultan responded, his voice rich and deep, loud and commanding. Unfortunately, I could not understand a word he said. Brother Illuminato and I exchanged glances.

The blue-eyed youth spoke in French, the language of my beloved mother. 'The Sultan requests that you accept his warm welcome and apologies for the treatment you received on your arrival.'

'We come in peace to share with you the stories and preaching of Our Lord the Father and His Son, our Saviour Jesus Christ.' I bowed my head and placed my palms together as a greeting.

The green-eyed youth immediately spoke to the Sultan, interpreting my words. The Sultan spoke again, and the blue-eyed youth listened, nodded his head and then turned back to face us.

'Sultan Malek al-Kamil is aware of you and your brothers as you go about your work, helping the poor and those in need. He has no argument with you and is happy to engage in such a discussion. First, you must refresh yourselves from your journey and the unfortunate welcome you endured, and then he will be pleased for you to join him at a banquet prepared in your honour.'

'We thank you for your hospitality. May God bless you.'

The second youth interpreted my response and the Sultan stood, bowed his head and swept out of the room. We followed the two youths, who escorted us to a small tent where two large bowls stood on stands, filled with warm perfumed water.

Our two interpreters were around sixteen years of age. They stayed and chatted with us while we washed the dust from our bodies, drank from bowls of cold water, brushed the sand and dust from our tunics, and rested on large tapestry cushions.

During our discussions, it transpired that they were originally part of the Children's Crusade. Both had been on one of the boats captured by the Saracens. They had been brought to the Sultan's camp to train as interpreters. I was horrified for them, but they assured us that they were well looked after. Most importantly the Sultan had respected their religious beliefs, and they had not been forced to change their faith.

We followed them back to the hall where the Sultan was overseeing the finishing touches to the banquet. It was with some trepidation that Illuminato and I surveyed the heavily burdened table. We had heard that the Infidels enjoyed such things as sheep's eyes and the roasted testicles of donkeys, but the table looked wonderful, covered with gold dishes containing different varieties of fruit, bread, and roasted meat, birds and fish. Illuminato caught my eye and grinned. I sighed with relief at the realisation that I could honestly thank our host for this appetising fare.

'The Sultan, Malek al-Kamil, requests that you make yourselves comfortable,' our blue-eyed escort informed us.

The Sultan waved a hand towards the cushions at his feet, and we obliged. Three young women in diaphanous white dresses arrived. They were such beautiful creatures with their exposed arms – dark brown and adorned with gold armlets, their slim ankles – encircled with gold chains, and their long black hair – woven into plaits and dressed with fresh flowers. As they served us from platters of food and delivered golden goblets of wine, their musky perfume wafted over us.

After the meal, we sat comfortably with the Sultan and the two interpreters. I explained to him about the life of Jesus, the Gospels, and our life lived in obedience, chastity, and poverty. I told him how we took the word of God out to those who were ignorant of it and explained how thousands of pagans had become Christians after hearing us speak. I begged him to convert to Christianity.

'The Sultan, Malek al-Kamil is impressed with the fervour of your faith. He wonders if you could demonstrate this further by walking across a carpet,' said the boy.

The Sultan clapped his hands, and a young male servant brought out a carpet which he unrolled at my feet, to reveal a pattern of crosses.

I realised that this was a test to see if I was prepared to defile the image of a cross.

'I am happy to do so,' I said. 'There were other crosses on the day Jesus died to save our souls. It is only the true cross that we should honour. It does not concern me to walk upon mere images.'

The Sultan listened to my response and smiled.

'I will walk through the fire pit to demonstrate my faith if your priest will join with me and do the same,' I said.

After the interpreter had explained my challenge, the Sultan's priest made a hasty retreat and disappeared for the rest of the evening.

'I could walk through the fire on my own,' I offered.

'Brother Francesco, the Sultan wishes me to tell you that he will not risk either your success at walking through the fire unscathed, or your failure. If you succeed, you will be hailed as the second Messiah. If you fail, people will claim that you were martyred by the Sultan's hand, and his people and yours will never find peace.'

Of course, he was right, and peace was essential if we were to end these senseless deaths.

The Sultan extended his hospitality and invited us to stay the night so that we could continue our conversation the following day.

We spent many days deep in conversation, assisted by our two young interpreters. We were joined by the Sultan's Sufi teacher, Al-Fakhr al-Farisi, as we explored each other's beliefs and discussed prayer and the Bible. After an initial attempt by each of us to convert the other, we quickly realized that such endeavours were futile. But we practiced holy obedience in that we each truly listened to the other. For three weeks we explored the differences and similarities in our religions and through prayer discovered much common ground in our experiences of God.

By sharing our beliefs and debating them at length, we realized just how similar they were. We both accepted that there was one omniscient, omnipotent deity who created and supported our world. We both believed in the messenger prophets: Adam, Noah, Abraham, Moses, David, John the Baptist and others. We both lived by the Ten Commandments, looked forward to the Day of Judgment and taking our place in Heaven. We both feared Satan and Hell.

The main differences were our interpretation of the prophets' messages, and that we Christians knew Jesus to be the final prophet and the Son of God, whereas the Sultan believed that Muhammad, who came after, was the final prophet.

The Sultan followed the teachings and believed in the miracles of Christ, and he believed that Mary, the mother of Christ, was a virgin. But he did not believe in the Holy Trinity, nor did he believe that Jesus was anything more than a mortal prophet, and therefore, should not be worshipped. We prayed and debated over this question endlessly throughout my stay, but I was unable to convince him.

I was interested in, but acutely disappointed by his argument that it was not Jesus who shaped the modern concept of Christianity, but rather Paul and the Romans at the Council of Nicaea. The Sultan believed that the Council had been invaded by Satan as it decided on what should, and what should not, be included in the Bible. He believed that pagan myths and beliefs were included to appease the Romans, new doctrines added, and other passages modified and corrupted. He believed that a holy scripture must be in the form inspired or revealed by God, not one polluted or created by human beings. Because he believed that the Bible became corrupted, he followed the Torah; the first five books of the Old Testament, given to Moses by God; the Psalms presented to David and the Gospels written of our Lord Jesus Christ. He also believed in the purity of the Quran, which he claimed was given to the prophet Muhammad by the Archangel Gabriel.

His dismissal of the concept of *Original Sin* concerned me deeply. He did not believe that every human being was born a sinner, bearing the burden of Adam and Eve, for two reasons. Firstly, because in the Quran, God forgave Adam; secondly, the Quran states that it is unfair for someone to bear the burden of someone else's sin or mistake. Therefore, he could not accept that Jesus was sacrificed to save our sins. This belief was so fundamental to me, but I was forced to accept that neither of us would change our opinions. However, I took great comfort from the fact that we were able to accept and be tolerant of each other's viewpoint.

We spent hours debating ways to bring peace between the Saracens and the Crusaders and concluded that dialogue was the route to ending this bloody war. The Sultan admitted that a negotiated peace was in his best interest. The whole of Egypt was suffering from famine, and he was concerned about the rumour that Frederick II, a formidable opponent, was about to comply with the Pope's demands to join the crusade.

I persuaded him to consider terms of a settlement that included the restoration of Jerusalem, central Palestine, and Galilee to the Christians. As an extra incentive, I urged him to propose that he rebuild the walls of Jerusalem. He also thought his cause was likely to be more successful if he agreed to hand over some hostages and a relic of the *true cross* in return for a thirty-year truce. We prayed for a successful outcome and prepared to take our leave.

The Sultan offered me many gifts, but the only one I accepted was an ivory trumpet, used to call the faithful to prayer. It reminded me of the Song of Roland, the *Chansons de Geste*, and Roland's magic horn of ivory which he named *Olifant*. It would be useful for waking those brothers who sometimes found their beds more comfortable than they should, especially when it came to attending the first service of the day.

My eyes prickled with tears as I said goodbye. The Sultan blessed me with words from the beginning of the Quran: "Praise to God, Lord of the worlds." He gave us a token to carry with us to ensure our safe passage and bid us a pleasant journey and long lives. My heart was tinged with sadness as we departed. Partly because I was unlikely to meet with him again to enjoy his friendship and intellectual debate, but also because I had failed to unveil for him the joy of living our lives through Jesus Christ Our Lord.

We walked back in silence until we reached the Crusaders' garrison. Illuminato decided to visit Elias and tell him all the news from our visit, but I was feeling unusually tired, so I begged his pardon and instead retraced my steps back to our lodging house. As I made my way through the streets, I was approached by a young maid of around sixteen years of age.

'You look sad, Father. Like some company?'

I looked at her, and a great sadness threatened to overwhelm me. She was still a child, and yet she walked the streets, selling her body to men. She ran the risk of abuse, physical violence, and exploitation.

'Follow me,' I said and led her back to my room.

Although the day was hot, the autumnal evenings could be cold, and I intended to light and enjoy the log fire this evening before retiring. I still took pleasure from watching a fire burn, as I had ever since those childhood days when my father returned from his trips and we sat before the hearth to hear his stories.

I used a spill, took a flame from the oil lamp and lit the fire, which quickly flared. Then I turned to look at the girl.

'Why do you lower yourself to this role of camp follower?' I asked. 'It saddens me greatly to see you offering yourself in this way.'

'I have to make a living, Sir.' She patted the bed, encouraging me to take a seat by her side. 'Come and sit here.'

'I am cold to my bones. I prefer to stay here by the hearth.'

'Do I not please you, Sir?' She stood and took a pin from the fabric on her shoulder. Her dress fell to the floor, leaving her completely naked. 'I could keep you warm.'

She looked like an angel. Her long brown hair framed her oval face. Large brown eyes looked at me as though she could see into my very soul. Her small young breasts were pale, with pink nipples. Improper thoughts flooded into my mind, before being quickly cast aside. I found that if I stood close to the fire, I was able to control my thoughts and resist carnal temptation.

'Shall I join you?' She edged nearer. 'Oh, Sir, how can you bear the heat? It scorches my skin just to approach you.'

I watched as her skin flamed red from the heat while I was able to remain close to the fire unscathed.

'You make yourself comfortable on the bed,' I told her. 'I will stay here to watch and pray over you tonight. Tomorrow we will go to visit some nuns who abide not far from here. They will employ you, feed and clothe you, and in time, if you hear the Lord's voice calling, you may decide to join them as a nun. If not, hopefully you will find a nice young man and marry. Either way, you will be safe from this dangerous and wicked life you now lead.'

The next day I delivered the young girl safely into the hands of some Benedictine nuns who provided care to the wounded

Crusaders. They were happy to give her shelter. With another soul saved, I left the brothers, turned my back to the horror of the Crusaders' behaviour, and made my way back to the Holy Land.

I was joyous and blessed. For several months, under the protection of the Sultan's seal, I was able to follow in the footsteps of our Lord Jesus Christ through Bethlehem, Jerusalem, Jericho, Galilee and Nazareth, before I made my return to Acre.

In Bethlehem, I stood beneath the Church of the Nativity, in the grotto where Jesus was born. I was overwhelmed with the significance of the event, the sense of place and the knowledge that I was standing in the stable where Christianity began.

That evening I sat around a campfire in the hills above the town and shared a meal with a group of shepherds. While we ate, the sheep foraged nearby. Their small neck bells softly chimed as they moved. I left the next morning and journeyed north to Jerusalem.

That first view of Jerusalem was unforgettable. Its walls, or the remnants of them, shone white in the early morning light. The spiritual calmness I experienced as I knelt to pray in the Sacred Garden of Gethsemane was overwhelming. In contrast, I was filled with a deep sadness as I walked up the Via Dolorosa, the street where Jesus had carried his cross on the route to Gol'gotha.

As the sun sank low over the hills, and the muezzin cried from their minarets calling the faithful to prayer, I walked through the olive-groves on the Mount of Olives to arrive at the mosque of Holy Ascension. The Muslim building had originally been an old Christian church until it was restored and converted by my new friend's uncle and predecessor, Saladin. My pass ensured I was made welcome, and I was able to pray on the very spot where Jesus ascended into Heaven.

A week later I climbed what had become known as the Mount of Temptation. It was still early morning, but already the temperature had risen to an unbearable level. The path was steep and covered with small boulders, making it difficult to climb. My eyesight had deteriorated considerably in the hot, dry conditions of the Holy Land, and I stumbled several times as I struggled to negotiate my way up the mountainside. I was out of breath but greatly relieved when I, at last, reached the cave and took shelter in its cool interior.

This cave was where Jesus had spent forty days and forty nights, resisting the temptations of Satan. Dust clouds billowed across the floor of the Jordan Valley. The mountains on either side were dry, bleached by the hot sun and devoid of vegetation. It was so unlike my lush green valley of Spoleto surrounded by the familiar mountains tinged with their bluish hues. And yet in this cave my life and the life of my Lord Jesus Christ were in sequence once more. He had faced His demons here, just as I faced mine. I knelt on the cave floor and searched for God's message in my recent dealings with the Sultan.

At last, I understood why my earlier attempts to reach the Crusades had failed. The arrogance of my younger self would have prevented me from understanding the lessons I needed to learn from the experience. I should have trusted that God would show me when the time was right.

My plan to convert the Infidels to Christianity, or be martyred in the process, was also arrogant. I should have listened to Hugolino; he was right to chastise me for sending my brothers into situations without proper preparation. Divine inspiration was not sufficient. God teaches us that life is valuable, precious, and not to be wasted. As Hugolino had suggested, God did not wish us to throw our lives away carelessly. Martyrdom was a risk we needed to accept if it was God's will; it was not something we should seek.

My quest, clarified by the Pope on my first visit to Rome, was to convert unbelievers and heretics to Christianity and the Roman Catholic Church. My visit to the Holy Land had always been to convert the Infidels to Christianity, and thereby to save their Godless souls. But my discussions with the Sultan taught me that they were not Godless. My new friend's intelligent debates had enlightened me to the truth: Muslims could be just as devout as Christians. They believed that they would experience everlasting life with God, just as we did. The Sultan, Malek al-Kamil, was not good and holy *in spite* of his religion and its scriptures, but *in response* to them.

The need to consider every person as an individual, and avoid generalisations, had been clearly demonstrated to me. I now realised that we all, every one of us, would struggle with adversity, with our faith, and with our understanding of what God expects of us.

These discussions enlightened me and provided great hopes for peace. But they also challenged my entire Ministry here in the Holy Land.

Was the route to peace in the Holy Land best achieved by converting the Muslims to Christianity? Or was it more likely to be realised through interfaith dialogue, sharing mutual beliefs, building understanding and practising tolerance, so that Muslims and Christians could live together in peace?

CHAPTER FIFTEEN
REVOLUTION AND CONFLICT

I arrived at the entrance of the small hermitage and knocked, desperately hoping that Elias would be in. I sighed with relief as the door opened.

Elias stood before me. A huge smile creased his face.

'Francesco, welcome back to Acre my dear friend. Come in.' He looked me up and down. 'Let me help you.' He took my arm and supported me as I staggered towards the bench and collapsed onto it. 'Whatever happened to you, Francesco? Are you ill?'

'I have been better.' I coughed, and then tried to catch my breath, but yet another bout left me desperate for air. 'The dust, it–' a further attack left me gasping.

'Here, drink this water.' Elias crouched at my feet and held the bowl while I drank from it. 'Do not try to speak. Sit here and rest awhile.'

His tender care reminded me of my mother, and my eyes brimmed with tears.

Elias lifted my legs up onto the bed and tenderly placed a cushion under my head. Gradually the pain in my chest abated, and I found myself smiling as Elias fussed around like a mother hen. He left the house briefly, but returned with a large bowl of water. Tearing a strip of cotton fabric in two, he soaked one-half and proceeded to wipe the dust from my feet.

'You have blisters the size of hen's eggs.'

He lifted my knees and placed my feet into the bowl of cold water.

'That feels good,' I croaked.

'Stay there while I get some dinner on,' he insisted.

I was too weak to argue. My head spun, and I must have passed out as the next thing that I remember is coming round. Elias had dried my feet and was gently pressing salve into the wounds.

'Let me help with the dinner,' I said.

'You will do as I tell you, and rest. I have prepared us a celebratory pot of lamb stew. It will take some time, but in the meantime, you must recover your strength.' He took the second piece of cotton, soaked it with water fresh from the jug and folded it. 'Here, place this over your eyes. It will cool them and reduce the swelling.'

I immediately fell into a deep sleep and awoke to feel refreshed. I removed the bandage from my eyes, sat up and watched Elias. He stood with his back to me stirring the food in a cauldron suspended over a log fire.

'Come on, Elias, let's have some of that stew, it smells divine.'

'Patience, Francesco. The longer it cooks, the more tender it will be. Anyway,' he turned to look at me, his eyes full of concern, 'it is so long since you ate a decent meal, I imagine the fumes alone will feed you.' He dipped a piece of bread into the gravy and handed it to me on a wooden platter.

My stomach groaned in protest while I nibbled on the tasty treat. Elias was correct. I was not used to such delicacies.

Elias paused in his stirring as there was a thundering on the door.

'Gracious. It's probably one of the brothers, excited to hear the news of your return.' Elias rushed to open it. 'Come in, come in, you are very welcome.'

He returned, followed by a young brother, unknown to me. His robes were tattered and frayed. The young man fell to his knees before me, kissed the hem of my tunic, and looked at me with tears in his eyes.

'Brother Francesco, I am so relieved to find you alive.'

'I am very much alive. Did you expect otherwise?'

'Brother Francesco, I am Brother Caesar, and I'm afraid I bring distressing news from Assisi. I am sorry to inform you, but Brothers Matteo and Gregorio became convinced of your death.'

'My death?' I gasped.

'I'm sorry, Brother Francesco, but the rumour is widespread. Brothers Caesar and Gregorio have announced that you no longer exist as head of our Order, and have made considerable changes.'

'But I have every trust in them. That's why I left them in charge. Whatever have they done to cause you such distress?'

'They have … oh, Brother Francesco, I hardly dare tell you.'

'Sit down, Brother Caesar. Share some food with us.'

'I cannot eat until I have told you what brings me here. Brother Francesco, you must return at once to Assisi. The brothers are torn apart by conflict. Brothers Matteo and Gregorio have accepted a Papal Bull, an amendment to your Rule, based on the Benedictine Rule.'

It was as if a knife blade had pierced my heart. So many times, I had resisted the urgings of the Church to make these changes, and now they had come about because of some premature mis-information of my demise. It was so unjust.

'Brother Caesar, your news saddens me greatly.'

'That's not all. They have created a rigid framework of monastic observance. Everything is far more prescriptive, with new rules about absolutely everything. There are rules about eating – we must abstain from red meat unless we are ill, and there are extra fast days, it's all very confusing. Then there are rules about main-taining silence, during meals, and in-between prayer times. The atmosphere is now so unfriendly. No one dares to speak. We are also told we must read books and study, so there's not enough time to attend to our ministry work.'

I could feel the anger bubbling up inside me. My head felt as if it would burst. 'Is that it?'

'Not quite. The Pope has insisted on yet another new rule. All future recruits to the Order must serve a year as an apprentice before they can be ordained.'

I sank my head in my hands and tried, but failed, to prevent tears of frustration from coursing down my cheeks.

'Please, Brother Francesco, please say that you will return at once.'

'Elias, let us devour that delicious lamb stew. Then we must make immediate arrangements to sail for Venice.'

We landed in Venice and immediately moved on to Bologna. On our arrival we discovered that the simple hermitage, built to provide overnight accommodation for brothers had been demolished. In its place, there stood a large building, bearing the title *The House of the Brothers*.

Hearing of my return, the brothers quickly gathered around to welcome me back, inviting me to enter the building and take refreshments, but I remained at the entrance, my fury poorly concealed.

'What is this place?' I demanded.

One young friar was pushed to the front by the others.

'Brother Francesco, it is our centre of learning, a legal and theological college affiliated with the University of Bologna. It contains an enormous library filled with books, and accommodation intended for both ourselves, and the patients sent to us for care.'

'Who is responsible for this ...?' I struggled to contain my anger, 'this atrocity?'

'Brother Pietro Stacia. But he will be devastated to hear you call it such.'

'Where is he?' I asked.

'He is on his way. Look, here he comes now.'

'Brother Francesco, we thank God for your safe return.' Brother Pietro knelt before me. 'I hope you approve of our building.'

'Approve? Do I approve, you ask?'

Pietro looked confused. 'There are some areas we are still developing, but even as it stands it does indeed rival the college built only last year by the Dominicans.'

'Rival? How could you believe I could ever condone such jealousy? How can I approve of your disregard for the Rule by this owning of property and the encouragement of learning? How can I approve of this extravagance and hoarding of books, which is totally against the Rule? I do not approve! I curse you and your lack of humble piety!'

Pietro looked crushed, but I was too angry to care. I swung around and pointed at the gathering of brothers, who were by now staring aghast at my outburst.

'Leave this place now. You should all leave.'

'But Brother Francesco, what of the patients?'

'Take them with you. Leave this grandeur, this corruption, this vulgarisation. I refuse to enter this building.'

The discussion – or rather, I am ashamed to say, argument – continued outside and might have lasted through the night had not Cardinal Hugolino arrived, summoned by one of the brothers to act as a calming mediator.

'Brother Francesco, how good it is to see you safe and sound. We feared you dead.'

His appearance somewhat sobered me, and although I was shaking with rage, I remembered in time to kneel and kiss his hand.

'I can see from your countenance that you are displeased with your brothers, who have all missed you and constantly prayed for your safe return. What troubles you? Your expression is like thunder.'

'Eminence, my brothers are vowed to poverty so that they may combat pride. I return to find this palace, built to promote learning, which as you know, I have always discouraged. Wisdom comes from experience, not books. The books have the stench of wealth and evil. Ownership of them, even in common, is contrary to our Rule of absolute poverty. They serve no purpose but to puff up the brothers with pride and arrogance.'

'Brother Francesco, please, calm yourself. Come inside and take refreshments.' Hugolino placed his hand on my shoulder and tried to steer me indoors.

'I will not enter this … this abomination.'

Hugolino relented and took me instead to a nearby Dominican convent. He sat me down, and with great patience explained that the new building belonged to the Church, with the Friars Minor granted its use in perpetuity.

'I know of your distaste for the ownership of property, even of common ownership. The Church is the registered owner.'

'That is a small comfort,' I told him – but it was a very small one.

I could not believe how quickly the brothers had turned away from our principles and beliefs, simply because they thought I was dead. It threw the future validity of the Order into question.

'Why so sullen, Francesco?' Hugolino lifted a jug, brought by our Dominican host who had tactfully retreated. My protector poured two goblets of water and pushed one towards me. 'It is not like you to behave like a petulant child.'

'You must excuse me.' I burned with injustice and felt incapable of containing my temper. 'I will speak with you on this matter again, but for now, I have the need for solitude.'

I made my escape. The Dominicans had prepared a cell for me, and I retreated to its sanctuary and contemplated my predicament.

Bologna, the chosen seat of learning by so many, would be the gateway to my downfall. I could see it clearly, as if in a vision. The learning created within those walls would invalidate our ideals, call into question our simple message and bring about the seeds of our destruction. My spirit was already changed into that of an avenging angel. I had lost my temper and sought to change the opinions of those present through ranting and condemnation.

How could my brothers forsake me and my simple message? The Friars Minor was my child, the brothers my chicks. I had written the Rule, taken it to Rome and established the Order. I taught them a way of life that had brought them closer to God, yet as soon as I left the country, they conspired against me to make their lives easier. They were treating me like an inconvenient elder. I had given birth to the Order, and now that it was successful, I was an embarrassment.

And what of Hugolino? Was he now my enemy? I knew he thought the Order incoherent at times, uncoordinated, driven by spontaneity. I had heard him express these thoughts on that day I had hidden behind the door and heard him talk to Father Tiberio. Even then I believed his intentions for me were honourable, but what of now? I realised that he had tried to protect my concerns about property, by ensuring that the Church retained ownership of the college. Was I not being a hypocrite? After all,

I had used a similar justification when I accepted La Verna from Count Orlando.

Hugolino tried to bring organisation where he saw chaos, compromise to maintain cohesion, and calm to troubled times. His actions were those of a true Christian, while mine, both my reaction and my outrage, were those of a sinner.

I knew in my heart that Hugolino still admired and respected not only me but also my loyal brothers who remained faithful to our simple message. I could see that he still wanted me around as a figurehead, but probably not in control as the Minister General. He wanted, and indeed needed, a level-headed, worldly man who would allow the brothers to live in sensible houses, to study in libraries, and to hold sufficient common property to make their lives more achievable. But then if this happened, the Friars Minor would abandon their commitment to poverty, hard work, and the nomadic life, to dedicate their lives to studying and prayer.

My head whirled in confusion. If I continued to fight this overwhelming demand for change, this revolt, this diminution of our Rule, those who opposed me would only redouble their efforts and grow in strength.

My appalling loss of temper might have already caused considerable harm. Many would now believe me to be damaged, deranged and incompetent. God forgive me if any witnesses to my descent from grace should fall away and stumble, for it would be my fault. Oh my God, what have I done?

And then I heard the consoling words from God, soothing my very soul.

'My son, you can only lead by example and gentle persuasion, never by anger, coercion or punishment. You cannot teach love through war, teach others to be gentle by being violent, or teach love and forgiveness through harsh words. You need instead to captivate their hearts.'

I lay prostrated on the ground, with my arms stretched out to form the shape of a cross and I prayed.

'My Lord, I realise I have sinned grievously. I thank you for such a gentle rebuke. Please show me the way to make amends.'

I prayed throughout the night.

The next morning, Cardinal Hugolino visited my cell. I thought he was attending to administer Mass, but he told me that first he had some important news for me.

'Brother Francesco, I did not wish to distress you further last night, but I think before you return to Assisi, you should be aware that Father Tiberio is dead.'

Thoughts of our various encounters raced through my mind. The shame and humiliation his words had brought, the feelings of injustice his actions had caused, and the sorrow he had inflicted upon me. What could I say? How, as a Christian, should I feel about this news? I looked at Hugolino. He was twisting his hands together; his mouth was a tight thin line, and I could see the pain in his eyes.

'How did he die?'

Hugolino sighed deeply, sank onto my bench and covered his face with his hands. 'Brother Francesco, I believe I was responsible.'

'You, but how could that possibly be?'

'When you came to me on that dreadful day of your mother's death I was so enraged. Although I gave you my blessing I was sure I was watching you walk away to the Holy Land and your certain death. I believed Father Tiberio was responsible – condemning you for the death of your mother like he did.'

Hugolino looked into my eyes, caught hold of my hand and pulled me down beside him. Still clasping my hand, he continued.

'I travelled immediately to Assisi and told him that I would preside at your mother's funeral and that this time, he was the one banished from the ceremony. I told him that if anyone had blood on his hands, it was him, especially if you failed in your mission and died at the hands of the Saracens. I said that he had displayed a heart of ice in all his dealings with you and demonstrated that he was a poor Christian. For his penance, I insisted that he should retire to the Cathedral for the night and pray for your successful endeavours in bringing peace to the Holy Land.'

Tears came to Hugolino's eyes and trickled down his cheeks. He quickly wiped them away with the sleeve of his tunic and sniffed. I felt a lump in my throat; I hated seeing him so upset and to think that his sorrow was because of me. I lifted my arm and placed it on his shoulder, giving it a slight squeeze of encouragement.

'Oh, Brother Francesco, I am ashamed to admit, I was so angry with him. I left him all night, and in the morning, when I went to find him in the Cathedral, I discovered him dead. He was still kneeling in prayer, but his body was cold. As cold as the icy heart, I had accused him of having.'

'My old friend, his death was not your fault. If anything, I was the cause.'

'But I was so angry.'

'I am sure it was more likely to be Father Tiberio's age and frailty that caused his demise, rather than your chastisement. And as for you being angry, who am I to comment on *your* anger after *my* display last night? God will know from our prayers that we are repentant. He will forgive us.'

'Thank you, Francesco. Your words are a considerable consolation. But what of you? How do you feel about his death?'

'Jesus taught us that we should forgive those that trespass against us. He must have had his reasons. I have already forgiven most things, but the one thing I still find difficult was his insistence that I refrain from acting as the Lord's instrument in healing the sick.'

'The one good thing that will come from his death is that it releases you from your vow. Now let us pray until it is time for us to join with the others for Mass.'

I was horrified when, a week later, I arrived in Assisi. In my absence, Brother Matteo and Brother Gregorio had accepted the offer of a wealthy businessman to re-roof the church with expensive tiles, which in my opinion were unnecessary.

As Brother Caesar had warned us, they had also accepted the Papal Bull that brought us more into line with the Benedictine principles. The Porziuncola had been such a happy, joyous place when I left, and now the brothers were bickering and taking sides. Some wanted things to be easier, and others wanted things, in relation to poverty, to stay true to the Rule.

The pain I experienced on returning to my spiritual home and finding things thus was that of a knife piercing my heart. My head hurt, my hands shook, and my knees became weak. I sank to the floor and wept tears of anger at the betrayal, and the shame of my emotional reaction to it.

Over the following months, the toll to my health was notable. Ever since my incarceration in Perugia, my health had suffered, but now my legs became swollen, making it impossible for me to walk long distances. My eyesight continued to deteriorate, and I could no longer see the Abbey of San Damiano as I looked across the valley from the Porziuncola. Always prone to doubts about my worthiness, I experienced serious concerns about my physical strength and my ability to continue in my role as Minister General. I prayed, pondered on the future and discussed my dilemma and frailty with Leo, my friend and confessor, and in correspondence with my beloved Chiara.

I was now so weak that I needed a chaperone whenever I travelled. My childhood friend, Elias, accompanied me on one particular journey, and the memory of that trip would remain with me forever. We were returning from the town of Viterbo, walking slowly along a track which took us towards Bagnoregio, when a young couple approached us. The man introduced himself as Giovanni di Fidanza. His wife, Maria, carried a small baby wrapped in a shawl. She stepped forward, knelt at my feet and held the child towards me.

'Brother Francesco, could you help our son, for he is blind?'

'I will ask God to help him.' I took the young child from her and cradled him in my arms. 'Dear Lord, bless this child.' I made the sign of the cross over his head. 'Lord, if it is *Thy* will, put to flight this darkness and grant this child the blessing of sight. *Amen.*'

I touched the baby's eyelids. He opened his eyes and looked at me, and then across at his mother. A broad smile played across his lips and lit up his face.

'He can see, look he's smiling at me,' the young mother sobbed.

I suddenly *saw* the baby as a young man, standing before a large group of friars dressed in habits such as mine, with cords around their waists.

'He will be a remarkable young man, very learned and holy. The Lord has need of him,' I blessed the child and handed him back to his mother. 'What is his name?'

'His name is Bonaventura,' she said. She sank to her knees with tears streaming down her cheeks and kissed the hem of my robe.

'You should thank the Lord for your son's sight. I am only His humble instrument.' I told her.

At last, with Father Tiberio no longer looking over my shoulder, I was free to do God's work.

More tribulations awaited us on our return to the Porziuncola. News reached us that six of our brothers, on a crusade to Morocco, lay slain and martyred.

Opinions were divided; some said martyrdom was a good thing, and that the six would, even now, be seated with God, surrounded by angels. Others thought that they had wasted their lives, taunting the Muslims about their faith, forcing the Infidels to chase and slay them. Some even thought that I was responsible for their deaths as I had encouraged their crusade. But the strongest criticism came from those who condemned me for the delay in delivering the message that I now believed, since meeting and debating with the Sultan, that tolerance and interfaith dialogue were the way to peace. Communication of my enlightenment had come too late for the six brothers in Morocco. Above all, this accusation forced me to reflect hard on whether I was still the right person to lead the Order.

My prayers and discussions helped me to come to the decision that I should no longer continue as Minister General. The Order was now so large that it required discipline and as I had once overheard Hugolino say, I could not rebuke a rabbit, let alone a fallen brother.

Although my eyesight was now too blurred for me to make out detail, it was obvious that once again a huge crowd had gathered for the Michaelmas chapter meeting. Word of my safe return from the Holy Land had quickly spread, and brothers journeyed over mountains and valleys to be here. A loud cheer rose from the crowd as I stood to address them. Humbled by their response, I gave the brothers my blessing and stifled an emotional sob.

'Brothers, I am no longer strong enough, in mind or in body, to carry this heavy burden and remain as your Minister General.' A loud murmur erupted, and I nodded to acknowledge their concern. 'You should be assured that this is not a decision I have taken lightly. I have come to this conclusion after much prayer, and after taking wise counsel from my brothers and sisters.' I placed my hand on Pietro's shoulder. 'From this day forth, Brother Pietro has agreed to take my place. Cardinal Hugolino has endorsed this decision. The Friars Minor will be in safe hands.'

My choice proved a popular one. Pietro was the obvious candidate to take my place as Minister General. He and Bernardo had been with me from the very earliest days of the ministry, and he had remained loyal to the Rule and my Lady Poverty. But perhaps even more important in this time of divided beliefs and opinions amongst the brothers, Pietro consistently demonstrated the considerable ability to maintain harmony.

The murmuring subsided.

I agreed to continue at the Porziuncola as a spiritual advisor only and pledged to become submissive to ecclesiastic authority.

Pietro, with his experience of being a priest before he joined the Order, showed himself far better placed than I could ever be to minister the more rigid and formal services imposed upon us by Rome. Unfortunately, the extra strain caused by all the turmoil contributed to the failing of his health. He died within the year.

We all felt his loss greatly, but for me, it was a personal tragedy. I would miss my loyal companion and his wise council more than words could ever say.

After first consulting with Cardinal Hugolino, I asked my childhood friend Elias to succeed Pietro as Minister General. Elias was not an inspirational leader or a priest, but he was an extremely effective administrator and therefore the natural choice to bring structure and organisation into the expanding Friars Minor. We were fortunate that he agreed.

My life became difficult as I struggled to maintain and preserve my ideals for our Order. Ministers were appointed, colleges established, churches built, and preaching transferred into the churches. We were constantly being deflected from our nomadic, apostolic life. I resisted these attacks as best I could, both by example and by pleading for concessions to the constant barrage of Papal Bulls arriving from Rome. Permission was granted for me to write the new Rule, but the Pope, despite my pleas, did not relent on his insistence that new entrants to the Order were to serve at least a year as a novice before they could be ordained.

I looked up as one of these young novices entered my cell.

'Good morning, Brother Francesco, I wonder if it is possible to speak with you.'

'Speak freely.'

He fidgeted as he stood before me. 'I have spoken with my Provincial Minister, and he has agreed, but I wanted to put my request to you directly, Brother Francesco. I joined the Friars Minor because of your example, for I hold you and your principles in high esteem. However …' he looked even more uncomfortable, 'I admit to a yearning to hold a Psalter so that I may read and learn the psalms each day. My parents are pleased with my choice of vocation and will be happy to purchase one for me as a gift. What is your opinion on this?'

'My son,' I sighed deeply, 'why do you want this Psalter?'

'I wish to improve my wisdom.'

'But you cannot know something simply by reading about it; we have to experience the facts. Wisdom comes from opening your heart and listening to the Holy Spirit. It comes when the heart, spirit and soul are as one with the mind. Learning flatters a man and fools him into believing he has wisdom and knowledge when in fact he has neither.'

I paused trying to think of an example. 'Think about the song of Roland and Oliver. They chose to die as martyrs, but others learn of their noble faith and aspire to the same level of glory, simply by having knowledge of their devotion. Others recite and preach the words of Jesus, the prophets, apostles or saints as if they were themselves responsible for them.'

I looked at him, so young, so fresh, and so eager. I knew he would take my decision harshly, but I also knew that I must hold true to my Lady Poverty.

'My son, learning is for decoration, not wisdom. It can bring pride and a yearning for still more. If you have a Psalter, you will then want a Breviary so that you may also learn the hymns and prayers. And when you have that, you will think of yourself as a great prelate, or a Bishop held in high esteem, rather than a humble Friar Minor. Pride will fill your heart, and you will sit on your throne and call to others and say, "bring me my breviary." My answer is; no.'

The young novice turned pale. He pulled his cowl over his head, knelt before me and kissed my hand.

'In humble obedience, I will accept your decision. Bless me, brother.'

He left me, but a few weeks later I was walking in the woods, close by the Porziuncola when the boy returned. He was no longer a novice and proudly wore his robe and cord to demonstrate his ordination.

'Brother Francesco, forgive me, but I beg you to reconsider my request. I am confident that I can resist the pride you speak of, and I still have a desperate yearning for a Psalter.'

I sighed, tired and confused by all this rebellion, this bickering among the brothers. My loyal disciples were still content to follow our simple Rule and live in complete poverty, but what of the others? They had sworn an oath of chivalry to our Lady Poverty. Why then, was there all this dissent? Why did they yearn for libraries? Why did they yearn for the opportunity to learn and acquire knowledge? Why did they need cloisters to read in when we had the woods and forests? Why did they desire to embrace a mendicant lifestyle, spending their time in prayer, rather than in ministry? Why did they shy away from hard work, which subdued any rebellious inclinations and prevented idle bodies from sinking into sin? Why?

'Brother Francesco, what is your answer?'

The young friar still stood before me, anxious for my reply.

'Do as your Minister says,' I told him.

The young friar smiled, thanked me and departed.

I watched him walk away, my shoulders slumped with the weariness of all these arguments, but then I remembered the words God spoke to me many years before:

Do not let your simple message and lack of learning make you afraid because your faith will uphold and sustain you. Your talents are manifold, and you will develop wisdom and grow wise with the grace of my blessing.

I chased after the young friar. 'Wait, wait for me,' I cried. 'Come with me, let us retrace our steps and when we get to the part of the path where I told you to go away and listen to your Minister, please, point it out to me. Here, this is where we were, is it not?'

The young friar nodded, looking confused. I knelt before him.

'I was wrong to advise you in that way, for I believe it is God's will that we continue to observe His simple message. A Brother Minor should own nothing but his clothes.'

I may have relinquished my role as Minister General, but I would not relinquish my belief in my Lady Poverty.

CHAPTER SIXTEEN
THE RULE, PERFECT LOVE, AND THE STIGMATA

The change in my role allowed for more time to pray and contemplate, but I was constantly troubled and wearied by the bickering that continued to divide the brothers. I craved some peace and quiet. It was also essential for Elias to establish himself as the Minister General, and that would be easier to do if I were not around. I escaped to the hermitage of Santa Maria Maddelena on Mt. Rainiero, to give me time and space to write the new Rule and prepare responses to the continuing onslaught of Papal Bulls generated by the Pope.

The hermitage is a beautiful place, originally a Benedictine garrison. The rustic stone buildings hug the side of the lush Mt. Rainiero, surrounded by a forest of ancient beech, ilex, and oaks. Many of the trees grow out of the bare rock. Their shiny roots clamber chaotically over the boulders like enormous snakes slithering their way through the rough terrain. The rocks and even the walls of the buildings are veiled with ferns. The building was a spectacular vantage point for the wonderful views over the valley Santa below – although my eyesight no longer allowed me to enjoy these as I had on earlier visits.

I retreated to the small cave below the building, where I fashioned myself a cross from two oak branches bound together with cord and spent my days in prayer and contemplation. It was in this wonderful undisturbed place, which I named *sacro speco*, where I found peace and tranquillity. I was able to pray for guidance and write the new Rule.

However, the presentation of my Rule at the next chapter meeting was not well-received. Even as I was reading it, I could see several brothers turn to each other and mumble behind their hands. There were deep sighs; some brothers fidgeted and avoided looking directly at me. As I finished speaking, Cardinal Hugolino took my arm and led me away, leaving Elias to close the meeting with prayers.

'Francesco, my dear boy, this is a wonderful effort, beautiful words, but I think you need to make it more concise before you submit it to the Pope for ratification.'

'Concise?'

He held my elbow and steered me towards the bench in the rose garden.

'Here, let us sit on this bench, Francesco. I know this is one of your favourite spots.'

He took his seat beside me. He looked uncomfortable, and I sensed he was struggling to find the right words.

'You are a visionary, there is no doubt about that. But the Pope will need to know how you are going to balance the need to mitigate the harshness of your Rule in a way that will enable most of the brothers to adhere to it. Since your very first visit to see our dear Pope Innocent III – God bless his soul – there were always concerns about the demands the Rule makes upon the brothers, as I'm sure you are aware. Although there is no doubt that you and your original recruits could follow such a severe oath of allegiance to poverty, the demands on those who come after you will probably prove to be a step too far. We have seen the result of that over the past few years. We need to find a happy compromise.'

'Is there such a thing as a *happy* compromise?'

'I have every faith in you, Francesco.' He stood up and patted my shoulder. 'I must return to Brother Elias, but be assured, I know that you can do this.'

Again I retired to the hermitage to write the new Rule. I took Leo with me as my trusty scribe, and Pacifico as my inspiration. Pacifico played soothing music on his lute while I dictated the words and Leo transcribed them. I was pleased with the result, but my perfectly scripted attempt went missing. Elias reported it lost somewhere between leaving my hands and being presented in Rome. I began to feel as though everyone transpired against me.

Snow fell in soft clumps as Leo and I struggled along the frozen pathway. We were returning from yet another of our visits to discuss the Rule with Cardinal Hugolino in Rome. I still found it difficult to understand why the brothers were resisting my call for complete poverty, or why the Pope was supporting their demands and insisting that it should be acknowledged in the Rule. Hugolino's parting words rang in my ears as we trudged through the snow: 'Remember, Francesco, the Pope will continue to withhold his approval until you achieve a happy compromise. Have faith, and do not forget – I *know* you can do this.'

We turned a sharp bend in the path and came across the *Cascata delle Marmore*, a spectacular waterfall built by the ancient Romans over a thousand years before. It was built to drain the wetlands created by the slow-flowing river Velino, which surrounded the city of Rieti. Many of the cattle and farmers who lived in the area suffered from a dreadful malady, thought to be caught from the flies that infested the stagnant water. A much-revered Roman consul called Manius Curius Dentatus investigated the problem and developed a solution. Folks in the area often joked that he discovered the way forward because he was Curius by name and curious by nature. Manius constructed a canal that eliminated the stagnation by diverting the water from the marshes and Lake Piediluco, over the natural cliffs at Marmore and into the river Nera, some three hundred and twenty cubits below.

Today, the waterfall was no more than a mere trickle, and the freezing temperature captured the water and turned it into long strands of ice that glinted and gleamed in the setting sunlight. Manius had found an answer to a problem and in doing so had created an object of considerable beauty: a solution that inspired perfect joy.

I halted before the beauteous sight while I pondered my problem. I was no longer able to cope with all this conflict, and yet the thought of compromising the Rule filled me with despair. But why?

God and the Sultan had helped me to accept that there was a better way to live among non-Christians; in peace, mutual faith and shared understanding. I recognised that the belief in our one true God is *not* exclusive to Christians, and is clearly visible in the way people of other faiths live their lives. Why, then, was it so difficult for me to accept that I did not have the exclusive right on interpreting the Rule on property? Surely the important issue was that the brothers were indeed true Christians, living their lives as humble servants of our Lord Jesus Christ. Through the brothers, the Pope, Hugolino, and the Sultan, God had tried to make it clear to me that I should embrace, tolerate and celebrate the diverse views of others in order to experience perfect joy.

'Brother Leo,' I said.

Leo looked up. Snow clung to his beard; his eyes glistened with frozen tears, and his body trembled from the cold. He wrapped his arms around his chest, first this way and then that, hugging himself tightly to create some warmth and comfort.

'Our brothers are spread across the world,' I told him. 'They are good examples of holiness and edification. But – note this down – this is not perfect joy.'

'Then what is?'

'Oh, Brother Leo, even if we restore sight to the blind, enable the lame to walk, restore speech to the dumb and hearing to the deaf, even this is not perfect joy.'

'No?'

'Oh, Brother Leo, even if the brothers could speak every language with the voices of angels and bring peace to the world, even if they knew everything about the sciences and the scriptures and could see and prophesise the future, this would not be perfect joy.'

'Brother Francesco are you going to tell me, or not?' Brother Leo blinked snow from his eyelids. 'What, then, is perfect joy?'

'If we arrive at the Porziuncola door, frozen, hungry and close to death, and we knock on the door, and someone comes and asks who we are, and we say "we are two of your brothers," and he says "you are two vagabonds who plan to steal from us, be gone from here." And if we invoke God's gift of the Holy Spirit, conquer our pride and willingly accept this cruel abuse, injustice, and dismissal with grace, then this will be perfect joy.'

Cardinal Hugolino and I exchanged letters on the next series of drafts and met on several occasions to engage in long conversations on the contents. Much of these exchanges were about the part in the Rule that stated: *take nothing with you as you go.* I kept putting it in as I still stubbornly believed it to be fundamental to the Rule, and Cardinal Hugolino kept taking it out as he did not believe that it was always practical. Eventually, exhausted, I conceded. After further redrafting by Cardinal Hugolino, the new Rule was finally approved by the Pope in the year of Our Lord twelve hundred and twenty-three: thirteen years after my very first attempt to have our simple Rule approved.

Two days before Christmas, Leo and I made our way to the village of Greccio. My health was still in poor shape; walking was even more difficult, and my eyesight was deteriorating, but I was in good spirits. My joy for life had fully returned, despite the disappointments, concerns, and compromises. We were welcomed and made comfortable by a good friend of ours, Giovanni di Greccio, a knight committed to living his life as a brother of the Tertiary Order. During supper that evening, I was suddenly struck by an idea.

'Brothers let us do something different this year – something that will make everyone as joyous as ourselves. Let us create the atmosphere of that first Christmas, when Our Lord Jesus Christ was born.'

'It sounds good, but how do we do that?' asked Brother Leo.

'Let us ask all the village folk, and especially the children, to bring their pets to the Christmas Eve midnight Mass. We must also find someone who will bring an ox, a donkey, and a sheep. We will help everyone to experience what it was like on the day the baby Jesus was born in Bethlehem.'

Giovanni offered to loan us animals and a cave on his land. He fashioned a crib and filled it with sweet-smelling straw. Invitations were sent out, and on the night of Christmas Eve, the population of the village and surrounding countryside, carrying rush torches and singing hymns, flocked to the cave. The children danced alongside their parents, leading dogs and carrying cats, birds in cages and even a lizard. I looked around the cave at the ox, the sheep, and the donkey. They nibbled at the straw, their breath gently billowing on the cold air. A brave mother wrapped her newborn baby in a shawl and laid him in the crib. A lump came to my throat and tears prickled my eyes. I could scarcely breathe as I realised that this was exactly how it must have been on that first Christmas morning.

The service was an absolute delight. The children laughed, danced and clapped their hands with glee. The donkey managed to deposit dung over Leo's feet, much to everyone's amusement. I led Leo outside and washed his feet while Giovanni swept up the droppings, and the festivities resumed. The villagers of Greccio were still celebrating as we left early on Christmas morning.

In August the following year, I felt compelled to visit the retreat at Alvernia, granted to us by Count Orlando. I intended to under-take a forty-day fast, in the company of Angelo, Masseo, and Leo.

We had not travelled half the requisite distance up the moun-tainside when my legs and my breath began to fail me. Masseo lowered me to the ground and propped me against a rock, carefully pillowing my head on his folded cloak.

'I will make haste and return shortly,' he promised, as he rushed back the way we had come in search of assistance.

Little more than an hour later he returned, trailed by a huge bear of a man, who was in turn trailed by a braying donkey. The man, even larger in stature than my dear Masseo, obliterated the sun as he bent over me and lifted me as you would a child: one arm around my shoulders, the other beneath my knees. The man, who turned out to be a farmer, perched me atop the donkey with a gentleness that no casual observer would suspect him capable of. But as he had carried me, I had looked deeply into his eyes and seen the pure goodness of heart that lay within him. He led me up the slopes, his patience with the rock-strewn path and the bad-tempered beast of burden a lesson to us all.

We travelled for a few hours, climbing higher and higher as the sun rose in the sky and our skin glistened with sweat.

'I am sorry to say it,' sighed the farmer, mopping his brow, 'but I am craving the simple gift of water.'

'I too have need of refreshment,' I admitted. 'Let us drink from that spring over there.' I pointed to an outcrop of boulders.

The farmer shook his head. 'I know this land well. There is no water around here.'

I smiled and pointed again. He shrugged and went to look in the direction that I had indicated. No sooner had he rounded the outcrop than we heard him cry out in surprise.

'Water. There is water. Come, look.'

A fresh spring flowed from the rocks. Each of us sated our thirst and cooled our over-heated bodies. The farmer palmed water for the donkey to drink, and then more to dampen its coat. The beast stamped his hooves and brayed.

As soon as we finished, fully refreshed, the gushing spring faltered, reduced to a trickle and then dried up completely. No matter: we were ready to press on with our journey.

After many hours, we reached the large plateau, used as the base camp for retreats. The farmer agreed to collect us on the feast day of St. Michael and then, waving, he led his donkey away back down the mountainside. The donkey's loud brays continued to echo up the slopes long after they were lost from sight.

Count Orlando, having heard we were on our way, rushed over from his nearby castle. He arrived shortly after us, bringing with him a couple of friends and a handful of his servants. They helped us to construct a shelter, to offer protection from the worst of the elements. They had also brought food, wine, and fresh water.

'Whatever you need to make your stay more comfortable, just send someone over to the castle. Remember, anything you need.' The Count left us in a far better state than he had found us, and made his way back to his home.

I told my brothers that we should not take the Count up on his kind offer. Instead, we should spend the next forty days in quiet contemplation and fasting. I also begged them to honour my desire for complete isolation and solitude. I wanted to immerse myself completely in prayer and communion with my Heavenly Father. Only Leo was to come to me each day to take Mass and hear my confessions, but even he was to call out to me when he arrived. I made it clear that if I did not reply, he must presume it was because I was at prayer, in which case he should return the following day. To assuage my brothers' anxiety, I agreed that Leo could bring me any supplies I might require, such as fresh water and a small amount of bread to celebrate Mass.

The brothers understood that this could be my last opportunity to spend forty days on a complete retreat in this spiritual place, and they agreed to respect my requests, although I could see they were concerned for me and would have preferred to stay by my side. Leo and I left Angelo and Masseo at prayer and made our way to a small level glade higher up the mountain. We discovered a narrow cave on the edge of the dell; an ideal shelter for me. We also found a large rock situated towards the edge of the plateau, which we used as our altar. I opened the Bible at random to provide us with a catalyst for our prayer:

'Proud men, one and all, are abominable to the Lord; depend upon it: they will not escape punishment. Proverbs, 16, 5.'

Was this a clear message to me? Was I guilty of the sin of pride? It was easy to do, as the apostle Paul himself discovered. Paul endured considerable pain but considered it to be a blessing. I recalled how he found joy in his acceptance of it. He claimed that it kept his pride and arrogance in check and made him more humble. He believed that it helped him to stay closer to God and placed him in a better position to undertake His will.

But the question remained: was I guilty of pride?

Certainly, pride and arrogance were sins of my youth, but then I had prayed to God in the cave that day, so long ago now, and I had experienced the warmth of His forgiveness and the outpouring of His love. Had I been guilty of pride since that time?

I recalled the day that Bishop Guido visited San Damiano for the Mass to celebrate its completion. Had a tinge of pride invaded my spirit that day? I believe that it had. I also reflected on how I had refused even to consider the Pope's original suggestion to combine with another Order. How stubborn I had been then – and since, whenever I had been asked to reconsider the complete poverty aspect of the Rule. I believed that the Rule was given to us by God, but was it pride that drove me to fight for our Rule so tenaciously? Probably so.

I was proud of my part in bringing peace to Assisi, but I realised now that, at the time, I had failed to give sufficient acknowledgement to the fact that the accomplishment was through God's interventions, not mine. What, therefore; was there for me to be so proud of?

I was also guilty of wallowing in self-pity over failures on my various Crusades. Had I been arrogant in thinking I could convert the Saracens and end the wars? It had taken me a long time to accept that there was a better way – through peaceful negotiation, interfaith dialogue, and tolerance.

And what of my reaction to the way my brothers had turned against me when they thought I was dead? I had collapsed in physical pain and suffering, but was that the pain and suffering of my body, or my pride? I knew it to be the later. I hung my head in shame.

So, what could I learn from all of this?

I had to accept that my views were not the only way to worship God. My failure to do so was indeed arrogant. I needed to embrace and celebrate the views of others to experience perfect joy. After all, what did it matter if some brothers fell short of my ideals, as long as they did not fall away from God?

'Dear God, I am guilty of the sin of pride. I thank You for showing me the error of my ways. I humbly beg Your forgiveness.'

Day's went by, spent in prayer, giving thanks for the insight into my failings and seeking forgiveness for them. And then it was September the fourteenth and we settled down to observe the Exaltation of the Holy Cross. I asked Leo to open our Bible three times and read the passage aloud. On each occasion, the book fell open at the passion of Christ. As I followed Christ in life, here was the confirmation that my prayers, to understand the mystery and depth of his suffering, was to be granted.

I prayed: 'My Lord Jesus Christ, please help me, before I die, to understand the suffering and pain that You endured when You were crucified on the cross, and the abounding love You experienced, which enabled You to bear such suffering. If it is possible, I want to experience these things in my heart, body and soul. May I share *Your* pain so that, like Paul, my pride and arrogance will be held in check and I will be better prepared to carry out *Thy* will? May *Your* will be done.'

As I prayed, I sensed a presence, and I looked up into the face of a Seraph enveloped in a diaphanous aura of bright light. When I looked more closely, I made out a six-winged angel with two wings positioned for flight; two more adorned his head, and the remaining two covered his body.

I recognised it instantly as the Seraph described in Isaiah, 6, 2. The Seraph looked at me with such generosity and compassion; that my heart pounded with an overwhelming surge of happiness. I realised it was my Lord Jesus Christ himself. He came as my mediator, to save me from the pit of Hell. However, as I gazed upon this vision, I realised that Jesus remained nailed to the cross, and my joy became touched with sorrow and anguish at the brutality. Why did He still suffer? Did our continuous capacity to sin contribute to His ongoing suffering? As I pondered this question, He smiled, reached out and touched me.

A searing pain pierced my side, my hands, and my feet. Christ had blessed me with the wounds that he suffered, as an answer to my prayers. The pain was intense. Filled with a passionate feeling of joy, I collapsed onto the floor. This pain was what He had experienced on the day He bravely faced His inevitable death at Gol'gotha.

The constant pain of the stigmata would not only serve as a continual reminder of His sacrifice for us, but would also prevent me from transgression in the future, by controlling my pride and arrogance.

Leo, who was standing nearby, saw me collapse and rushed over to help. I tried to hide my feet from him, covering my hands with the sleeves of my habit, but he had already witnessed the stigmata. He tore cloth from his tunic and gently bound my feet and then lifted me from the cold ground and staggered back down the mountainside towards the others.

Masseo saw us struggling and ran towards us, took me carefully from Leo's arms and carried me to the shelter. He laid me gently on the floor. 'What happened to you, Francesco? Are you ill?'

Leo and Angelo fussed over me and helped position me comfortably.

'God has blessed him,' Brother Leo told them. 'He has received the wounds of our Lord Jesus Christ.'

Having inspected my wounds with wonder and awe, Masseo clasped his hands in prayer. 'We must return at once and share this miracle with everyone.'

I groaned and lifted my head from the floor, before collapsing back.

'No,' I begged. 'I am reluctant to reveal this honour, in case others believe that I am boasting, or it is false and think badly of me. I must never again be guilty of the sin of pride.'

Leo gazed down at me and smiled, his love for me a bright light that bathed the whole mountain in a warm glow. 'Brother Francesco, when God honours you in this way, it is not intended for you alone, but for others as well.'

I promised to sleep on it, and I did for several hours. When I woke, the sun was lower in the sky, and a gentle warmth soothed my sore body. I beckoned Leo to my side.

'Please, I would ask you to return to the rock that we were using as an altar where the Seraph descended.'

'Of course, Brother Francesco. And then?'

'I want you to anoint the rock with oil, in recognition of the part it has played on this remarkable day.'

He patted my arm. 'Consider it done.'

I clutched his hand and held his gaze. 'I believe that we should not routinely talk of the stigmata.'

'Routinely?'

'I have listened to what you have said, but I believe that we should only reveal it to others if the spirit moves us to do so. Let us trust Him to tell us what, if anything, we should say.'

He squeezed my hand and left to do my bidding.

My heart filled with gratitude when, two weeks later, the brazen braying of a donkey reached our ears, and my friend, the farmer, lumbered into our camp, exactly as previously arranged, it was Michaelmas Day, the feast day of St. Michael. He surveyed my poor state with concern, lifted me without help and transported me with great care back down the mountain.

However; it was obvious to us all that I could not continue on foot. Leo arranged for the loan of a horse from Count Orlando, to take me back to the Porziuncola. The pleasure the Count clearly derived from being allowed to assist me in this way reminded me that I should not let pride in my independence prevent me from enabling others to give. To accept help and support, when graciously offered, is a great gift to offer in return.

As we were leaving, I turned and blessed the mountain.

'Sacred Mountain of God, I give you my blessing. Farewell. Alas, I will never see you again.'

The journey was not without pain. Every sway of the horse's flanks jarred my wounds, but I embraced the sensation. Lost in thought, I looked up some time later to discover an unexpected landscape. Instead of sandy paths strewn with rock, I saw lush green vegetation and undulating hills.

'When do we get to the town of Borgo San-Sepolcro?' I asked.

'Brother Francesco, we passed through there an hour ago,' Masseo said in an exasperated voice. 'How could you fail to notice, it is beyond belief. The whole town came out to greet you, pulled at your tunic, cheered and shouted your name. I know you are distracted, but that is unbelievable.'

I laughed.

'What?' Masseo wanted to know.

I held out my arms to reveal the bloody wounds on the palms of my hands. 'What is truly unbelievable is this great honour, received directly from God.'

Masseo nodded. 'I can see how that puts things into perspective.'

I smiled, and as the horse plodded on I slipped back into my thoughts. I would never be able to express my gratitude, no matter how much longer I lived. I resolved to try by returning to my ministry and work for as long as I remained on this earth.

CHAPTER SEVENTEEN

THE CANTICLE TO THE SUN AND THE FINAL QUESTION

On the way home, a group of people came to us and begged me to turn back to tend to a woman. She had endured labour for several days and was becoming very weak. Her husband had carried her from their home, and was making his way towards us, but they were still some distance away. Too weak to make haste myself, I asked Leo to remove the harness from the horse, and make his way quickly to the woman. I stayed with the horse and continued to pray. I prayed to God to grant me strength and channel His healing powers into this woman. I prayed that I was not yet too old and weak to carry out His work in His name. Leo returned and told me how he had run to the woman's side and placed the harness on her swollen belly. The child was immediately born and let out a loud cry to announce his entry into the world. I praised God and thanked Him for allowing me to continue to act as his instrument.

We reached the hermitage, our shelter for the evening, but we were alarmed to find a young priest in a poor way. His body contorted and thrashed the ground. His legs lifted one moment, and the next twisted sharply beneath him. The force of the attack caused him to buck off the ground with each wave of the seizure. His face distorted into a manic grin and he frothed at the mouth. I laid my hand on his forehead and in the name of our Lord Jesus Christ asked the evil spirit to leave his tortured body. We all prayed over him and immediately he became calm. His eyes met mine and he smiled. He fell into a deep sleep and the next morning, when he awoke, we were relieved to find him completely restored.

'Thank you, Brother Francesco. Thank you for my recovery.'

'The Lord healed you, and may the Lord give you peace.'

We arrived back at the Porziuncola, but I was aware that there was very little time left, and I was eager to take the gospels to as many people as I could while I was still able to do so. Masseo was able to negotiate the loan of a donkey from a local farmer, and we travelled on as quickly as my frailty allowed. Sometimes we were able to visit three or four villages in a day. But after three months, I grew so weak that I was forced to agree to Masseo's entreaties, and return to the Porziuncola.

I was enjoying the September sunshine and refreshments with my beloved Sister Chiara. Although we constantly corresponded, this was our first meeting since Pope Innocent III, at the instigation of Father Tiberio, had made her convent a closed Order. Realising how ill I now was, the Pope Honorius III gave his permission for me to stay at San Damiano under Chiara's care. When I had arrived a few days earlier, the brothers constructed a small shelter for me in the grounds. Already my health was so much better.

Chiara was reading from a letter from Brother Agnello, who had travelled to England the previous year with eight of our brothers. Five had set up a hermitage in Canterbury. Agnello and the other three had gone first to London and then on to Oxford, where they had built another hermitage. Under the changes made by the Pope that now positively encouraged learning, several of the brothers were taking courses at the University.

'They have recruited some eminent people,' Chiara informed me.

'I knew he was destined for great things. Just look at what a good job he did in France when Cardinal Hugolino persuaded me to send him and Pacifico in my stead. That was a difficult job with all the heresy they encountered.'

'Yes, but none of us could have achieved what we have without your guidance and example.' Chiara folded the letter and placed it in her pocket. 'Here, Francesco, take some cool water. The sun is hot today and we need to look after your health.'

'Thank you, I will take a quick drink and then I will read my new poem to you. It is called the *Canticle of the Sun*:'

Most High, all-powerful, good Lord,
Yours are the praises, the glory, and the honour,
and all blessing,
To You alone, Most High, do they belong,
and no human is worthy to mention Your name.
Praised be You, my Lord, with all Your creatures,
especially Sir Brother Sun,
Who is the day and through whom You give us light.
And he is beautiful with great splendour;
and bears a likeness of You, Most High One.
Praised be You, my Lord, through Sister Moon,
and the stars,
in Heaven You formed them clear and precious
and beautiful.
Praised be You, my Lord, through Brother Wind,
and through the air, cloudy and serene,
and every kind of weather,
through whom You give sustenance to Your creatures.
Praised be You, my Lord, through Sister Water,
who is very useful and humble and precious and chaste.
Praised be You, my Lord, through Brother Fire,
through whom You light the night,
and he is beautiful and playful and robust and strong.
Praised be You, my Lord, through our Sister Mother Earth,
who sustains and governs us,
and who produces various fruit,
with coloured flowers and herbs.'

Chiara clapped her hands together. 'Oh Francesco, what a joy you are – a true Troubadour.'

'I must send for Pacifico, and have him compose the music.'

'And then we must teach the song to our brothers and sisters,' she said, ready as ever to support and encourage my every ambition.

My sight was getting even worse; I could no longer see the doves as they flew back to their nests, although I could hear them. Nor did I did know which brother had arrived in my shelter, until he spoke and I was able to recognise his voice. It was a great sadness to me. I had always enjoyed the beauty of nature, the animals, the countryside and our beautiful Porziuncola. It also made it difficult for me to manage day to day, without support from my brothers. It saddened me to think that I was a burden to them, although I constantly reminded myself of the need to accept their offers of help with good grace.

'Brother Francesco,' Elias said when he brought me some supper. 'I think the time has come for us to do something about your eyesight. The Pope has heard of your condition and has offered you the services of his physician. We will go to see him.'

I travelled by donkey and we eventually arrived in Rieti at the papal apartments. The physician was a kindly man and examined me carefully before he gave his opinion.

'The swellings in your legs are caused by dropsy. We know not what causes it, nor do we know how to cure it, but if you sit with your legs higher than your chest whenever possible, and sleep with a pillow under your feet at night, you may see some improvement.'

He reached over and used his thumb and finger to ease back my eyelid.

'Your eyes have become covered with a membrane, like a layer of skin. Again, we know not what causes it, but we see it mostly in people such as you, who spend time outside in the sun, wind and dust. The only cure is to cauterise the eye. It is painful, but it can be effective.' He lifted my arm, re-examined my palm and sighed deeply. 'As for the weeping wound in your side and on your hands and feet, I have never seen anything like them before. The Pope did tell me he has heard of them, but I am afraid I can do nothing to ease the discomfort.'

'Fear not. They are a joy. A permanent reminder of our Saviour's sacrifice.'

I agreed to the procedure for my eyes, but the following day I relapsed once more and was moved to the quiet and peaceful hermitage at Monte Rainero.

The physician kindly arranged to visit me there to carry out the procedure. Although I remembered his warning that it would be painful, I was completely reconciled to the idea; after all, as I was already living in constant pain, the thought of more did not frighten me. However, I must admit that I was somewhat apprehensive as I entered the room to find a brazier burning, with a thin iron wire glowing white hot in the embers. I prayed and lay down before the physician, prepared to receive his treatment.

'Treat me gently, Brother Iron,' I remember saying before I passed out.

When I woke the following day, I felt the need for some soothing music to comfort me and asked the young brother, tasked with my care, if he could find an instrument and play for me. As he left the room on his quest, a wave of pain swept over me. I could bare it no longer, and I lost consciousness.

I came to, surrounded by the most wonderful music. He must have found a full choir and an orchestra to create such a heavenly chorus. I slipped into a peaceful sleep.

I woke several hours later. The young brother was sitting by my bedside. He was frowning and looked agitated.

'I thank you so much for the music. It was truly divine, and brought me much comfort.'

'But Father Francesco, I failed to trace any instruments. I was unable to satisfy your yearnings to hear the music. I beg your forgiveness.'

He may not have been able to satisfy my frivolous fancies, but my Lord Jesus Christ had clearly decided to satisfy my desires with a magnificent celestial chorus. Once more His kindness overwhelmed me, and my heart swelled with gratitude.

By July, although there was no improvement in my eyesight, I was sufficiently recovered for the Pope's physician to agree that I could return to Assisi. However, he was not happy for me to stay in our primitive lodgings at the Porziuncola and instead arranged for me to dwell in the comfort of the Bishop's palace.

I was unsure on the prospect of taking up residence with Bishop Guido III. He was a different personality to my old friend, the Bishop Guido, who had preceded him. Elias persuaded me that it was for the best and arranged for the loan of a cart, pulled by an ox, to take me back. The Pope arranged for us to have an armed guard, to protect me from kidnappers. He feared that if people heard of my condition, they might be tempted to kidnap me to collect relics after my death – or even before.

I was sad, but not surprised, to hear on my arrival that Bishop Guido III and Don Oportula, the Mayor, were in dispute. The quarrel had escalated to such a level that the Bishop had excommunicated not only the Mayor but also the rest of the dignitaries who governed the town. In retaliation, the Mayor had ordered a blockade of the palace, and we were now under siege. War had returned to Assisi, threatening the permanent peace negotiated sixteen years before.

How could I face my death knowing that I had failed?

I prayed for guidance and gave thanks for this second chance to bring peace to Assisi. I resolved that this time, I would be sure to acknowledge that any triumph belonged to God and that I was merely His instrument.

My prayer was answered when overnight I stumbled across the seeds of a possible resolution. I summoned Pacifico.

'Pacifico, we have a considerable amount of work to do if we are to follow God's guidance and restore peace to our beloved town.'

'What can I do to help, Brother Francesco?'

'God has shown me the way. We need to encourage love, tolerance, and forgiveness between the Bishop and the Mayor. We must write a new verse to our song, the *Canticle to the Sun*.'

We spent the next day preparing and practising the new verse. I wanted us to be word-perfect and note-perfect. The following day I summoned the Mayor and his corporation to appear before the Bishop's palace, and I also requested the Bishop's presence. As everyone gathered, I asked the brothers to sing the Canticle and enjoyed seeing the look of surprise on everyone's face when they heard the new verse:

> *Praised be You, my Lord, through those who give pardon*
> *for Your love,*
> *and bear infirmity and tribulation.*
> *Blessed are those who endure in peace*
> *for in You, Most High, they shall be crowned.*

I looked at the Bishop and was pleased to see tears streaming down his cheeks. The Mayor stood motionless, looking down at his feet. Then he wiped his eyes, approached the Bishop and knelt before him.

'My Lord, these words have filled my heart with love, pardon, and tolerance. I beg your forgiveness, for the love of our Lord Jesus Christ, and his humble servant, Brother Francesco.'

The Bishop reached down, took the Mayor's hands, and pulled him to his feet. 'No, Don Oportula, I should have known better. I have behaved badly. It is me that begs your forgiveness.'

The two men embraced. I led the prayers as we gave thanks to Almighty God for restoring peace to Assisi once more.

I did not fear death, but I was concerned about what would happen to the Friars Minor after I was gone. I recognised that the success of the Order and the considerable growth in their numbers, together with my inability to maintain contact with them as they multiplied across the world, had contributed to my downfall. Hugolino had been correct: order and discipline were necessary to sustain the Order. Perhaps there was still time, a way to reach out to every one of them.

I called for Elias and asked him to write down my words.

'Adieu, my brothers, I will soon depart from you to abide with our Lord God Almighty. I am sorry to be leaving you at these difficult times, with many trials and tribulations before you. There will be scandals and divisions to contend with, but you must always give complete and implicit obedience to your superiors and the Holy Catholic Church. Continue to observe the Rule, especially those aspects relating to property and your duties of manual labour, and you will find peace and happiness. I still believe this is the true message from God himself, who revealed to me that we should live according to the example of the holy gospel and our Lord Jesus Christ. May the Lord give you peace.'

As I pondered on my forthcoming death, I was reminded of the day my mother had brought me news of my father's. How I wish we could have made our peace before he died. I realised now, too late, that I could think of him fondly. It was our differences that had caused us to argue. He strived for wealth; I craved poverty. He enjoyed the formality of the Catholic Church service; I preferred the spontaneity that we humble preachers embrace. He was a proud man; I pursued humility. He enjoyed being treated like a lord and having servants; I enjoyed being a servant of my Lord Jesus Christ. I thought how, as Enricho had suggested, my father had shaped me into the man I was, if only because I totally rejected the life that he wanted for me. Poor Father; he had never understood me. We made each other so unhappy and yet, in his way, he was a good father, and I a poor son.

By the autumn, when it was clear there was very little time left for me, the Bishop agreed that I could return to end my days at my beloved Porziuncola. As the brothers carried me down the hill, I asked them to pause and turn me around so that I could look back on the town and give it my blessing. By now my eyesight was so hazy that I could hardly make out the town of Assisi as it nestled into the slopes of Mt. Subasio, the delicate pink rustic walls reflected in the subtle light of the Umbrian skies, a blurred vision of spiritual peace and tranquillity.

'God bless this town; may it give peace of mind and serenity to all who reside here.'

I lay in my cell that evening singing the *Canticle to the Sun* with Pacifico and Leo. The melody and the simple joy of the words helped me bear the pain of the stigmata wounds. We reached the end of the last verse – the words which were instrumental in restoring peace to Assisi. As I prepared for my day of judgement, the last judgement, from which there is no escape, new words formed in my mind and I sang what was to become the final verse:

Praised be You, my Lord, through our Sister Bodily Death,
For whom no one living can escape.
Woe to those who die in mortal sin.
Blessed are those whom death will find
in Your most holy will,
for the second death shall do them no harm.
Praise and bless my Lord and give Him thanks
And serve Him with great humility.

I was writing a letter to my dear Jacoba of Settesoli or, as I jokingly called her, 'Brother Jacoba.' I hoped she would visit me, and I also requested that she bring with her some ash-coloured cloth and candles for my burial, together with some of the sweet Mostaccioli biscuits that she always created for me. Before the letter went, she arrived with the items. She told me she was at prayer in Rome when she heard my voice asking her to come and telling her exactly what I wanted.

I lay on my deathbed and welcomed Brother Jacoba to my cell. She knelt and kissed the stigmata on my feet.

Bernardo, Elias, Leo, Rufino, Masseo and Angelo joined me that evening as we celebrated Mass. I asked them to remove my habit and to lay me on the ground so that I could leave the world naked, just as I entered it. Someone covered me with an old cloth and my heart rejoiced as I kept faith with my Lady Poverty.

I summoned my strength to speak to the brothers one last time.

'I have done my part. Now may our Lord Jesus Christ support and guide you to do yours. Love our Lord God with all your heart, follow the Rule and always respect the Catholic Church and her priests. May the Lord bless you now and in the future. I want you to give your full support to Brother Elias as he continues with his role as Minister General. I also want you all to take guidance from Brother Bernardo when I am gone. He will serve as your spiritual leader, and I urge you to follow him as you have followed me.'

I must have lost consciousness for a brief while because the next thing I remember was waking to find Elias bathing my forehead with a cloth soaked in lavender oil. Again, his care reminded me of the times my mother had cared for me in this way.

'Francesco is there anything I can get for you?'

'Will you read me the Passion from the Gospel of St. John?'

Elias read the familiar but still moving passage, ending with the words, 'Having received the wine, he said: "It is finished." He bowed his head and gave up his spirit.'

Tetelestai: it is finished. Such moving words. My Lord Jesus Christ, who knew no sin, took our sins upon Himself so that we could enjoy forgiveness and eternal life. His declaration that mankind's debt to His Father was obliterated for all time: the debt of sin. He had fulfilled prophesies of the Old Testament and finished the work He had been sent to do. He experienced injustice, antagonism, betrayal, pain and suffering – and now, *telelestai*: it is finished. He gave up His spirit and took His place in Heaven: perfect joy.

And now, for me also – *Tetelestai*: it is finished. But I am still confused. Why did God choose me as his instrument? Why me?

I believe it's because I am so insignificant. I did not have nobility, great wisdom or good looks. I think God chose me because then it was obvious to everyone that every good thing I was able to achieve came from Him and not from me. I was His humble servant, His instrument.

Was I worthy of His faith in me? Would my life make a difference in the future? Had I accomplished everything He wanted me to achieve? I could only hope so.

Would the Order survive my death? I knew my loyal disciples with me here tonight would continue to keep our principles. But would the changes introduced by Rome divide the Order and dilute it? I took comfort from knowing that Hugolino held the Order in his heart and would continue to guide and protect them after my passing. I also took comfort from the *showing* on the day that sight was restored to the baby Bonaventura. I recognised it as a promise that the Order would continue and that, at some time in the future, he would lead it.

Should I have gone to the Holy Land? My ambition to convert the Saracens and bring the bloody wars to an end had resulted in failure. My approach was arrogant, and it had taken the patience and friendship of the Sultan and the guidance of my Lord Jesus Christ for me to understand that dialogue and interfaith tolerance were more likely to succeed as a route to peace over time. My arrogant message of conversion, taken up by my brothers in Morocco, had resulted in their untimely deaths. My brothers were right to blame me for this senseless loss of life. If I had returned directly from Damietta, instead of indulging my desire to travel in the footsteps of Jesus, I might have persuaded them to take a different approach, and they might still be alive today.

Even my visit to the Holy Land was an indulgence; I saw that clearly now. I should have realised that the growth of the Order left it exposed to rumblings of discontent. If I had remained in Assisi or even Italy, those rumbles might have been quashed, but instead, I pursued my selfish childhood dream of becoming a knight and joining the crusade. I left the Order vulnerable, resulting in the current arguments and the erosion of our original simplistic principles.

I had made mistakes, but I had learned from them at last, and now it was time for me to step back and let go, I was ready to move on.

Tomorrow, without pain I will meet my Lord God, my Father in Heaven. Tomorrow I will experience the second death, the day of judgement. Tomorrow He will answer all my questions. My body will be carried by my loyal brothers to San Damiano so that my beloved Chiara and her sisters can say their last goodbyes, before I return through the town gate into my beloved town of Assisi.

EPILOGUE

Francesco, otherwise Francis, died in the infirmary cell of the Porziuncola at St. Mary of the Angels, on Saturday evening, 3 October 1226, surrounded by Jacoba and his loyal brothers Bernardo, Elias, Leo, Rufino, Masseo, and Angelo. In 1228, Francesco was canonised as St. Francis of Assisi. Pope Gregory IX (formerly Cardinal Hugolino) laid the foundation stone for the Basilica in Assisi that became the final resting place for the remains of St. Francis.

His purpose was achieved: to rekindle the love of God in the hearts of men and women across the world. The harvest of souls he had so carefully reaped multiplied, spreading seeds of love, peace, and perfect joy.

Elias continued his role as Minister General following Francis' death. He was responsible for the original design of the Basilica, oversaw the fundraising and coordinated the building work. He strengthened the discipline of the Order, even in remote provinces. Despite his endeavours, five years after being elected to Minister General by Francis, and less than a year after Francis' death, the chapter meeting of 1227 appointed Giovanni Parenti as his replacement. Elias was furious at this treatment, refused to accept the decision and carried on as before while lobbying for his re-election, which he achieved in 1232.

His next few years as Minister General were plagued by conflict and conspiracy against him. He continued with his strict regime and determination that the Basilica would be opulent, which many believed would have been against the wishes of the Saint. By the time the chapter of 1239 opened, Pope Gregory IX had realised that his protégé would have to go, and demanded Elias's resignation. Elias refused, so the Pope was forced to depose him. Eventually, totally rejected and embittered, Elias continued to cause trouble until he was excommunicated from the Order, and was only reconciled with the Pope and the Franciscans on his deathbed.

Elias's legacy in the Holy Land continues to this day. Brother Elias, at Francis's request, became Provincial Minister in the Holy Land and established the Franciscan presence in Syria. After Elias had returned to Italy with Francis, this presence was maintained by the Friars Minor until it became formally recognised by the Catholic Church. The role of Custodian of the Holy Places and provision of care to the visiting pilgrims was conferred upon the Franciscan Order in 1342 by Pope Clement VI. The Custodians' jurisdiction covers Israel, Palestine, Jordan and Lebanon, parts of Egypt, Cyprus and Rhodes.

Following the death of Francis, the debates, arguments, and disputes over various aspects of interpreting the Franciscan Rule continued. As a result, there are several different branches in existence, the main ones being: the Friars Minor (OFM), the Friars Minor Conventual (OFM Conv), and the Friars Minor Capuchin (OFM Cap).

Chiara, otherwise known as Clare, died in 1253 and was also venerated as a saint. On two separate occasions, she was credited with saving the town of Assisi from attack. The first occasion was in 1240 when Frederick II battled against the Pope for control of Italy. A group of his Saracen mercenaries ransacked the valley of Spoleto and were about to scale the walls of St. Damien when Clare appeared at an open window holding a chalice. The soldiers were dazzled, fell from their ladder and in their confusion made a hasty retreat. The second occasion was in 1241 when General

Vitalis d'Aversa was about to attack the town. Clare gathered her sisters at the town gate and prayed for the safety of Assisi. A violent storm broke, scattering the army and their camp, and the attack was averted.

She is entombed in the Basilica of St. Clare in Assisi and the Order of Poor Clare (OPC) continues today.

The Third Order of St. Francis, the Tertiaries, or, as it is sometimes known, the Third Order of Penance, also continues with many members, some living in religious communities and some living by the Franciscan principles within their normal family lives.

Bonaventura became Minister General of the Franciscans in 1257, just as Francis had seen in his vision. He wrote the first official biography of the Saint. Confronted with the problems that threatened to tear the Order apart, Bonaventura adopted a moderate position, attempting to remain faithful to the ideals of St. Francis but adapting them sufficiently to bring reconciliation. He became known as the second founder of the Franciscan Order because of his successful endeavours. He was venerated and became St. Bonaventura two hundred years after his death.

The Basilica of St. Francis is built on the hill that was known as the *Hill of Hell* when Francis was alive. The hill where he prayed to God before the stinking corpse of the thief, '*Dear God, whatever happens, whatever your intention for me, do not let me end up here.*' Ironically this is exactly where his final resting place is situated, surrounded by opulent artwork created to celebrate the life of the Saint.

Assisi is an amazingly pretty, calm and tranquil town, an inspiring and spiritual place to visit. It hugs the mountainside with steep, narrow streets and stonework that reflects the changing light, at times a pale golden honey tone, at others a light blush of pink. The small houses are delightfully decorated with exquisite and intricately woven ironwork, flower baskets and balconies with terracotta pots and flowers tumbling everywhere. The churches and basilicas are painted with frescoes depicting the life and times of Francis and Clare.

Paul Sabatier in his excellent biographical book *The Life of St. Francis of Assisi* makes an interesting statement about the Basilica of St. Francis:

> *Go and look upon it, proud, rich, powerful, then go down to the Porziuncola, pass over to St. Damian, hasten to the Carceri, and you will understand the abyss that separates the ideal of Francis from that of the pontiff who canonized him. (p. 354).*

It's a compelling point.

THE CHILDREN'S CRUSADE

Éloise would never forget that first day she saw Stephan. He was preaching at the entrance to Saint-Denis Abbey, surrounded by hundreds of young children. He was tall for his age, which she guessed to be around twelve.

His voice, already beginning to deepen, was strong and assertive: 'I was minding my father's sheep when I noticed a strange light on the horizon. I thought I must have fallen asleep, that it was dawn already. But then I realised that the light was getting bigger, brighter, taking form – and behold, the Lord Jesus Christ appeared before me.'

'What was he like?' shouted a child from the crowd.

'What did he say?' another cried.

'He had the gentlest eyes I have ever seen and a beautiful smile. He lifted His arms towards me. His voice, when it came, was soft and tender. He told me that I must travel to the Holy Land and take you children with me. Between us, we will stop the fighting. With His help, we will end the bloody wars.'

'But how would we cross the sea?' shouted Éloise.

'Fear not, I have the Lord's promise that the seas will part to allow us safe passage, as the Red Sea did for Moses.'

'What of our families?' a young girl called out.

'We will be a new family. Our Father in Heaven will watch over us, and we will be brothers and sisters to each other. Our parents and siblings will miss us, but their sorrow will soften with the knowledge that we go with God's blessing to bring peace to the Holy Land.'

A small boy sitting beside Éloise on the Abbey steps gazed up at Stephan; his large dark brown eyes gleamed in stark contrast to the pallor of his gaunt face. Éloise watched as Stephan walked towards him.

'Will you join me in this crusade?'

The boy pointed to his wooden crutch. 'I wish I could, but I am unable to walk far. I was born a cripple.'

'God will be your support on this journey. Stand by my side, give thanks to Him and throw aside your crutch.' Stephan reached down for the boy's hands and pulled him to his feet.

The crowd gasped as the boy took one tentative step on his crippled foot and then, realising that he was no longer lame, threw his stick aside. The children cheered.

Stephan waited for the cheering to subside. 'For those who wish to join us on our Holy Crusade, come here tomorrow at noon. Bring a water bottle and as much food as you can carry, for it will be a long and arduous journey.'

Éloise watched him walk down the steps; pausing now and then to shake hands with many of the young audience. He could only be a year older than her, and yet he was so sure of himself. As he disappeared from view, she was overwhelmed with a feeling of loss. She had no family. She had never known her father. Her dear mother and younger sister had died of the fever two years previously. Life, when you are alone in the world, is difficult. The decision to leave her damp, derelict stable and straw bed to follow Stephan was easy.

Éloise arrived in the square early the next day, but she was not the first. Hundreds of children mostly eleven or twelve, but many considerably younger, had gathered before the steps of the Abbey. By noon there were perhaps close to a thousand excited children, skipping, dancing and cheering.

'Thank you, every one of you,' called Stephan from the Abbey steps. 'Today the Children's Crusade will begin the march towards Marseilles. We will pass through Tours and Lyons, where we will share the message of this vision and recruit more children to our quest. It will be a long journey: many weeks of hot and weary travel with little food to sustain us. We will all endure harshness, as good soldiers of Jesus Christ. Fear not, for God, will provide.'

Éloise was filled with excitement as their expedition began. She noticed that some of the wealthier children had horses and that one had brought a trailer that became designated as Stephan's carriage. Someone tied a banner, depicting the white crusaders cross, to the trailer. It flapped in the light breeze, and the sound mingled with the applause from those who lined the street to wish the children well.

She joined in with the other children as they followed on foot, singing hymns to maintain their spirits. She preferred to stay close to the trailer so that she could watch Stephan. He would always wave and greet the children who rushed out from their homes to see what was happening, encouraging them to come and join the crusade. They made good progress, and their numbers swelled. By lunchtime on the third day they reached the city of Tours.

Éloise sat on the dry sandy ground and watched Stephan as he preached to a large crowd of children that had gathered to hear his words. Even though she had heard his story several times by now, she remained enraptured. His voice reverberated through her body, making the hairs on her arms bristle and her toes tingle.

Éloise felt a hand brush against her arm. She turned and noticed a small girl who sat beside her. Éloise watched as a crimson flush crept over the young girl's pale cheeks, and tears swam in her startling blue eyes. She looked up at Éloise and held out her hand, in which there was a crumbling biscuit – one of Éloise's.

'You dropped this,' the young girl stammered.

Grabbing her wrist Éloise snapped. 'You stole it from my bag.'

'I meant no harm. I was hungry, and I have nothing to eat. Oh, please.' Huge tears rolled down her cheeks, streaking the fine dust that powdered them. 'Please do not report me as a thief.'

Éloise looked away and watched Stephan once more. She still held the girl's wrist, and she could feel the girls fragile frame tremble with fear.

'Very well, you are welcome to the biscuit,' she sighed. 'What use would there be in reporting you? None of us will have anything by tomorrow. We may as well share what little we have.'

'Thank you, Miss,' her sobs gradually subsided to a snuffle.

'What's your name?'

'It's Adelais, Miss.'

'What are you doing here? You're far too young for such a journey.'

'I'm six, nearly seven – and I have nowhere else to go. I used to live in Paris with my parents and younger sister, but they all died of the fever a month ago. My mother – before she died – told me to travel to St. Denis and find my aunt, who she said would look after me.' Adelais' tears began to fall with renewed intensity.

'Come Adelais, dry those tears.' Éloise placed her arm around Adelais's small shoulders and hugged her frail body to her. 'I understand how it feels to be alone in the world. Were you unable to find your aunt?'

'I did find her, but she told me to go away. She already has four children to provide for, and she said she had "no space for her sister's brat." I went to pray at the Abbey, and that's when I heard Stephan say that if we joined the Children's Crusade, we would all be brothers and sisters to each other.'

'Dry your eyes, Adelais. I will be your new sister. Now, eat your biscuit and listen to what Stephan has to say.'

Éloise had realised that by the time they left Tours the next morning the army of children had grown by several hundred. Food supplies had dwindled to nothing. Hunger forced Éloise and Adelais to join the other children and beg for food in the villages and towns they passed through. Unfortunately, the area was ravaged by hot and dry conditions, which resulted in famine and food shortages. Although the people, driven by compassion, gave what they could, in reality, there was little to spare.

Adelais remained cheerful, but each day she grew weaker through lack of nourishment. She struggled to keep up the pace. Éloise frequently had to carry Adelais on her back, to prevent them from falling behind. Adelais weighed so little, but Éloise was also weak with hunger, and the journey became more and more difficult.

On several occasions, the procession was brought to a halt as a child collapsed, died from exhaustion, and was buried under piles of stones by the roadside. Others, who were unable to continue, were more fortunate and taken in by families prepared to offer them new homes.

The children reached Lyons, a month later, Éloise was completely exhausted. She looked around and felt overwhelmed by the huge wave of sadness that engulfed her. The once angelic faces of the children had become disfigured with open sores: their hair was matted with dirt and grease and speckled with lice eggs; their skin darkened by the hot sun and ingrained dust; their nails broken and blackened, and their bellies had swollen with hunger. She wondered if anyone would survive.

Éloise stroked Adelais' hair and sang her a lullaby as they took advantage of a small tree and sheltered from the unrelenting heat of the midday sun. Stephan had organised this campsite on the edge of the town. A small stream provided sufficient water to drink, but there was very little food.

Adelais stirred. 'Leave me here, Éloise. I cannot go on anymore.'

'I will not leave you, at least not for long. Rest here in the shade a while and I'll go and find help.'

Éloise made her way over to the trailer where Stephan was resting.

'I wonder if I could speak with you, Stephan.'

'I have seen you before, have I not? You have a young sister with you.'

'Yes, Adelais is my adopted sister, but she is unwell. I have come to beg for your help.'

'Take me to her.'

As they reached her side, Adelais opened her eyes and smiled. 'Éloise, you came back.'

'I told you, I will not leave you. We are sisters now. Look, Stephan has come to see you.' She turned to face him and saw his handsome face distorted by a frown.

'She is beyond help,' he said in a low voice. 'I have seen this several times already. Your sister is so weak from lack of food that she is unable to fight off the fever.'

'But surely, if she could ride with you on the trailer–'

'No.'

'But–'

'If I say yes to you, others will ask the same. It would weaken the horse, and it is pointless. She will die anyway. It is best you just make her comfortable and leave her here to let nature take its course.'

He turned his back on her and walked away. How could he be so uncaring, so callous? Éloise had followed him without question. She loved him, worshipped him. Her dream was that one day they would be together celebrating victory in the Promised Land. But he had refused to help and had shattered her dream.

'Please, Éloise, you must leave me here.'

'Hush my sister; I will always be here for you.' She held Adelais' hot little hand and stroked her damp forehead. Stephan has been right about one thing; she definitely had the fever.

Éloise watched the Children's Crusade, with Stephan at the helm, as they left Lyons to make their way to Marseilles. Tears ran down her cheeks as they disappeared from view. She was filled with disappointment but determined to nurse Adelais through the fever crisis.

A woman approached. She smiled and spoke in a warm, comforting voice.

'Have they left you behind?' The woman asked.

'I could not leave my sister Adelais. She has a fever and is too weak to continue.'

'We have a stable at the farm. It is so run down that we do not use it anymore, but you are welcome to use it as shelter.'

Éloise thanked the woman and carried Adelais the short distance to the farm. The stable was dry and offered them shade. Éloise made a bed of straw for them both and made Adelais as comfortable as she could.

The woman brought them a container of goat's milk every day and Éloise was able to dip her handkerchief into the cup and dribble the creamy liquid into Adelais' mouth. But it was of little use; Adelais became delirious on the third day. Éloise continued to do everything that she could, but even though Adelais was a fighter, she died four days later.

Éloise and the farmer's wife buried her in a shallow grave with boulders on top to keep her safe from wild animals and stray dogs. Éloise carved a piece of wood with Adelais' name and formed it into a cross to mark her grave. She was too exhausted to cry, but as she resumed her journey her heart was heavy with grief for her dear sister, Adelais.

Her plan was to catch up with Stephan and the children before they reached Marseilles, but the delay of over a week made that impossible. As she trudged down the dusty track, she occasionally passed by small mounds of boulders, some marked with crosses, others unnamed. Another life lost. On several occasions, she met small groups of children who had turned back and were beginning their long weary journey to return home.

At last, she arrived in Marseilles, but the children were gone. She heard that they had been received generously by the citizens, who provided them with food and shelter for the night. The next morning the children had rushed down to the harbour expecting the waters to part – as Stephan had predicted. They lined up along the beach and prayed, but nothing happened. The children prayed all day but to no avail. Eventually, they were forced to accept the offer of help from two merchants, Hugh the Iron and William the Pig, who gathered together seven boats to provide the children with carriage to the Holy Land.

Éloise had arrived too late. The children had sailed the previous day. Distraught, she sat on the harbour wall and gazed out to sea. She continued to sit on the harbour wall, over a period of several weeks. The townsfolk would provide her with food and fresh water. Then news came. Tragically, two of the boats were shipwrecked in a storm and the children all drowned. The other five boats were captured by, or even worse, sold by the merchants to the Saracen army and the children taken into slavery. Éloise was distraught. She refused to eat, and then one day she simply disappeared. No one knew where she went. Perhaps she returned to the kind farmer's wife in Lyons and made a new home there. Perhaps she returned to her derelict stable in St. Denis. Who knows? Whatever happened to her, the people of Marseilles did not forget Éloise. They kept her story alive and the story of her heroic struggle and her compassion for Adelais became a legend.

ACKNOWLEDGEMENTS

This book is a work of fiction, but it is based on the character of St. Francis, a real person. However, the various biographies and facts relating to his life often conflict on the exact year of his birth (1181 or 1182), the dates and nature of certain incidents, and the names of his early companions. There is disagreement on where exactly he was shipwrecked, how he first became acquainted with Elias, and whether Brother Pietro, who joined the Friars Minor at the beginning with Bernardo, was the same Brother Pietro who became Minister General and died in 1221.

There is also conflicting evidence on when Clare's father died and if it was her father, Count Favarone di Offreduccio, or her uncle who tried to return her to the family home. Others argue that Clare's family name was Scifi. There is disagreement on who granted Francis the Indulgence for the Porziuncola, as it happened somewhere around the death of Innocent III and the appointment of Pope Honorius III. I chose to attribute this to the latter. Because of the multitude of different interpretations, artistic license is taken throughout.

The development of the Cathar movement is another area of disputed history. Some believe that the faith had spread across Italy by the time of Francis, while others state that this did not happen until much later, in the 1240s.

Many sources claim that Francis became a deacon when he visited the Pope in Rome and gained verbal approval for his

Order. It is, however, more generally believed that this was an invention of more recent history. It is unlikely that the office of deacon existed in the time of Francis.

Some people doubt that Francis wrote the prayer of St. Francis. Did he write it, did he not, does it matter? Again, I chose to embrace artistic licence and included it within the story, where I believe it belongs.

Bonaventura was a famous philosopher, a scholastic theologian and for a while became Minister General of the Order. He later became a saint, but at the time that Francis met him as a baby, he would have been known as Giovanni.

Place names have changed over time, and I have tried wherever possible to remain faithful to historical accuracy. For example, I have placed the shipwreck in Slavonia, which is now Dalmatia; Acre in the Holy Land is now Akko in Israel; Alvernia is now La Verna; Monte Rainero is now Fonte Colombo, and Gol'gotha in Jerusalem became better known as Calvary.

I also chose to write Francis' story in the first person as I believe this created the opportunity to explore his possible thoughts, beliefs, and reasoning in greater depth. Much of this self-deliberation is indeed fiction, but I hope I have not attributed anything to his personality or thoughts that would have caused him offence or that might detract in any way from his life or the contributions made by this remarkable man.

I offer my heartfelt thanks to my husband Harold and our daughter Rachael; without their encouragement, this book would never have been completed.

I am also indebted to Kath, my creative writing guru and guide, and to our beta-readers group, Elaine, Joy, and Laura; I will be eternally grateful for their helpful advice, endless cups of tea, fun, and encouragement.

I also appreciate those who have taken the time to read, critique and proofread earlier drafts of the book, including Francis, Ken, Maureen, Clare; and fellow writers at Writeword. Thanks are also due to Barbara and Sarah at Cornerstone, who helped with my final draft. Also to my friends who I have sadly neglected at times over the past four years.

I will be forever grateful to the Order of Friars Minor Conventual (OFMConv) in Oxford, and in particular to Brothers Daniel, Gerard, and Benedict, who read and critiqued my manuscript and especially Brother Paul (now based in Manchester) who gave detailed feedback and ongoing support on the manuscript as it progressed. Our meetings to discuss various aspects were invaluable, and their prayers, hospitality, and support were an inspiration.

All errors that remain are mine.

Thank you, one and all. X.

REFERENCES

Armstrong, R.J., Wayne Hellmann, J.A., and Short, W.J., (1999). *Francis of Assisi: The Saint.* New City Press, NY.

Bonaventura, (St.)., (1904 edition). *The Life of St. Francis.* J.M. Dent, London.

Catholic Encyclopaedia online. *St. Francis of Assisi.*

Giandomenico, N., (2004). *Art and History – Assisi.* Bonechi, Florence.

Moses, P., (2009). *The Saint and the Sultan.* Doubleday, NY. *The New English Bible, Pocket Edition.* (1975) Oxford UP/ Cambridge UP.

Okey, T., (translator), (2003). *The Little Flowers of Saint Francis.* Dover, NY.

Raymond, E., (1938). *In the Footsteps of St. Francis.* Rich and Cowan, London.

Rega, F.M., (2007). *St. Francis of Assisi and the Conversion of the Muslims.* Tan Books, Illinois.

Sabatier, P., (1894). *Life of St. Francis of Assisi.* Scribner Press, NY.

Thompson, A., (2012). *Francis of Assisi – A New Biography.* Cornell University Press, NY.

Vauchez, A., (2012). *Francis of Assisi: The Life and Afterlife of a Medieval Saint.* Yale University Press, London.

Walsh, M., (ed.), (1987). *Butler's Lives of the Saints.* Burns and Oates, Kent.

Wikipedia, where would we be without you?

EIN HERZ FÜR AUTOREN A HEART FOR AUTHORS À L'ÉCOUTE DES AUTEURS MIA KAPΔIA ΓΙΑ ΣΥΓΓΡ
UN CORAZÓN POR FÖRFATTARE UN CORAZÓN POR LOS AUTORES YAZARLARIMIZA GÖNÜL VERELIM SZÍ
UN CUORE PER AUTORI ET HJERTE FOR FORFATTERE EEN HART VOOR SCHRIJVERS TEMOS OS AUTO
SZÍVÜNKÉRT SERCE DLA AUTORÓW EIN HERZ FÜR AUTOREN A HEART FOR AUTHORS À L'ÉCOU
ВСЕЙ ДУШОЙ К АВТОРАМ ETT HJÄRTA FÖR FÖRFATTARE Á LA ESCUCHA DE LOS AUTO
ΓΙΑ ΣΥΓΓΡΑΦΕΙΣ UN CUORE PER AUTORI ET HJERTE FOR FORFATTERE EEN
SZÍVÜNKÉRT SERCE DLA AUTORÓW EIN HERZ FÜR
ACÃO ВСЕЙ ДУШОЙ К АВТОРАМ ETT HJÄRTA FÖ

The author

Wendy enjoyed a successful career in health service management, educational strategy and lecturing, and has previously published several education-related articles in various magazines. She began writing fiction when she took early retirement. She now lives in Cornwall with her husband, Harold, who supplies endless support and cups of tea while she writes. Her daughter, Rachael, and her family live close by, and also provide never-ending encouragement.

The publisher

He who stops getting better stops being good.

This is the motto of novum publishing, and our focus is on finding new manuscripts, publishing them and offering long-term support to the authors.
Our publishing house was founded in 1997, and since then it has become THE expert for new authors and has won numerous awards.

Our editorial team will peruse each manuscript within a few weeks free of charge and without obligation.

You will find more information about
novum publishing and our books on the internet:

w w w . n o v u m - p u b l i s h i n g . c o . u k